Everlan Trilogy

Ancients' Roulic and Ravenna fall in love, but war, a curse, and time itself keep them apart. Thunder ensues when the witches of Doth enter their lives...

The witches of Doth have a score to settle.
Roulic wants to find his family and be with his beloved Ravenna.
Together, can they break the curse of Mayem?

~

Where the Witches Dwell (Book One)
Searching for his family, an orphaned Ancient makes a pact with the witches of Doth.

Charming Tomorrow (Book Two)
Roulic treads the dragon's door, chased by Mayem's ghosts of Onan.

Everlan (Book Three)
Cursed, sibling witches stir the pot on the path of star-crossed lovers.

SPECIAL EDITION

Everlan Trilogy Omnibus (Books 1-3)
    Everlan Trilogy Omnibus bonus content includes: anagrams, the Black family tree, a timeline, and more.

A curse, a war, and time itself keep lovers apart in the land of dragons

EVERLAN TRILOGY OMNIBUS

Charming Tomorrow

Everlan Trilogy
Book 2

Conor Jest

JEST PUBLISHING

PAPERBACK EDITION

• **ISBN-13** : 979-8992506518

For Ryder, and Madison

'TIS NOT WHAT YOU SEEK, 'TIS NOT WHERE YOU WEND

CHARMING TOMORROW

When all that was and ever is
stops marching tomorrow,
there shoots a changeling
out dancing doors to endless shores;
starlight's never ending
For the will of we, calm
amid ireful storms,
coax the odd and wheedle the norm
from head to eye to heart to horn

Where taken, lent, even borrowed,
time's memory retreats,
charming tomorrow
on her way to remembering
if not for us old souls,
but for the good of Doth;
whose true kingdom
lies in ancient dragons who birth
air to water, fire to earth

UPPER KINGDOM OF

SOARING HILLS

EVERLAN

BELIEF

MOUNT
NOCTURNE

TOP OF
THE WORLD

DRAGONFALL

WOODS OF
EVERLAN

OLD ROCK ROAD

DRAGON FYRE

TRUMP

DANDO

GREAT ORIENT

H

DANDLING OARS

OCEANS INN

CASSAVA

LARGEN

OUTCAST

MAYEM'S CAVE

BLACK SHADOWS
BEACH

MIDWAY

THE NINE OCEANS

THREE FURROWS

ON WELLS

THOSE

Contents

Chapter 1

In Mayem's Shadow

Mayem hit the foggy beach, running. No stranger to a portal dive, his rebound rivaled a fox's. Yet his graceful gait slowed, then stalled, giving in to the Ancient's old injury. He cursed his wound, a nasty singe inflicted by a young dragon named Baby. The telling scar wrapped around his right heel, leaving the Ancient in agonizing pain and shoeless for a year. At first, he took the burn as a reminder of the futility of raising an infant dragon. But this, he grew to refute, as it only hounded his ongoing woe: that of her utter rejection. Now, alone in a foreign land, he had no way of getting back to Doth without the portal key. And so he kept moving, hopping like a feral gray fox.

This barren shore has no people to plunder, no fishers, no nets, nothing. If only I had taken the key from Roulic. It would have brought me some-place pristine, like Gadbanti's island. I've got to get back to my island; Dandling Oars. But how?

A plastic water bottle grounded by the tide rolled over the beach. He read the soggy label: Please recycle.

Nothing but refuse littering the sea!

Mayem dropped and stepped on it, squishing the bottle with his boot until it was buried in the sand.

Damn that Roulic! I'm going to step on him and crush his skull. Rip

out his heart. Dance over his body. Take the Pearlytok from his hands.
We'll see how long it takes before he does something he shouldn't. He's no
saint. Just like his father. A failed do-gooder.

Nearing a line of waterfront homes, his head stayed low, obsessing his predicament. He trudged along the beach like a caught fugitive, reluctant to inhabit his cell.

I've no future here. I'd have to start all over. I'll be a prisoner unless I
get that key. Damn him to Doth.

Because of the fog, he couldn't see the cargo tankers on the horizon or the jets taking off from Long Beach Airport. Had he been able to see the island thirty-one miles offshore, he might have realized he'd been to this future world before. Nothing registered until he heard the jangle of keys. It came from hands unlocking a back gate. He stopped, studying the corner house, and his next victim.

"You're not supposed to be here!" the old man growled. "This is a private beach." Mayem's pitchy eyes went from vacant to icy, staring at the man's home.

"I'm sorry I've trespassed. Forgive me," Mayem said. "Could you find it in your heart to bring me a glass of water? I've a terrible thirst."

"No! Now, get off my property or I'll call the police. It's bums like you who ruined this beach years ago." The old man slammed the gate, dropping his lock and keys into a planter beside the fence. He bent over to retrieve them. Mayem kicked sand, bolting over the beach. He shoved the gate open, knocking the man into the bushes.

"Get up! Give me those keys. And get inside. I'm your lord now," he sneered at the old man struggling to stand. "And I'll have that water now," he flouted, revealing a horrific smile. The man hobbled through his patio garden to the kitchen door. Drops of blood smeared his hands and the back of his balding head.

"That's better," Mayem said, drinking the man's water, "but courtesy won't make you live any longer. What else have you for me!?" He left the kitchen for the living room.

"I've got money. Lots of money. It's in my safe. You can have it all," the old man pleaded, "please take it and go."

Mayem commanded from the sofa: "Go get it. Bring it to me now. I've not got all day."

The old man returned with a walrus hide valise full of cash. Mayem licked his lips, unimpressed with the quivering hands stacking green notes on the coffee table.

"Have you no gold?" Mayem grilled.

"This is all the money I've got. It's my life savings," the old man trembled.

"Don't count on currency saving your life," Mayem raged. He jeered at an easel standing by a wide window lined with oil tubes, overlooking the ocean. "What's this? Have we an artist? A painter of the sea? Well then, let's see what you can do."

"Why are you doing this to me?" the old man shuddered, his anguished eyes teary.

"Let's just call it my daemon's whimsy, shall we?" Mayem's eyes rolled back.

He leaped to the window, and the paintbrushes kept in a cup by the easel. Grabbing the longest brush in the cup, he stroked the blank canvas.

"How 'bout I paint you?" Making sure the old man could see him, Mayem turned, holding the brush in his palm like a dagger. The man gasped. His eyes never left Mayem's back. "Let's see, I'll need plenty of red," he taunted. The man crossed his hands over his heart in agony. Mayem howled, then spun around screaming, "Have you any red??!!" But he turned too late. The old man lay slumped on the carpet, having died from fright.

"I didn't think so." Mayem threw the brush in the dead man's lap. An hour later, he got giddy drinking the painter's scotch, amusing himself by flicking every light switch in the house. But that mood went dark after tinkering with the old man's stereo record player. Turning up the volume of Frank Sinatra's crooning amplified his private agony; the shunning of his brother Meyrick's late wife, the beautiful Ancient, Grace.

"Her rejection has damned my soul more than any act for which I'll ever be damned!" he broached.

Drunk at the easel, he played ballads by candlelight, painting grotesque portraits of her. Stupefied in self-pity, he wallowed, venting from his ruined heart.

"If only I could undraw the soul birthed in black rain,
I'd forget the unspoken name, long since uttered on the battered banks
of the world's pain
The seasons I've endured, can't measure the value of her comely
company; an imperishable paint,
brushing this wanton heart, mislaid unto today, yet
her soft edge remains, forever faint beneath the stain of my endless
shame
And so I chase her winded cries, with a lean and yellowing tint,
swipe fading stars in the desert's diamond glint
My utmost lament; my unrequited folly
And dying, never again held by the heart who colored over
my black canvas in the rain.."

He passed out at the easel. Fine-woven showers crept over the light-less ocean, pattering against the old man's beach house window.

In the autumn of his youth, Roulic vanished. He fell over a waterfall on Dandling Oars Island. No one dreamed of his descent, not even the witches of Doth. Had he not fallen, he might have ambushed and killed the abominator at the island's citadel, or even at the Edge where it all happened; Mayem's watery playground of torture. Both Ancients fought there for Doth's golden portal key, the Pearlytok. And both fell, lost in the Master's magical hatch hidden in the roaring falls.

Now, after surviving the liquid portal, Roulic knew he'd clash with Mayem again. He could feel it in his bones. He just couldn't feel his leg. But a numb leg didn't stop him from sitting upright on the unknown beach. He got busy testing the sleeping appendage. Pinching his right limb brought no response. So, he waited until a wave crashing on the sand made his left leg twitch twice. In the din and quiver he thought he heard the flock of herring gulls over his head, squawking:

"Get on your feet, Mayem's coming!"

"I can't, until I feel my leg," he grumbled at the gulls. He looked left and right for Mayem, wiggling a toe.

I've got to get back on my feet, he thought. He kept pinching and wiggling, urging the blood in his heart and head to meet in his leg. When it did, he licked his lips. "Salty...," his sandy hand clutching the cool gold of the sacred key.

"I'm alive!" he testified to a disapproving jury of shore walkers. Their glaring verdict stung in the ocean air. He pivoted, pocketing the key. "At least I kept Mayem from it," he proclaimed to their head juror. He had received that silent sentence a thousand times as a young orphan: the pitiful looks given to the homeless and hungry. "If you only knew where I've come from," he shook his fist at their taciturn backs, rattling his enchanted bracelet.

It tinkled, as it did the day Alison gave Ravenna its matching necklace. He cupped and jingled the gifted charms with a wishful hand. *She'll hear me and get me back to Doth.*

"Ravenna!" He squeezed his wrist, shaking the bracelet in vain. "Ravenna, are you there? It's me, Roulic." He rose, shaking off the sand. "Nothing. I suppose even a witch's talisman could fail when thrown into another realm," he said.

His vest pockets were still wet from his fall with Mayem from the Edge. Digging in, he tallied a palmful of coins, bits of tobacco, and a wet, wrinkled map of Doth. The fall's finality also cut off all sight of Ravenna's longing eyes. Eyes he lived for and would die for.

I guess I'm not in Doth anymore. Damn Mayem for all he's done. Mayem! His neck spun. He rose, scanning the beach in every direction. Mayem wasn't there, but a congested, two-lane highway ran alongside the coast, carrying strange horseless carriages. Some paused at a stoplight. Most sped by. His mouth opened when the signal changed color from red to green. He understood the system, but couldn't fathom what powered the lights and cars.

Between the beach and the busy road lay a wide wooden boardwalk bordering a 100-foot-wide park of bright green grass. He passed the boardwalk sign: Main Beach. People lounged on towels and beach chairs, watching their children play in the water. Some picnicked, some sat on benches, reading. Others napped in the mid-morning sun. Two gray-bearded men played chess. A shirtless, ponytailed surfer stood over them, engrossed in the game.

Well, at least I've landed in a place of learned citizens. But where have I landed? Nothing here resembles the villages of Doth.

At the end of the boardwalk, a lively court game was taking place. Two-man teams bounced a big orange ball and ran it to the far end of the court. They rallied around a netted hoop attached to a backboard set on a 7-foot steel pole. One man jumped, dunking the ball through the hoop. A cheery crowd of spectators clapped and clamored.

"Do you like basketball?" A scraggly-faced beggar loomed in, catching Roulic off guard. He jumped back from the dirty cloak, ready to defend himself. The beggar jumped back as well, creating a safe space between the two. Realizing the man meant no harm, Roulic lowered his arms. "Who wouldn't like basketball? A better game this world has never known."

"Don't tell that to a football fan." The disheveled man laughed and walked away. The Ancient One wandered, unwilling to show his ignorance.

I shouldn't trust just anyone, he thought. *If only Demeter or Jillian were here. They would help me get back to Doth. The witches understand the secrets of traveling through portals better than anybody. Except maybe, Mayem.* He scanned the boardwalk nervously.

Roulic destroyed what Mayem spent centuries killing for. And he'd carried the Pearlytok and the love of Mayem's own niece. In her suffrage Mayem sought to quell the dragon power passed to her from Grace. At least that's what he told himself as he cursed her at the Bridge of Belief in Everlan.

No, Roulic thought, set on fulfilling his second obligation to the witches of Doth. *I must first return the Pearlytok to King Vim at Trumbleton in the Inner Realm of Doth.*

I've already restored the Divine of Doth,—delivered her home. Next comes the key. ...Aurora said, "Regarding your third and final challenge; commit a selfless deed of dire consequence, the act of which includes the engagement of Death." Haven't I already met this request on more than one occasion? How many times must I face death?

I've got to get back to Ravenna and see my family. I'll need a portal to get back... But what if there are none? And where to find one if there are? Now that I've got the key, I've no clue how to use it. It won't be so easy without the witches guiding me. Maybe we could meet in a seance. It might prove impossible but I've got to try to connect with them somehow. His mind rattled. *Is this a remote future—or some distant past? I need a safe place to regroup until I can find a way back to Doth.*

Music playing snapped him out of his head. Three girls sang a ballad broadside, reminding him of Raine, Jillian, and Marlee. Two played guitars, accompanied by a wind instrument that shone like the Pearly-tok. Ten feet up the boardwalk, a blissful blonde woman with an easel painted a beach scene. *Ravenna would enjoy this sunny society,* he thought.

Endless streams of cars drove past the idyllic park. *Still no horses!* The technological culture shock tapped at his cheeks, begging him to be wary. He told himself: *Remain an observer in this strange place.* So, noticing a group of young women come off the beach wearing what appeared to be nothing more than tight, colored underclothes, he observed them much longer than he probably should have. Even for innocent bathing sports, scanty beach apparel was unheard of in 1699. His long curiosity earned more than one harsh look from the bikini clad group. They shamed him off the boardwalk and onto the sidewalk.

After the crosswalk light turned green, he followed a small crowd. They scattered into the art galleries and eateries along Forest Avenue. He dared himself to enter the Candy Baron, where barrels brimmed with saltwater taffy. *What heavenly aromas!* He sniffed the cherry, apple, and maple barrels. His mouth watered. He passed the raspberry, grape, rum, orange, peppermint, pear, and pomegranate. The banana barrel, irresistible. Watermelon, mango, licorice, and coconut, bypassed to smell the mysterious key lime. Catching him elbow-deep in the bubble-gum barrel, a flinty voice summoned him.

"You need to use a basket," she said, looking at his condition, "so we can weigh your taffy at the checkout." A small woven wooden basket found its way into his hands.

"Yes. Of course, please forgive me. It seems my sweet tooth preceded my manners." She glanced at him with a look of disdain, prompting his exit from the shop. Spotting his haggard reflection in a window, he recalled the tatterdemalion from the boardwalk.

This won't do. He ran across Forest Avenue, back toward the beach. Hurrying past a pub, he halted. A news shop's outdoor display stopped him. The wall of colorful magazines hit him all at once. Racks of wild animals, glamorous fashion, gourmet food, guns, guitars, and gadgetry. But he refrained from scrutiny, rushing to round the corner. He hustled in front of the ice cream shop and passed the movie theater, stopping at the corner gas station on the coastal highway. *Too many people, I gotta keep moving, gotta get cleaned up, wash my face.* Cars parked at the station, drivers outside each vehicle, each car with a hose connected to a pump. *So that's how they power them.* Noting the fueling process, he jaywalked across Broadway Street, stopping in front of a window display. *That's nothing new. A timeless tool.* The site of an ordinary shovel eased him. He entered the hardware store, knowing it would hold useful and strange items.

Power saws, clocks, lawnmowers. Modern nails. 20th-century innovations. *So much under one roof.* He looked up. *How is this light emitting from ceiling fixtures? What powers the street lights? The lights on the coaches?* Blood left his brain. Living nine centuries among the mortals of Doth, he thought he'd seen everything. He left, circling the block, lightheaded, before catching a whiff of rich vanilla pipe tobacco. The familiar aroma triggered welcome thoughts of Doth's hearty folk and rugged countryside.

Finally, a familiar place. The room enveloped his nervous system. Inside the quiet smoke shop a stout man enjoyed a robusto cigar at a table for two. A chocolate crocodile skin attache case occupied the chair to his right.

"Do you mind? I've come a long way and need to sit, if just for a moment," Roulic said. The man accommodated, setting his case on the side of his chair.

"A long way can do that," the man agreed.

Roulic tried to ignore his anxiety by watching passersby through the shop's window. Double-checking his vest and coat pockets revealed that his beloved pipe, marked with an "R," was gone.

"It must have fallen out of my vest when I fell into the falls with Mayem," he inadvertently recounted aloud, puzzling the man.

Aside from Alison's charmed bracelet, the pipe was all Roulic had of his beloved Ravenna. The thought of never seeing her again saddened him. He twisted in his chair. The thickset man flashed a nervous look.

"Try this one; it will calm what ails you." With an awkward smile, the man offered a slim cigar. Roulic accepted, having never seen, let alone smoked, a cigar before. The man helped him light the tight-rolled tobacco. Drawing in smoke, he took in too much, distracted by the man's briar-shell butane lighter. He choked, coughing his head off.

"Don't inhale! It's not a cigarette, you know," the man struggled to get out of his chair. He came back with a cold drink from the shop's mini-refrigerator. "Try this. It'll soothe your throat."

"Thank you," Roulic said, knocking his head back. He gulped half the sweet drink, dowsing his dry throat. "Yet another wonder. This bubbly beverage is most pleasing," he said under sugared breath. The eccentric response only further agitated the man. Roulic stared out the big window, sipping his Coke with glazed eyes.

The man leaned over. "Hey buddy, Coca-Cola went global half a century ago. Where'd you fly in from? I don't know how far you've come, but it's 1999 around here."

"1999?!!" Roulic spilled Coke on his knee, then laughed it off, hoping to recover the conversation. "Where did I fly in from?" He chuckled, facing the man. "Oh. Well, the Kingdom of Doth. Ever heard of Doth? Or Dandoorthose? Do people fly in here often?" Within seconds, he'd gone from a peculiar traveler to a laughing nut.

The heavy man lost all tolerance. He grabbed his attache case, got up, and left. But not before barking, "There's a fortune teller *and* an astrology shop up the street. They might be able to help you — but I doubt it."

Roulic's head dropped. He knew he sounded mad. And looked out of the ordinary. *What am I to do? I don't know a soul here and I've nowhere to go.* So, he finished his Coke and walked up the street. *Good gods! It's 1999! I'm three centuries ahead of myself. I hope you know what we're doing, Destiny, because I am completely lost!*

Chapter 2

Olde Fortune Teller

The cigar smoker proved to be right. Up Glenneyre St., he found a vacant astrology shop. Next door, an antique shop with a "resident psychic" sign in the window read: open for business. He entered the Olde Fortune Teller, pleased to find the store of familiar objects. But it was strange to consider them antiques.

A glass case containing Late Renaissance era knives slid open for inspection. He reached for one in particular, a burnished, long-handled dagger. The blade's price tag: $325.00. Its carved ivory pommel, a buxom mermaid, the kind a seafaring desperado like Salty the Slaver might have gripped. He shut his eyes and squeezed the knife handle, imagining the Hurling Gal slicing the sea at full speed. Holding the weapon so consumed him that two minutes passed, forgetting where he was. He stopped at the front desk's 1913 National cash register. A 1905 gold-plated pocket watch shined atop an autographed edition of H.G. Wells's "The Time Machine." He chuckled at the book's title.

"The watch is in need of repair but the book is ready to read." A weathered-looking woman with a warm smile approached him at the register. "May I help you?" Her wrinkles rippled.

"I hope so. That's why I'm here. I need to find someone as soon as possible. An old friend."

"Is this friend still living?" She read his face, navigating his nervousness.

"I don't know. I'm not even sure of their whereabouts. But it's imperative I find them. A matter of life and death, and I'm afraid I haven't much time." His tense tone and tightened face didn't strike her as disingenuous. And yet she winced from a twinge, hiding her gut reaction to his portentous plea.

"My readings are forty dollars per half hour session," she stated. Roulic nodded, handing her a small gold coin, of which she assessed, assayed, and then accepted, despite its dubious origin: *Realm of Doth.*

"Come, sit with me, dear," she said, amid her growing doubt about the stranger. She led him to the back of the shop, past a doorless closet cluttered with vintage boots and frilly jackets. Sacks of used clothing put on boxes of old records stuck out between two filing cabinets. A horseshoe-shaped red leather booth, illuminated by soft light, surrounded a Formica table. Bleeding from a low-volume boom box mounted behind his head, the Rolling Stones sang "Time Waits for No One." He slid into the supple booth, analyzing the eerie lyrics. The fortune teller's jaded face divulged a similar story of glory and gloom.

"One of my favorite grand old songs." She rolled deep set eyes, hinting that wisdom comes in superior ironies. "Hot java or tea?"

"Java, please, that is most kind of you." She disappeared, returning with a hot mug and a burning candle. The leather booth soon smelled of coffee and lilac.

"What is your name, son?"

"Roulic."

"May I read your hands?" He blinked with approval, and extended arms. She turned them over, gazing into his palms. "Have I seen you here before?"

"No, ma'am, you haven't."

The old woman leaned over his arm. She scrutinized his palm before running her thumb and two fingers over his lifeline. "No, I don't think I have..." Goosebumps covered her body as she turned his hand over. Her complexion turned white. "It's withered at the wrist, crosses the hand, loops through all the fingers, and weaves back along the head and heart lines, meeting itself at the wrist." She let go of his hand, her complexion rivaling the shade of her braided gray hair. "Your lifeline wraps around your entire hand."

"A journey written I must travel to reach my fate, I suppose. It is merely the circle of life, like time," he said, referring to the Stones' song.

Leaning back, the fortune teller froze, fixed upon the young man sitting at her booth. It had been decades since she'd encountered any ill-wishers or protesters of her trade. And it wasn't his odd manner, period clothing, or antiquated speech that unnerved her. It was the lifeline circling the entirety of his hand and wrist.

"I wouldn't believe it if I hadn't seen it," the diviner said.

"You wouldn't be the first to see I've got too much time on my hands."

"I've never seen such lines. And I've seen a few." Her face remained in need of color.

"I've either got too much or not enough. That seems to be my fate."

She vacillated, rethinking his getup similar to that of Laguna Beach's Renaissance actors. But the lines around his hands and wrists confounded her as they weren't artificial.

"Are there more of you here now? People with...?" She pointed at her wrist.

"I can't be sure."

"Where did you get those lovely ankle boots? They're absolutely medieval," she said, mindful of her probing.

He peeked at his old brown boots. "A dear friend gave me these," he said, recalling to himself the day he got his new boots, three hundred years ago. "Alastar's more than a friend."

"Are you trying to find Alastar?"

"No. The one I'm looking for is a witch."

"A witch? I see. A witch in Laguna Beach?"

"A *family* of witches, actually. If they're still alive and living together. I'm hoping you might know of them. You're their type of friend. Someone with a unique perception. They are seven sisters, one boy, and their great-aunt and grandmother," he paused, "and a big black cat."

"Hmm, a family of witches, that's most interesting," she said, color returning to her face. Squeezing his hands, she slid out of the red booth.

"I'll be right back. Don't leave; I'm going to make a quick call." She hurried to a hallway, where he heard a door closing.

A 'call.' Okay. But what if she calls someone harmful? Can I trust her? If I leave, I lose an opportunity to find the witches. I'll stay on the ready to run if necessary. Two long minutes passed. He was standing by the shop's front door, examining a dragon tarot deck, when she reappeared.

"I've got good news. A friend of mine knows your family of witches."

"Where, and who, is this friend? I must meet them. It's a matter of…"

"It always is, isn't it?" she said. "He's on his way now. He'll introduce you to them."

"Where? And how far?"

"Not far. They live in town. Up the road, in the canyon. They're well-known here in Laguna." His sigh of relief made her press his hand and ask, "He said they have been expecting you. Are you all right?"

"I'll be all right when time returns me back home and to my love. And for that, I thank you, my dear lady."

"You know, Roulic," she recited, as if from a treatise, "It's as if *time*, that triangular beast put forever in our minds, got caught and captured. Its fleeting existence is bound in both tamed memory and bewildered projection."

"I've not heard it put quite that way. But I agree, you can catch and hold time by dividing and measuring it. Most folks seem to see it that way. Still, there are some who revere time, taking it as the fluid agent of opportunity. Neither here nor there, it exists everywhere, regardless of its form or function."

"We shouldn't live our lives carrying around yardsticks. That's the oldest mind trick, an ancient trap set that few ever escape," she stated.

"Now, that trap I have heard of, but I've never considered it as much of an ancient trap as the trapping of us Ancients."

She didn't pretend to understand his rambling mention of the elder race. "Escaping Time's trap might not depend on where or when you go. *Whenever* you arrive, keep on fighting, regardless of life's uncertainties. Your life decisions are yours to make, and yours alone." He nodded, appreciative of her advice, but mostly her maternal concern.

The Old Fortune Teller's front door swung open. A lanky young man with black hair took off his black sunglasses. He wore Vans checkerboard slip-on shoes, black jeans, and a Crayola-red t-shirt. It promoted a band called "The Strokes."

"Roulic, it's you! They'll be so excited to see you!" he said, bedazzling magnetic velvet-blue eyes.

Roulic stuttered, "Are... are you Jax?"

Jax's laughter had a rich, full quality. "Yes. I am Jax. I know it's been ages since... how are you, Roulic?" They hugged like brothers who hadn't seen each other in a decade. For Jax, it had been three centuries since he had last seen the Ancient. For Roulic, a matter of days had passed since he last saw the child witch.

"But, how did I end up here? That portal on Dandling Oars could have put me anywhere."

"But it didn't. It brought you here. This is where you belong now. C'mon, we've got to go! My sisters are waiting and we've got lots to do. I'll explain it all on the way home."

"Thank you so much, Tarina," Jax turned to the palm reader. "Once again, your service has been impeccable. We cannot thank you enough."

She smiled walking them to the door, baffling the scope of her 'service'. "Nor I you, Jax."

"Time to go, Roulic!" Jax beamed, prodding him out, but Roulic managed to squeeze Tarina's hand before slipping through the door. She tugged the Ancient's hand, this time whispering in his ear. "Love never gives up on its journey—or destination."

Chapter 3

O' Jessamine House

"I'd warn you to put on your seatbelt, but this car has none." Jax opened a windowless door and slid on the worn red leather seat. Roulic mimicked him, settling into the sleek, white roadster. Wire wheels burned rubber, peeling out, but the curvy coach babied up Third Street in first gear before revving up Park Avenue.

"Meet my 1954 Jaguar XK120," the young witch boasted. "I just got her. She'll sing like an exotic orchestra when she hits ninety."

"Ninety, what?" Wind whipped over the windshield, blowing their hair.

"Miles per hour," Jax purred, "and no electronics, just p-u-r-e heaven." Roulic cringed up the winding hill.

"You'll get used to it. We all had to. Automobiles replaced horses a long time ago." Jax shifted into third gear. Roulic took a chance, letting warm California air glide over his arm out the window.

"I've never moved this fast!" he said.

"It's great, isn't it? — the power of a car? A motor fueled by gasoline made from the oil of Earth. Engines power the world, Roulic," Jax stated. Roulic rode exhilarated. *The world has changed so much. Time has sped up. It's as if I've entered a quickening.*

Jax rolled the Jag through the stop sign at the top of Park Avenue.

He veered left on Alta Laguna Street, parking at the dead-end's precipitous lookout. Sweeping views of Catalina Island and the famous little city of Laguna Beach took Roulic's breath away. Tennis courts, a baseball field, and a playground stretched out between the lookout and an Olympic sized soccer field. Hiking and biking trails wove across the crest and back of the city's foothills. They stopped by a bench on a walking trail that circled the park, surrounded by chirpy sparrows and sagebrush.

"Do people play schnaball here?" Roulic considered the wild foothills on the other side of Laguna Canyon Road.

"Yeah. They call it football and soccer, but we haven't seen any gnomes around here."

"Where are we, Jax?"

Jax turned, pointing at the sea. "We're still in the 3rd dimension, on the west coast of a land called America. And...believe it or not, they call this neighborhood Top of the World." Roulic stopped walking. "We are in a new timeline," Jax stated. "Same universe, different world. Think of it as another version of its former self."

"A planetary metamorphosis?" Roulic waxed supernatural.

"Where did you even learn that word?"

"From an old poem."

"Gram put it this way once, 'He uses mojo in sea'... — describing Creator's way of turning infinity into today's and tomorrow's. Heavy stuff, I know."

"I guess time waits for no one. And changes all."

"Time hasn't changed the world as much as people have. Time is merely a space for people's imagination. A space to change things. And a space to make things undone. To *reimagine*. As you well know, once a thought's entertained, it'll stick around as long as it's thought about." Jax enjoyed discussing what he knew Roulic had pondered for centuries.

"You're aching my brain, little brother," Roulic exhaled, shaking it.

"It's all in your head," Jax grinned, "but that's where the real action happens: when you change your mind. Reality lives or dies in the power of our imagination. I hope you know there's a reason we've waited so long for you to get here."

"What reason?" Roulic's head cocked.

"We want you to return to Doth and destroy Mayem," Jax said, watching two squirrels scolding a blue jay. "If you don't, Mayem will destroy Doth. And everyone you love."

"How do you know this? Have you seen the future?"

"I've seen the past," Jax said. "Remember, Mayem still breathes because you brought him into this timeline. We would have killed him, despite the curse, had you not fallen through the gate at the Edge."

"If I go back in time, isn't there a chance he will kill me there and use the key to destroy Doth?"

"There is that possibility. But we won't let that happen to you. Or Ravenna."

"Where is she?" Roulic blazed.

"She's in Doth, waiting for you."

"Where is she right now? I need to know, Jax."

"That, I can't say. We haven't seen her in this timeline. To see her again, you must return to Doth."

Roulic's head lowered. Jax put an arm around his shoulder, "Come on now, Roulic, it's gonna be all right. We've got a plan. I'm taking you to Jessamine." The Ancient One nodded, half relieved and half scared, hoping for the best and preparing for the worst. He braced on the dash of the Jaguar leaving Top of the World, thinking about his return to Doth.

R acing down Park Avenue, Jax sped through Laguna Canyon Road. They pulled onto a gravel road, easing up a steep driveway. A 10-foot-high black wrought iron gate, with gold stars and silver half moons, stopped the Jag. Two lewd, open-mouthed gargoyles leered from either end of the gate, happy to rid runoff from the lot. Jax extended his arm, typed a password into a hidden keypad on the gargoyle, and the gate slowly swung open. Roulic's mouth opened as well, awed by the electrical entry.

"Wait until you get inside her," Jax coasted through the round-about, idling in front of the mansion. Roulic's first impression of Jessamine House was a mesh of canary-yellow flowers and vines. They clung to the home's wraparound porches like aging, needy children.

"How many floors does she have?"

"One for every season." Jax hopped out in a hurry. Roulic followed, grateful to be in the company of a friend.

Her dark exterior held up well with her side-slant roofing, Victorian trim, and stylish oak window frames. Her flamboyant Gothic arches brought an old-world solidity that he found charming. Lofty pines and eucalyptus trees cradled the lot's lush lavender and herb gardens. But it was the monarchs wafting over her tailored railings that led his mind to Gypsy Wynd.

She thwarted Gadbanti with the help of the butterflies. Without her help, would we have escaped the giants? That seems a lifetime ago. Indeed, a world far from this one.

"And now, for the historic tour...," Jax chuckled, opening the wide oaken front door. "Can you believe we've lived here since 1905?" He pointed up at "her chandelier." The foyer led to an airy, circular anteroom perforated by three arched hallways. "That way leads to the master suite—my bedroom," he said. "And that way leads to the living room and den. But this way," he pointed again, "will take you past the Craft Room to our state-of-the-art kitchen. Are you hungry? You must have a giant's appetite," he winked.

"I could eat a horse," Roulic said.

"You'll suffer no such fate," Jax led him into the long hallway. "We offer a fine table where you'll sit and eat a fine meal fit for an Ancient."

Roulic poked his head in the Craft Room. "Ravenna would love those," he said, looking at a row of three Singer sewing machines. Projects lay about the room in various stages, laid out on end tables, chairs, and on the cedar floor. Wood and felt figures. Painted stones. Cloth gnomes. Acrylic scenes in progress. Stained-glass boxes, hearts, frames, stars, birds, and moons nearing completion. Bricks of beeswax beside Tupperware filled with stones, beads, and sandy seashells. A glass grinder on a Husky workbench. And matching the room, its tool-laden, powder-blue pegboard.

Deep in the hall, a long bench upholstered in padded purple velvet hid against the wall in a concealed alcove. A matching alcove hid an 8 x 6-foot mirror hanging in an ornate, foliated frame brushed in gold on the opposite wall. Neither the anteroom nor the kitchen offered a view of the hidden bench and mirror.

"After Gram and Demeter died, they popped in through this mirror, not two months after Marlee bought it. That was during the so-called roaring twenties. It came to us perfectly intact, from some famous magician's estate in India, leaning against this very wall—in this very spot. Scared the life out of Marlee, seeing our departed turn up unannounced in the mirror like that. All my sisters laughed, saying the elders took her unawares just to keep her on her toes.

"Before renovating, we called this 'the kitchen hallway.' Now, because of *this* grand old thing," Jax drummed his fingers on the impressive mirror, "we call it Glassy Hall." Roulic joggled at the ghoulish image of his host shifting in the glass. "Besides our hand mirrors, this is the only mirror in the house. I guess you could say we've become superstitious about what we choose to reflect on. Okay, enough of the secrets, moving on to Jessamine's legendary kitchen! Let's get you fed."

The mansion's busiest room, although over 100 years old, remained august and elegant. As with all quarters of the residence, the witches spared no expense restoring its quaint Victorian flourishes. Alison and Agnes renovated the room in fits of fury, taking great pride in their handiwork. They lovingly refurbished its courtly, freestanding honey oak cabinets, installed white jasmine Corian countertops, checkerboard flooring, and a matching island with antique barstools. Modern amenities, like filtered water and the concealed luminescence of under-cabinet lighting, intrigued Roulic as much as their electric can opener and meat thermometer. The contemporary kitchen well served the family, their old mahogany table reflecting the grandeur of Jessamine.

"This is our 1952 Wedgewood; it's a white porcelain double gas oven, see?" Jax demonstrated the magic of natural gas, turning on all the knobs, heating up the stovetop with blue flames. Roulic stepped back, delighted. "And this is our 1966 Sunbeam toaster. We burn bread in it every day. Oh, and this fine appliance," he said, pointing to the stainless steel French door refrigerator, "it's our latest and greatest. We just got it a week ago."

"What's in there? I mean, I have an idea, but..."

"Go ahead, open it. See what's inside," Jax said. Roulic pulled out the bottom drawer, numbing his fingers in the freezer compartment.

Among frozen steaks, ground beef, chicken, and pork products, he chose the ½-gallon container of chocolate ice cream.

"Dare to try a chocolate shake?" Jax was met with nodding puppy eyes. "Good choice. Okay, let me show you how this works." Jax had him retrieve milk, a bottle of chocolate syrup, and a can of Reddi-Wip. They stood around an old Beehive blender until the shake got thick. Roulic didn't say too much besides, "Ooh, that looks good." Tasting it, he uttered, "Yum," several times and requested more whipped cream on top. After their shakes, Jax slid a plate across the table. Roulic reclined in the corner chair, his back against the wall, devouring a microwaved bowl of Progresso New England Clam Chowder and a pile of Ritz crackers.

"I can't thank you enough, Jax."

"You're too easy, old friend." Jax put the bowl in the dishwasher, saying, "It's good to have you back."

"Your great-aunt Demeter was kindly to me. Have you seen her lately? In the mirror?"

"Last night, actually. She's been waiting for your arrival as much as we have."

Jessamine's hallway, running between the dining room and kitchen, ended in a seven-step stairwell. When the sisters rushed to the kitchen, the hardwood stairs sounded the flock's flurry; a stampede corralled like swans in a broken-pen-roundup.

"Roulic!" They reunited, taking turns hugging him in bursts of girlish glee. After all, it had been three hundred years since they'd seen him. Agnes and Madelyn fought for either side of the Ancient. Raine, Jillian, and Marlee followed, spilling into their chairs. The kitchen became a curious six-cat circus. Family familiars paraded, performing acrobatics and meowing from their counters. Even Jax's new Harlequin Lionhead rabbit joined in. But when Aurora entered, the felines and hare calmed in an eerie syntony. All eyes landed on the loveliest of them all. She wore a short, purplish dress, her trademark look, and a camellia flower in her hair. Having learned to accept fascinated looks, she felt appreciated for her beauty rather than annoyed by the attention. But today, she fixed *her* eyes, eager to let the Ancient presence enthrall her.

"It's so good to see you again, free from the perils of Everlan!" she said.

"I'm not so sure about my freedom. Or perils. I may be in a dream that never ends," he embraced her, struck by the look of liberation swimming across her face. It was far from the distraught visage he'd seen, immersed, ashen in the pools of Everlan.

"Perhaps our dreams never do end. Perhaps they only continue," Aurora whispered, a tear in her eye, "Welcome to our home, dear Roulic." Several sisters raised their arms to the ceiling in praise of the reunion.

Marlee, the family's high priestess, entranced him, "Close your eyes, Roulic." He obeyed, immediately delighting at multicolored feathers, floating before his mind's eye. Their glissade released a trailing band of hues from baby pink to fern green. *Green as the forests of Everlan*, he thought.

"Are you viewing this as well?" his eyes scrunched.

"Yes, we are," Marlee said. "Lovely, isn't it?"

"It makes me think of home."

"It is home. Now, tell us what else you see."

"I see a magnificent tree. And a radiant grapevine circling its trunk."

"That would be our kindred; those of us who are thriving here, there, and everywhere," Marlee said. "The tree is a living image of our home, whether it be here or in Everlan." It made him think of Everlan's countryside.

"It's beautiful," he said. *But why are they showing me this? Am I under a spell?*

Without thinking, he opened his eyes. The nexus split and Everlan vanished, the vision replaced by watery eyes set in a cherub-like face he had never seen before. And with kind blue eyes, but so close to Roulic's, that he jumped back. The women laughed.

"Don't be afraid, Forby won't bite you," Marlee chortled.

"I didn't mean to startle you, nose to nose like that. I'll wait outside, by the trees..." the lean gentleman apologized.

"Oh, nonsense!" Marlee said. "Roulic, meet Mr. Nagnee, Jessamine's one and only groundskeeper. Forby's lived most of his life here. He's been tending the grounds since his tenth birthday."

"That was the day we dubbed him our 'Charming Gardener'. In 19?..." Raine hesitated.

"—43," Agnes stated.

"January, I believe it was," Madelyn wagered.

"It was the 11th," Jillian clarified.

Marlee continued, "O' Jessamine House, our chosen abode,—like us, she's a bit of patchwork. Part Queen Anne, part Spanish, and part Italian—most of her renovation completed after Jillian came home. *But*, as you've not a clue as to these goings-on, I will bore you no more. Relax and get settled. Tonight, we'll discuss your next steps. Roulic, will you invite Mr. Nagnee to show you around outside?" He nodded. "I'm sure you'll find him quite helpful. Enmeshed as we are in this revolving quandary, we need all the help we can get." She gestured, walking the men across the hallway into the dining room.

H e followed Mr. Nagnee out of the dining room's sliding glass door. Marlee closed the slider on the long, wide patio of herb and rock gardens. Dotting the space were round glass tables, leisure chairs, and cantilever umbrellas.

"I understand you've come a long way," said the stoic Nagnee.

"My head is still spinning," Roulic said, noticing gray sprouts in the gardener's stubbled chin. "And the clock is still ticking." Nagnee pulled a verdant leaf from his breeches and handed it to him.

"Chew on this mint. It will settle your nerves."

"No, thanks. The last time I tried that, I ended up having a long conversation with myself."

"Have you got the key?" Nagnee's hand sprang from his pocket, palm open.

"Yes, why?"

"See that lil ol' well?" Nagnee pointed to a pile of dirty red bricks in the shade of a mulberry tree.

"Yes," he answered, espying a colony of webs presiding over the bricks.

"Jillian and I planted that tree to complement the old pit."

"That's nice," Roulic said.

"You and I are going in there," Nagnee said.

"I'm not going in there." Roulic became clear.

Nagnee's blue eyes pierced, "You will if you wish to see Ravenna." Roulic quickly produced and presented the Pearlytok to Mr. Nagnee, who brushed it aside.

"*You* hold the key, but don't let go of my hand until we're out of the portal. By my hand, we will land in a stable place."

Roulic looked back on the way to the well, sizing up the stature of the maturing residence. "They sure have waited for this moment a long time, haven't they?"

"More than any of us would care to admit, sir," Nagnee said.

"Well, I guess this is it. May good luck be with us a day longer than we need it," he looked back at Jessamine, his head spinning at how fast things were moving.

"Good and ready. Let's go."

No sooner had they dangled their legs into the old well than a white light shot from the damp hollow. A thicker beam of similar cast followed the former's path into the hanging shrubs. The portal became visible, drawing a thin curtain around them. Eyes went black. Seconds later, the curtain opened. The well vanished, and they were beside a creek beneath a ponderous canopy of conifers. When they walked from the spot, the portal began sealing itself in a mist.

"I know this place," Roulic said, exhilarated in the heart of the forest. "I've been here before." He leapt onto the embankment of a road winding above the creek. Mr. Nagnee nodded, moving toward a neat stack of stones set beside an ailing trunk. From the road, Roulic watched him stop at the marker and treat the distressed bark using an oily ointment from a small glass jar.

He must be making his rounds. Treating this forest as his own. Strange...

The Ancient's world broke when a doe bolted from a thicket. Hearing the sound of pounding hooves, Nagnee called out, "You can't talk to her now. If you do, you'll upset the timeline and may never see her again."

Roulic jumped off the road. Crouching against the steep bank, he poked his head up to peek over the leaves when she came through. He refused to blink. He wanted to catch every motion of her being, to see her face, alive and well. And the stalwart eyes he fell in love with on the Bridge of Belief.

Is there any part of her that senses me?

She fleeted like a dream, in a gust of rustling leaves. Her long red cape and cocoa brown boots passed so close he could have reached out and touched them. But she didn't see him. She focused fiercely on the path, galloping on her beloved Arrow. He reached for his stomach, flipping like a fish out of water, his heart banging like a drum, returning to Mr. Nagnee.

"Where was she going?"

"She was going to meet *you*. That is why you can't see her today."

"Why did you bring me here? If I can't be with her now, I want to leave. Can't you bring us *together* in time?"

"That all depends," Nagnee said.

"On what?"

"If you are a prisoner or a fugitive. We are all prisoners of time but fugitives fight back," Nagnee said, shaking a fist. "First you fight Mayem, then you'll find Ravenna. Now, follow me. And don't look back."

They stopped at the creek's end; where the forest met the mountainside. Sunrays splintered across the sleek slope and falling water. Across the sky peaked the proud cap of the highest mount in all of Doth: Grand Pekoes. Loftier than his father's eminent refuge at Merelands. Looping the mountain, a valley river wrenched its magnific base like a liquid serpent. Treacherous dunes, rife with snakes and cactus, faithfully courted the river's pneumatic turns.

"Remember this cradle in the trees; its window is just a few miles from the dragon's keep; where the gods created the first of their kind. Should you pass here again, be thankful for even the slightest graduation, for the steps behind you will have been well earned."

Nagnee's advice triggered him to a fruitful anamnesis: *Alastar had spoken of the value of graduation.*

"The Masters split the Realm in two, then created spaces here and there as gateways to graduate from realm to realm."

Alastar's elucidation stirred his speculative mind. *Is there a connection between portals and our journey through time and space?* He took it all in, pondering the meaning of Nagnee's advice, Alastar's explanation, and the looming alp.

Across the creek, the conscientious caretaker crafted a wreath from a leafy vine. Two chunky squirrels scrambled onto a mossy rock halving the stream. They froze, staring at Nagnee from the stone, then scurried, splattering water on Roulic's boots.

"Nagnee, have I been here before?"

Mr. Nagnee blessed the wreath before tossing it into the water. Golden light spilled between the evergreens, nurturing the moist forest floor. "You'll be scaling Grand Pekoes soon enough. It's time to go forth now."

"Forth? Or back?"

"Forth, Roulic, always forth. Now, take my hand." He took Nagnee's hand and held the Pearlytok in his other hand, stepping into the amber shafts of forest light. The chance of reuniting with Ravenna made his stomach flutter and his heart race.

S urging through the portal as fast as thunderbolts, they landed dizzy, two yards from the witches' well. Across the patio, a beguiling woman, whose fine features rivaled the arresting qualities of Aurora, reclined in a high-back rattan chair. She studied his approach like a cat wanting to play. He shook his head, pocketing the Pearlytok. *Who is she?* Her sensuous stare challenged him, especially when their eyes met up close. But as her worldly gaze remained, he looked elsewhere, taking in the shiny auburn hair spilling to the elfin waist. A prick in his chest, a pang of guilt tolled for thinking a thing he shouldn't. She reveled in the torment coming from his obvious brown eyes. Hers; an alluring caramel color, getting creamy during the melt-up.

"I've been waiting for you," she said.

"Well, here I am," he said, not knowing what else to say. "Mr. Nagnee has brought me back all in one piece. Please forgive my green face. It seems I'm in need of a quiet corner."

"By all means, sir," Nagnee said, "Lilith will show you to your room." Nagnee bowed his head and left. He disappeared along the side of the house through a blue picket gate laced with pink rambling roses.

"For a lifelong gardener, that man seems to know a lot about the ways of the woods," he said.

"Forby's more than a man. He's a king. King of the forest," her eyes batting, "our regal ruler of gardens at Jessamine."

"Do you live here as well?" He asked the safest question he could think of.

"I do," she said, leading him by the hand toward the sliding door. "The witches took me in some time ago—during 'Yule', as they call it. They pulled me from *that* Gehenna; countless seasons accompanying Arthur in his never-ending toil with Time. Had they not, I'd still be the casual companion of that wandering beast."

"Beast?"

"100% male. Mr. Black is a busy rover, always looking for a better time."

Madelyn and Agnes cut Lilith's rant short. "Time for supper, Roulic!" they tittered in tandem, squeezing through the patio sliding glass door.

"And just what is so funny about that?" Lilith grilled the sisters' frivolity with a po-faced expression.

"Oh, nothing. We were just laughing about something," Agnes said.

"Come, Roulic, join us for supper. We've so much to catch up on," Madelyn said.

"Thank you. I will join you after a much needed nap; I promise."

"All right, but don't nap too long," they smiled, tottering off.

"You must be exhausted," Lilith said. "Follow me." She led him, gliding up the creaky stairs without making a single creak. "Those two are always up to something, cackling up a storm."

"I'm sure they could if they wanted to," he said.

"Oh, they could." She opened the first door of three along the second-floor hallway. "You'll find peace in this room. Unless the brats plot otherwise." She lit a tea light candle and set it in front of his bedside lamp. After he took off his boots, she put them at the foot of the oak and walnut four-poster bed. "Sleep well, Roulic."

"Thanks, Lilith," he said from the bed, watching her back out of the room and close the door with sultry eyes. Her combination of angst and beauty had disarmed him. So, he reminded himself she could only ever imitate Ravenna's complete beauty.

Lilith seems a troubled soul. Restless. And what of this Arthur Black? That will have to wait. His goal of returning to Ravenna was foremost on his mind and he didn't want to think about confronting Mayem, at least for a few hours.

Under his pillow, he found and skimmed a worn-out paperback book called Practical Magic. He fell asleep in minutes, dreaming of the same woods Mr. Nagnee had shown him an hour prior.

Creeping along a trickling brook, he followed the old gardener. Two does bolted, leaping across the nettled path above the stream. "Ravenna! Where are you? Ravenna?" Roulic chased the deer through the mist, never finding her. Returning, he found Nagnee had altered; his coarse chin hair had grown a yard. Roulic shouted from a safe distance. "Take me back, Nagnee!" The long beard touched the forest floor when the hideous jaw dropped, showing off chiseled teeth and forbidding fangs. Sweat rolled from Nagnee's swelling forehead, wetting his expanding brow.

"Nagnee! Come back!" Roulic howled in horror. Dropping to his knees, the morphing creature reverted to the groundskeeper's angelic face. The wild features melted like ice in a fire. However, the reborn Nagnee hadn't freed his transmogrifying host. It transmuted him into a shaggy white dog. Roulic extended his hand and took the dog's paw.

"I know you, but you aren't Nagnee."

The captive dog spoke, uttering in guttural distortion, "You'll never go forth. You'll only go back."

Roulic ran to the forest's edge and settled on a slab of rock. He pondered the peak beyond the valley. The white dog followed, curled up, and fell asleep beside him. The nightmare broke when the white dog stood on its hind legs and barked.

Chapter 4

The Circle Room

"Time to wake up, my love," Lilith whispered, tugging his sleeve, "you've missed both dinner and dessert. The family's upstairs in the Circle Room, waiting for you.." The white dog vanished. Lilith hovered, her satin robe brushing his ear. She led him to the landing on the fourth floor. He expected her to enter with him but she twisted on the last stair, "Whither thou goest I cannot."

A stranger day I cannot remember, he thought, trying to push her out of his mind. He nodded at her, anxious to see the fourth floor.

His first impression of the Circle Room wasn't exactly what he expected: *It's a witch's museum dripping with motley things and hermetic color.* Lit displays featuring odd masks, elaborate wands, and colored crystal balls blazoned the room, as did open trunks containing various weathered weaponry: daggers, spears, guns, ammunition, and even a small cannon, although no part of the prismatic room smelled of death or decay. The entire floor smelled alive, like a queen's garden. And there were no less than four designated areas of the room, he noted, that held the trappings of spent candles and the like, his general expectation of ritual magic, the practice of which he knew little.

. . .

"Welcome to the Circle Room," Marlee introduced, "where chaos can be transformed into order..." His eyes widened, affected by the scope of the spiraling room.

"We replaced the original walls with these helical panels and partitions before Jillian's last return," she said. As chief guide, she walked him through the floor, explaining how its rectangular symmetry was aimed at capturing 'the essence of the divine proportion.'

"Nooks for all," Jillian said. "And not as cramped as our old farmhouse at Black Shadows beach."

"Has mortalkin ever caught a glimpse of it?"

"Oh, yes, many a student. Times have changed, even for our kind," Jillian informed.

The sisters took turns explaining each exhibit in the multifaceted room. Jax sat aloof, comfortable behind Gram's old birch desk in an open corner office by the landing. He checked the price of gold: $283.40 oz. and made after-hours stock market trades in the light of earthen oil lamps. Studying three 15-inch flat-panel monitors, his disinterest in Marlee's tour wasn't because of boredom. After all, he knew everything she would say. But he had work to do. He'd overseen the family's investments and financial affairs since they moved to Jessamine House. If he hadn't taken over, they would have lost the house, his sisters always managing to spend more money than they had.

"The cats abhor this room," Jillian said. "Can't stand the Calla Lily. So, they never pass the third floor unless they dare climb gutters or vines to reach the fifth."

"There's a fifth floor?"

"Technically, no. But the cats come and go as they please. The sky's the limit where there isn't a roof."

Roulic thought about her explanation, wondering if the cats of Jessamine flew off into the night sky from the rooftop. *That would explain a lot. Natric would be privy to this mode of travel.*

Reaching the far corner of the mazelike room, Roulic discovered a familiar pleasantry: that of an eclectic collection of esoteric books and literature, neatly sheltered in a row of three Victorian bookcases set on matching oak cupboards against the wall. Scented candles graced the end tables of two sofas and four chairs, the little library giving off the congenial warmth he last enjoyed at Meyrick's castle the night he brought Ravenna home. In a cozy step-down beneath the floor's parquet de Versailles motif, he found a triad of intertwining pentacles inlaid with bands of silver detailed with tiny crystals and gems set into the oaken flooring.

"I'm taken aback. Jessamine is wondrous."

"She's been good to us," Raine said, "and we are ecstatic living here. We've put ourselves into her hearth."

"Fond of these?" He pointed to nine two-foot long planter boxes set on wooden legs. They lined the low wall where three large stained-glass windows, overlooking the patio, let light in over the planters, each box brimming with yellow Calla Lilies.

"We give these to newcomers during new moon gatherings," Marlee said.

"—Our favorite flower for ages," Raine said.

"They remind us of ourselves," Aurora said.

"Born to live and die, and be reborn," Alison said.

"There's no end to it," he agreed, perusing the collection of herbs, potions, cauldrons and broomsticks.

"Is it true, as the priests claim, that you ride on these?"

"Take your pick," Marlee tendered. "On All Hallows Eve? On Sabbath's and full moons? Or when hexing and vexing?"

"I'm afraid to ask."

"Don't be silly. We display these artifacts to educate about bygone days," she lingered, "but there was a time when..."

Madelyn cut in, "When people stereotyped us — marked us as wicked beings — they killed us off, one by one, two by two, as you well know and remember. Many times in droves. Only because we were different and they were afraid. But here, we've stopped hiding, and in recent decades, spoken out against the witch-hating madness. Our efforts have led to a growing community, in this violent place, —a community learning to accept our kind."

"It's been a good era," Agnes remarked. "For the craft. The dawn of a new age beckons, full of unexplored possibilities." She pulled a small stone from a stitched pocket on her white summer smock. "Take this with you Roulic, it will ease your journey."

"It's a pretty one."

"It's called fancy jasper, and it brings both passion and courage to its holder." Grateful for Agnes' help, he squeezed the stone and put it in his pocket. He saw on their faces a century of hardship and joy he knew nothing about, yet thought only of himself.

Falling into that portal on Dandling Oars robbed me of three hundred years. Three hundred years away from Ravenna.

"Will you help me get back to Doth? And the Pearlytok back to the gnome king in Trumbleton Wells?"

"Yes, but first you must kill Mayem." Marlee's words silenced the room.

Roulic tensed hearing what he knew the witches would ask of him. He knew Mayem was searching 1999 for the Pearlytok and would hunt him until he got it. Only by going back in time to kill Mayem could he break the curse and reverse the war started 300 years ago.

"So, you're sending me back to 1699? To Mayem's fortress on Dandling Oars island?"

"No. You must go to the Bridge of Belief in 1649. To the time when Mayem curses Ravenna. But the hour to the gate is getting late. The portal's window is closing in this timeline. You must enter it by tomorrow night."

Chapter 5

The Froth of Life

"Shouldn't I rescue Ravenna first? Before killing Mayem?"

"No," Marlee said. "You must kill him *after* he binds her to the bridge. He won't know you are tracking him. You'll ambush him and his men near Aspired Mountain."

"Or die trying and never see her again."

"Try to reimagine your ideas about the word never. At no time have we not been meticulous in determining when to eliminate Mayem, as it stands today — just after he cursed Ravenna on the bridge."

"Cursed? Or curses?" Roulic addled.

"Both," Marlee said. "If he hadn't already, you wouldn't be here now; Your pact with Aurora would never have required you to rescue Ravenna in the first place."

"Why wait to drag Ravenna out from beneath a bridge!? Why keep Alison in exile, Aurora mirrored in the pools of Everlan?" Roulic steamed. "Why didn't you kill him after he killed your..?" Tongue tied, he couldn't finish his sentence. Alison and Aurora gazed into his eyes. Gentle voices entered his head. Waves of strange words crisscrossed his mind that he couldn't decipher, yet the solemn message was clear, sent in soft tones through his pituitary gland. The irreformable realization passed through the left side of his brain and lodged, pulsing at the center of his heart:

What must be, must be done. What must be undone, must be done.

He snapped out of their trance. "What becomes of me—the other me? The one questing to the Bridge of Belief riding on the back of Ally?"

"As long as you rescue Ravenna before he does, your paths shouldn't ever cross. He can search the Inner Realm for his family, but he'll never hear of witchcraft on Mt. Nocturne. Destiny will never send him to Aurora to break a curse you've already broken. You had to go through it all to get to a certain point in time where you won't ever have to go through that again. Arthur made sure of that. You'll be able to stay with Ravenna and live out your lives, as the curse will die the day Mayem dies. And all of this, this 1999, will become a much different place."

"How long has this been going on, Marlee?"

"We don't know. Or care. To us, knowing that number is nugatory." Of all the siblings, Jillian, Marlee and Jax were the only ones who kept journals chronicling negligible but often strange and sometimes consequential effects occurring in their timelines.

"What *would* happen should I encounter my former self in my new life with Ravenna?"

"Peculiar consequences, one might think. Welcome to our compelling conundrum."

Marlee looked out the stained-glass windows above the lilies. The witches turned as well, leaving Roulic at their backs, their reflections taller in the colored glass. The room went quiet again. Marlee turned with urgent eyes. "Mayem's reign of terror will devastate Doth unless you go back and kill him, so let's rid the world of him together."

His breathing slowed processing Marlee's warning. Failing the realm, losing Ravenna, and his family, only reinforced the weak moment. His head fell.

Agnes took his hand. "Come, Roulic, let us ascend to fresh air."

"I could use some," he said, lifting his head. "Your lilies are taking my breath away."

Agnes led him up the right wing of the room's bifurcated staircase. Either wing led up to a ceiling landing where a redwood banister circled the roof. Decorated in colored chalk, a wide pentacle covered the roof's center .

"So this is where you make it rain these days?" he joked.

"Yes, it is," Agnes said, fondly recalling how in 1699, Aurora's gift of watercraft brought a great storm upon Mount Nocturne, all the while being distant, cursed, and bound to the pools of Everlan. Until the day Mayem fell from the Edge on Dandling Oars Island. That day, of Aurora's splendid release and the epic flight of dragons, the Black family hailed as pivotal to their navigation of time.

"Would you care for another demonstration?" she telegraphed, tapping her amulet necklace.

"Do your worst, little sister. But remember, I weathered the last storm you threw at me, as bad as it was," he volleyed back.

"How 'bout I draft a less devastating, more suitable example?" Agnes said. Before he could respond, she raised her palms to the sky, sang two indiscernible words to the heavens, and swung her arms to the ground like a windmill in a hurry. Wind whistled over the roof. He bemused when she caught an airy bounty of eucalyptus leaves followed by drops of rain.

Emerging from the dark, a figure appeared amid the jested wind and wet, chuckled leaves, sliding along the roof's railing. Roulic's hands closed and clenched as the figure slid closer. Marlee dropped her minty leaves and reached for his hand, releasing from the handrail a well dressed, well-kept, aging man.

"Roulic, meet Arthur Black, our gentleman on the inside. He can bring you to Everlan."

Their hands met in the moonlight, Roulic unsurprised by the firm grip coming from the quivering hand. Arthur moved slower than the swift Nagnee, yet carried himself with an air of joviality. He wore a fine black suit, powder blue shirt, carried a carved brown cane, and wore a beaver fur hat that leaned to the left.

"But, I thought Mr. Nagnee..." Roulic started.

Agnes shook her head. "Mr. Nagnee took you out for a ride. Arthur, —Arthur can show you the world. A world only Arthur knows."

"The *only* world Arthur knows." Lilith strolled over the roof, vixen-ish, in her amaranth-red cotton summer dress. She carried a black hoodie for the rippling evening breeze. Sensing confrontation, the startled witches reacted by forming a half-circle around her. Mr. Black receded into the shadows, keeping eye's on the dress. Roulic kept his eyes on the circle of sisters. *The tension between Lilith and my seven wary witches is a telling testament to her power..*

Alison spoke up in defense of Mr. Black, "The only world he needs, or wants, to know."

Lilith recited, for Roulic's benefit, what the witches were well aware of. "Arthur has chosen his path. He's spent lifetimes altering the lives of others and not even the Fates know where he will land. Then again," she faced the railing, "His artistry in the field of portal jumping is nothing short of lionhearted. All on this roof lauds Arthur's dedication to exploring the vast immeasurable: time; The froth of life that..."

"Unites us," Alison said, taking offense to Lilith barging onto the fifth floor.

"Who knows where it begins or ends?" Lilith said. "Frankly, I don't care anymore. I want the best for you, Roulic,—and Arthur, too. Fortunately, time is on both your sides.

"Arthur's the world's greatest portalist," Aurora said. "He knows the way to Everlan better than anyone. He'll show you the ropes."

"That's right," Jillian's green eyes flickered. "I can't tell you how many times Arthur brought me to where I needed to be."

"To Callian?" Roulic ventured.

"Yep. To Callian," she said, her eyes becoming moist. "Arthur appeared when the risks of returning became overwhelming. He guided me for years, each time holding my hand, as we said our goodbyes."

"But not forever, Jill," Madelyn lifted the conversation.

"No, sister. Not forever. This is true." Jillian said.

"Speaking of forever, this is exactly why we've brought Arthur to the equation," Aurora said. "I assure you he will take precautions on your behalf, for your safety and that of the mission," Aurora said.

A kaleidoscope of anxieties rolled in Roulic's cranium. For one,— *Why are they trying so hard to instill my confidence in his expert abilities?*

This question caused a collision among the dominos of doubt assembling inside his head.

"That's reassuring," he said, "but what happens to Doth if something goes wrong?"

"Something has already gone wrong, seriously wrong." Aurora took the tone he'd heard at the pools of Everlan. "In this timeline, dragons no longer exist as we knew and loved them in Doth. They've never been. They only exist in our memories. Here, the dragons have been reduced to that of mythical creatures, their legacy hidden, their history rewritten as unbelievable creatures, only briefly mentioned in ancient history books."

"Ancient, indeed," Arthur said. "Pardon me, the wind has caught up with me. I've been standing in that dark corner, waiting to speak to..." The group on the roof froze in respect, except Madelyn and Agnes, who nodded in praise to the sound of his solid steps.

"Roulic," his eyes shined, "your biggest concern shouldn't be 'what could go wrong?' For when it comes to humming the tones of time, it is a matter of 'what pitch?' that decides who sings the song. Better to wade a thousand seas in harmony, than to drown in dissonance, never to reach an island of notable melody." A brisk wind blindsided the house, grating a pine bough against Jessamine's sleek backside, the wailing pine scratching her, indelibly.

The sisters crowded around Arthur when he said, "Goodnight. My apologies for being so blunt. Tomorrow will be quite a journey and..."

"Of course," Agnes said, gingerly walking with him, arm in arm. "It's been a big day. You can go over details with Roulic in the morning. Jax will see you to your room." Arthur nodded and shook Roulic's hand a second time, bidding him a good evening.

"Silver sand on golden shores awaits the vigilant heart." He smiled and turned toward the landing. Left behind, Roulic wondered. *His speech carries an air of the Old One's with yet another nod to Alastar. He spoke about vigilance using the exact phrase. I wonder if the two ever met? What is Arthur trying to tell me?*

Jax bound up the stairway to escort Arthur to his room, across from Alison's, on the third floor. "Goodnight, uncle Arthur, I love you,"

Madelyn whispered. The witches retired, leaving Roulic and Lilith alone on the roof.

"Uncle Arthur?"

"Oh, yes," Lilith stated. "Their paternal uncle. Arthur is a pure witch, too, but he never took to the family's quixotic form of wizardry, as did his brother, Frane, who spent his life conjuring 'for the good of Doth'. Their paternal grandfather, Fraser, passed down that legacy. After the girls were born, Frane and Damira wasted no time in teaching their babies to practice the family craft. By the time Captain Salty killed them, the girls were well aware of their inherent abilities. Gram and Demeter have guided them ever since."

"So, Arthur isn't adept in the ways of magic?"

"Oh, he is, but he rarely calls on Spirit as the others do. His unique gift enables him to change vibration at will. That's why it's so easy for him to navigate the portals. He can manipulate frequency and vibration using his mind. His mind over exotic matter."

"That explains the grand reception," Roulic said, sharing the night sky, beside Lilith.

"No one in the family can jump like Arthur," she lit a long menthol cigarette but didn't smoke it. "But what you witnessed has more to do with the family denying the decline of his gift than it does boasting the prowess of his past. Not one of them would talk about it until I made them."

"This sounds serious," he said.

"It is. All of Arthur's troubles started after the Blacks moved to Jessamine. He and I were far from here, over the eastern sea, visiting a town called Winchester. He read about the biggest ship of its day and booked an opulent cabin for us during its maiden voyage to America. It sunk four days into our trip. Only a few survivors are still alive. I thank God the Carpathia rescued our lifeboat and brought us to America. Luckily, authorities counted us 'lost at sea' because Arthur used fake identities to board us on the ship. Smart witch. So, we disappeared in New York City. Arthur had to sell his watch for food until he could find us a portal. We made it home, three days later, penniless."

"Was your portal jump home affected?"

"No. But he's never been the same since. It wasn't long before we found ourselves at the wrong place in the wrong time."

"My biggest fear," said the Ancient.

"He nearly froze that night, enduring the cold sea," she stared at the stars. A chill set into his bones that he's never been able to get over. That's why he's always bundled up. His jumps never were prone to mishap, missing the mark either in time or place, until the Titanic sunk in 1912."

"Should I be worried about tomorrow?" Roulic's brow lifted.

"You don't have to go tomorrow. They'll find another gate and window. They always do." She put her hand on his. "It would give us time to..."

"It would give Mayem time to find me. I've got to go before this window closes. Get him before he gets me."

"I know, it's what you men do. Run back and forth. I wouldn't worry too much about Arthur. With your heart and his touch, I'm sure the two of you'll make it to your promised land in one piece. Arthur lives to ride and guide. He's a born protector." The ash on her unsmoked cigarette had grown long, so she took a puff and put it out.

"A *Protector*? As in the ways of the Ancients?" Roulic perked up.

"No, not so much. But he did adopt the ways of Frane and Fraser, years after *they* took the vow of Lycus."

"I'm listening," Roulic said, avoiding her eyes. Windswept branches continued to rub against Jessamine, breaching another layer of paint.

Lilith put on her hoodie and moved closer, speaking softly. "In the nomadic days before countries and kings, Lycus excelled in tending dogs." She lit another cigarette, smoking *too much*, he thought. "He traveled vast areas, acquiring, breeding, and tending a great many dogs—balky dogs admired for their strong-willed nature and unique hunting skill. But when his dogs started disappearing he, unwittingly, led the pack straight to the wolves of Smeringal. At least that's how the story goes."

"Dogs against wolves? Doesn't sound fair," Roulic said.

"It wasn't. The Smeringal wolves were a united tribe of many wolf packs. They dominated the high woods until food sources became exhausted. That's when they took to hunting in the lowlands, and took on the dogs."

Lilith's sprightly manner and vigorous speech enthralled him. *She's a volatile mix; throwing her inimical disposition alongside the temperate witches.* Nevertheless, he enjoyed listening to her, and catching her sheeny eyes, like meteoric suns, when he thought she wouldn't notice him looking.

"Lycus never wanted conflict with the wolves. He knew they were a much stronger force. But when his dogs got caught in a terrible storm, he sheltered them in a cavern that ran along a riverside. In wolf country." Sadness dimmed her face, the sheen in her eyes.

"It was there, at the great cave, when the Smeringal wolves attacked the dogs. All of Lycus' dogs entered the cavern, but none came out alive. The wolves waited along the river for them to come out and fight. When they didn't, the wolves provoked them at the edge of the cave. One by one, the wolves lured the dogs out." She flicked her rose gold Zippo lighter twice to accentuate her story, dropping it next to a clay ashtray on the redwood railing. Casually squashing her cigarette butt, its little cherry perished beneath a final plume blown over their heads.

"What happened to Lycus?"

"After watching his last dog meet a terrible death, he ran out of the cave with twin spears, killing the oldest male and female in the pack. The younger wolves didn't dare attack while their parents were fighting."

"Leaders perished at the hand of his rage, and yet their offspring didn't retaliate?"

"One did, and was defeated. After killing the elders, the next wolf in line attacked him, but in his exaltation, Lycus' strength became that of a god. He made a violent example, before the entire tribe, by squishing that wolf's skull. This terrified the wolves and earned him their respect.

"Many of the wolves sympathized, hearing the moans of Lycus over the slain bodies. His grieving carried on, joined by the mourning wolves, howling for their loss and that of their canine cousins. By dawn he had won them over. And as the sun came up, he transformed into a magnificent alpha wolf. That's how Lycus became the leader of the Smeringal wolves."

"That's quite a story. And his vow?" Their eyes met like a falling fire. "The vow goes like this."

> *Nevermore shall I turn from wandering wolves, restless*
> *dogs, or banshees on the move*
> *In deep caves, I will meet howls and wails, defying the*
> *bottomless bale*
> *With eminent repose, I will guide the wayward and the*
> *righteous*
> *whose meek account doth humble my toll; to heed cries of*
> *the lost, in heart or soul*

"So, Arthur took an oath on behalf of the lost and lonely?" He said, taken by her recitation.

"He did. He vowed to help people who get lost in their lives and find themselves in a corner. People who don't know whether to stay or go."

She grabbed his hand and led him inside, to the warmth and sanctity of the Circle Room's far end. Gram's old 4-bell grandfather clock chiming midnight announced their entrance into the library. Lilith turned, pulling the chain on a Tiffany table lamp, wishing he'd see the secret in her eyes.

"The question remains: What vow will you uphold?"

Chapter 6

A Thing Thrice Said

"Not a witch in sight," she said, settled in the library's step-down on a pile of luxuriant throw pillows. "I ask again, my love, what are you going to do?" He said nothing. "Why let those old hags keep telling you what to do? You're a big boy. You've made it this far on your own. Can't you see they just want to get their hooks in you to do their bidding? That's what they've been doing all along."

He didn't like hearing Lilith speak against the witches. All his doubts aside, he didn't want to hear what he had long avoided to consider. Since meeting Aurora at Dragonfall, the witches had influenced his actions and led him to where he was now. *For the good of Doth.*

"If it weren't for the witches of Doth, Mayem would still be there tearing it apart," he said, brushing aside the pillows. "Not going back to kill him means he will find and kill me here. I can't see it any other way, Lilith."

"Why not wait awhile before you go? I could show you things in this world you never dreamed possible. Unimaginable places." Her eyes blazed like tiny torches. Torches he didn't mind watching. "What does it matter if you wait to leave? The world behind you isn't going anywhere. You can always go back to it, my love." He liked it when she said 'my love,' but knew he shouldn't.

She stared at him as she repeated the two words a third, magical, time. "My love..." His heart stopped and restarted, stirring his soul. "There. It's done. I'm sorry, but I couldn't help it, Roulic; I had to say it. And now it's 'a thing thrice said that unlocks the head.' We can both thank Marlee for that little charm."

"Wait...Lil...," he stammered. Stunned, he couldn't speak.

"It's not what you think," she said. "I would never do that to you, my love. And believe me when I say those old crones put a jinx on me. They call it the Forever Spell. I was young and in love and couldn't bear losing you, even in death. They promised me I would live again, and you'd come back to me. So, I trusted them and drank their potion. Can you see me now? Recognize my voice? My face... Roulic?" Tears wet her cheeks, her head held high.

Shaking hands covered his drooping head. His mind blurred focusing on a scar, its wound in remission, on his heart. Days and nights he'd buried centuries ago came up and out like a living painting. Pictures hidden from the palette they'd never gotten to amalgamate, never gotten to render. Thoughts and memories of a love destined to die before getting the chance to live.

"I remember now... I do," he whispered. "We were living in a wagon. We stopped at a drink hole in Altlan called the Fidgeted Wand."

"Yes, that's it," she sobbed. "What else do you remember?"

"We shared a meal, danced to a fiddler, and drank a potent drink that we called...?"

"Loud Lesson. We drank far too many," she sighed. Searching eyes locked as they had when he proposed to her at the Fidgeted Wand.

"Oh, Lilith, sweet Lilith." He sensed her anew, remembering their joy and the playful light that once dared from her innocent eyes. Her tawny hair, delicate fragrance, and the way her slinky body slid and teased, all surfaced in remembering his first love. "You were the first joy let into my heart after a youth spent motherless and alone, wandering in hardship." He cupped her temple, their lips brushing when her head went back. Sparks flew from the old flame, erupting hot out of the cold wound he'd pledged to forget centuries earlier. He pulled away before their lips met.

"You died 500 years ago! I watched the Black Death take you," he said. "I buried you at the foot of the old ash we used to picnic under."

"I blame your friends, the witches. They assured me I would see you and be by your side again. They just didn't say it would take forever."

"They *are* my friends. I can't believe this is happening."

"Believe it," she said, "this is happening to both of us."

"I'm thunderstruck. I mean, I know it's you, but I can't believe you're here right now. I put your memory to rest—because of my hurt in losing you—so hard to bear. I buried you as far from my heart as possible. So much so that when I met you today, I couldn't even remember the Lilith who died when we were kids. How can that be? But we were just kids. You were barely 16 and I not much older, in my own time."

"It never would have been had the witches not interfered. But I was desperate and sought them to extend my life. They promised me eternal life if I obeyed their instructions."

"What instructions?"

"They made me drink their bitter brew. To this day, I endure their dreadful mazes until they get what they want. Their instructions?—deeds I must perform for them. Always for them. Deeds that keep you and me together, but always apart. I still hold them in contempt of God for that, but there's nothing I can do about it. I once believed that if I would see the light in them, I would find my way through this. I never did. It's like they've made me blind, having to wait all this time to be with you. For what they did to me — to both of us — I'll never forgive."

Dazed, Roulic nodded. But he was reluctant to trust flashing memories of their tragic story, his or hers. "I was a wreck after you died. I blamed the gods. Had I known the witches were to unite us, I wouldn't have blamed the gods so much when you became ill. We always knew I would outlive you, but I never imagined you leaving so soon. You were my world; we were so happy, and then you were gone. And I found myself unequipped to face the loss of you."

"I know, my love. But our misfortune is over. We're together now, and that's all that matters," she said.

But he held her hand with a cautious heart. That he loved, lost, and then found her 500 years later only complicated his already addled chemistry. He wasn't sure if the pain of losing her or his splintered memory had erased her from his world. *Maybe both,* he weighed. *Either way, the witches got involved, but for their own aims? I think not. I hope not.* He feared that confronting the witches would cost him Ravenna and his family. So, he resolved to consider the accusations only if, and when, he was ready.

And although he felt drawn to Lilith, he knew in his heart he belonged to Ravenna. *Our vow is precious; I won't allow myself to fall to the whimsy of Lilith's charm. Or illusions of our cloudy past. My history with her is just that: history. Whatever morbid afterlife she endured has jaded the young lass I once loved. We're not the same people anymore. And never will be again.*

She turned her face, but he caught the chill of death claiming her eyes. *There's icicles melting behind those dancing torches.* Then he waffled. *Still, she captivates. Her playful verve, hidden in red-hooded lambswool,...* Thoughts like that made him wonder things he shouldn't. There was no denying her seductive nature. She'd always had that effect on him, but he knew better than to act on heated passion. *That would bring nothing more than deep regret. And why am I getting the inexplicable feeling there's more between us besides our history? What is she hiding?*

Lilith ended the long silence with a sweet nothing. "Red was my color. You preferred it to blue. Our patterns spun as we slept, spent, and rekindled." She closed her eyes and kept them closed until he responded.

"I am so sorry, Lilith," he said, recalling his memory. The flash dressing of their salad days had turned brackish. "But I can't remember much of our time together. When we met, I'd already spent my entire life running from my past. Losing my family in the Inner. Then, after losing you, I kept on moving, hiding from myself. Centuries of running from my own shadow. Until my father found me and took me in. I didn't know it then, but he was protecting me, healing me, teaching me how to live again. When I left, I stayed in the Outer realm, hidden, living among mortalkin. Even while acting upon the calls of Destiny, which gave me a new life, a new way of living."

"Do you believe Destiny brought us together?" Lilith purred, her eyes afire.

"I believe she did," he said. "But..."

"You don't think the witches had anything to do with your Destiny? Why did they make you run all over Doth looking for the Pearlytok? I'll tell you what I think. I think they've been using you to kill two birds with one stone. To get rid of enemies like Mayem and that Captain Salty. And to keep the key for themselves. With Mayem dead, who could ever oppose them? Keep them from gaining immortality? Anyone possessing magicality can locate a gate. But even a single trip takes a bit of life with it. That's the cost of jumping through portals. That's why they're desperate to get the key. The Pearlytok takes no toll on the body as it passes one through time and space."

"Then why didn't Demeter keep the key when I brought it into her home in Three Furrows?"

"She owed a favor to the fae," Lilith said.

"A favor?"

"More like a debt. Look, there's a lot you don't know about them. Or the lengths they will go to to get what they want. I'm telling you they want you to kill Mayem so they can keep the key. Who will challenge them once he's gone?"

"But I have the key. It's in my pocket. Why haven't they taken it from me?"

Her eyes batted. "It's not that simple. You, my love, are the chosen one."

"You don't think the Masters aren't watching all this?"

"Shadows aid a witch's desire."

"Shadows have their place. Mortalkin will go after a witch in broad daylight. Giants, too. As well as pirates and gnomes. Not so easy in the shadows."

"They have allies," she persisted. "Here and around this house. That's why they chose Jessamine House, knowing of her portal. Jessamine suits their needs. They didn't rush out of Doth all at once. They spent a decade searching for a haven capable of combating Mayem. It's lucky for them, for when life in Doth finally did come "How did you come to know so much about the witches? Weren't you off and about with Arthur for centuries?"

"That's complicated. My new life under Arthur's watchful wing came with certain obligations."

"I'm no stranger to owing them," he said, hoping to avoid any embarrassing implications. She looked the other way.

"Despite it all, ever since I took their drink, I've never stopped observing them... or you."

"Words can't convey my sorrow," he said. "It seems your heart carries what we once shared, while mine hides a hint of what might have been. I'll always keep a place in my heart for you. But I must return the Pearlytok to Doth. My family, my life, and love are all in Doth."

"Your 'dragon girl,' Ravenna," Lilith pouted, blurting the name.

"Yes, Ravenna. But today, I leave to kill Mayem. At the proper time and place," he said, diverting talk from Ravenna.

"Don't worry about that. Arthur's windows still open with precision. I'm hoping you'll change your mind and stick around a while. With me. Lots to see and do in 1999." With a kiss on his head, she bid him goodnight and went to her room.

Roulic didn't want to believe Lilith's words. Words that scratched a hole in his brain, letting in doubts he didn't want to confront.

What if she is telling the truth? The Masters would frown upon the witches. Punish them. The Masters made the key, after all. And they gave their blessing to the gnomes for acts of peace during the War of Realms. I can't blame her for hating them for what they put her through. I'll give her the bitterness. That should be her right, considering all the centuries she's endured. But Demeter and Gram have shown their good intent all along. They proved that by helping me rescue Ravenna. They led me to the Pearlytok. And they've treated me as one of their own. Did they make an effort to kill Salty? Yes, but who can blame them for that after he murdered their family?

Waking on the floor, he maneuvered from the library's throw pillows, and from the Circle Room. In the watery gloaming, he heard a stirring in the depths of the sleeping house. It sounded smaller than the cats but bigger than a mouse. He thought of infant fins rippling fields of sea at dawn. He plowed into bed, refusing to germinate Lilith's tidal charges. And no matter how much they wrestled, sprouting in his mind, he refused to feed them until satisfying a deeper concern: *What if I can't kill Mayem?*

Chapter 7

The Dragon's Fate

Jax broke Jessamine's silence, flopping into a kitchen chair. Roulic handed him a cup of coffee. Jax pointed at the cabinet over the stove, grunting, "Tea."

"What kind? Your cupboard is brimming," Roulic said.

"The Indian Black Tea. No—today I'll have the lemon-ginger. "It's in that glass jar. By the Royal Cup Orange-Pekoe," Jax mumbled, finger-brushing his messy hair. "It's a probiotic. Good for the soul and all of that."

"I may need to try it. I didn't sleep much."

"You didn't eat Jillian's cooking, did you? When she gets it right, it's right, but when she gets it wrong, it can stop your heart." Jax flashed a wicked grin.

"No, it's not that. I didn't eat last night. I stayed up late talking to Lilith," he said, pouring hot water into a cup.

"Oh, I see. And how did our lovely lady affect your mind?" Jax sipped. "Foul words frequently frequent those pretty lips."

Roulic saw Mr. Nagnee, pruning a magnolia, through the dining room sliding door. He whispered. "She said Gram and Demeter tricked her into a life of despair. She also said that they want to keep the

Pearlytok for themselves after Mayem dies. What do you say about that?"

"Classic Lilith. She's had it in for my family for as long as I can remember," Jax said. "It's not like anyone forced her to drink from the Tree of Life. That concoction would never have worked even if ten men and a monkey poured it down her pretty little throat. She took it all on her own. The spell only worked because her heart wanted it to work. No matter the price."

"The price of forever?" Roulic sighed.

"Nothing lasts forever, old friend," Jax said. "The so-called Forever Spell dictates that Lilith can't pass until you do. Not a day sooner. And not for ages, I hope. I'm sure you'll both outlive us all. But isn't forever only as long as it takes to make things right? Look at Grace and Mayem..."

Roulic glared, "What about Grace and Mayem?"

Jax recoiled. "I wasn't supposed to say. We only found out late last night. My sisters were going to tell you this morning, but they've slept in and, well, there you have it. I'm the youngest witch in this house, and I can't keep my mouth shut."

"What has Grace got to do with me going back to Doth?" Roulic barked.

"Stay cool, there's been a slight hiccup, that's all. Nothing new, really. The wind changes all the time around here."

Roulic leaned over the kitchen table on his elbows. "Tell me, Jax.."

"Okay, okay, I'll tell you. We found a dragon's egg. And it's not just any egg..." Jax winked.

"Tell me this isn't Grace's egg! From the dragon's nest on the craggy mount?" Roulic flustered. "How is that even possible? I saw Baby spit fire on Dandling Oars Island!" His face turned red. Jax went to the fridge. He pulled out two eggs, a container of ham, and a jar of Martinelli's apple juice.

"A close associate has verified the specimen. It's a dragon egg."

"Who is this close associate? I have questions, Jax!" Roulic paced the kitchen table.

"Didn't my sisters tell you Arthur is the world's greatest portalist?"

"Why didn't he mention the egg last night on the roof?"

"He hadn't found it yet," Jax said, dropping toast into the toaster.

Roulic's jaw hung. "What!?"

"So, last night, my crazy uncle jumped the backyard portal to go poking around Catalina Island. The Catalina of long ago." Jax toyed with the frying pan.

"Yeah? I'm listening."

"Had he showed up this morning, nobody would have been the wiser of his late-night jaunt. But after finding the egg — with a fracture in its shell, he won't risk bringing it back through the island portal. It already endured one jump when he returned it to 1999. It must endure another before the portal closes tonight with you. *So*, he's not taking any chances bringing it home. He's getting the egg here the fastest and safest way possible. By plane."

By airplane. "Okay, so, now I'm guessing, instead of killing Mayem, you want me to return the egg to the dragon's lair on Grand Pekoes?" That question brought to mind another: *How the hell did the egg get to Catalina in the first place?*

"By Jove, you've just won the grand prize!" Jax sang, topping his plate with toast.

"But wouldn't it be better to kill Mayem *before* he finds Grace and the egg on the mountain?" This scenario bored Jax.

"No. And I want you to listen to this part carefully. If you kill Mayem before he finds Grace, she will die on the mountain. And Ravenna's brother, Thaniel, will never be born. And if the egg isn't there for Grace to find, she'll never receive the gift of the dragon. Nor will Ravenna. Ravenna will never have the power to heal and save all those lives in Dandoorthose during the war. These things must not come to pass."

"But if I kill Mayem before he brings war..." Roulic started.

"No, no, no," Jax's head shook. "Mayem is a born killer and will always be a killer. No science can change his genetics. He's been warring with the gnomes in both realms since before you were born. This is what he does. Besides, you were born to return the dragon." Roulic's stunned look had no effect on the witch standing in the kitchen, eating breakfast over the sink.

"Well, now my sisters won't have much to tell. I've already said so much; I might as well tell you all." Jax took a breath between mouthfuls of egg. "It has to be you, Roulic, because you were born a Dragon Protector. So were Ravenna and your father. When the Masters created mortalkin, the creatures of Doth were already here. The Masters knew mortalkin would kill them, so they created your kind; those born to protect. They deemed dragons sacred creatures. And people treated them as such for thousands of years. Until the likes of dragon haters like Hogan Darter, Mayem, and Nagendra came along. Those men slaughtered the dragons to near extinction."

"Wait, you're telling me that I'm a Dragon Protector?"

"Yes, I am," Jax nodded, swigging his juice, "—as directed by the Masters. Your father served the dragons for centuries. During the War of Realms, he prevented the death of many creatures. The Protectors have always fought for the greater good of Doth." This news shocked Roulic as Alastar never mentioned his being a Protector. He spoke of the great battles of Doth, but never the details of his role in the war.

"Some good it did. Look at mortalkin now. If Mayem gets the key, he'll use the dragons as agents of death."

"That is Mayem's doing. He changed the Universe. He imagined a world in chaos," Jax said. "But you can change the Universe, too. Picture a world where war is a thing of the past, remembered by none. Here, the mortals keep wars raging year after year. They have no respect for the nature dragons represent. It's just a matter of time before man and technology annihilate this timeline. They're well on their way to wiping out life as we know it. With or without Mayem's help."

"I'm sure he'll have a hand in it," Roulic scoffed.

Jax reiterated, finishing his last bite of ham. "If he gets the key in this timeline and brings it back to Doth, he won't rest until he finds a portal large enough to transport a..."

"Not if he gets killed first," Roulic said, paying attention to his shirt cuff. "Didn't Gale Guthrie and our stouthearted forces take a toll on his flickering armor?"

"They did, which changed the course of events." Jax put his plate in the sink. "But their dent in Mayem's metal only postponed what we've recently come to know. There lies an exact point in time when Doth will no longer exist. That's why it's critical for you to be where you can finish

Mayem——without him finishing us first. There are only hours left before the window closes."

"I know, I know, Jax, we've been over all this," Roulic ranted. "If I go back too soon—or too late—we all die. I'm beginning to question whether tampering with the past can ever serve the greater good."

"Every ship in this harbor has had a good go with that bit o' wonder. No doubt about that," Jillian trumpeted. She rounded into the kitchen, followed by Alison, Raine, and Marlee. "But life always brings us times we can't be sure about. You know, Roulic, it's not like we're asking you to do anything we wouldn't do ourselves. It's just that we can't." Jillian sat by her brother. The older sisters went about making breakfast. "We're only asking you because you're the only one who can. This we are sure about. There's just one thing we aren't so sure about."

"What's that?" He pierced her sea-green eyes.

"When the egg will arrive." Everyone laughed except Roulic.

He rolled his eyes at Jax. "So I've heard."

"It's coming by courier," Jillian continued, despite her visible irritation with Jax. "It seems that after Arthur left us last night, he went to Catalina Island. Back in time—searching for traces of giants."

"Giants? I didn't hear that part."

"Oh, yes. We were here when they unearthed their bones."

"1930," Raine said. "It was in all the newspapers. An act of desecration to a sacred lineage of giants. In 1990, the Native Americans gained the right to claim the remains of their ancestors. We thank the gods for that, at least."

"That's right," Jillian nodded. "We've long had an interest in the giants, so, naturally, Arthur has spent a lot of time exploring the island. Of course, he started looking for bones on the island long before that Glidden fellow came along. And light-years before the internet."

Roulic's face couldn't hide his curiosity. Jillian explained, "The internet connects information anywhere in the world in moments. It's quite a new thing, but like radio and television and so many other things these days, it's catching on fast. Pretty soon, the whole world will be using it. Jax handles the family finances using it. His computer is sitting on his desk in the Circle Room. He can talk to anyone, anywhere, anytime."

"As long as the person on the other end has got one," Jax said.

"A lot of people own a computer these days," she said. "It's like having the world's library at your fingertips. We even shop from home. And communicate, in online forums, about things we're interested."

"And things you're not supposed to be interested in," Raine said.

Jillian leaned across the kitchen table. "So, now that 'the younger' and I have got Roulic up to speed," she turned, "Jax, why don't you show Roulic the World Wide Web? I'm sure he'll find it interesting to see what has happened here over the last three centuries." Roulic followed Jax, locking eyes with Jillian.

She read his mind: *I'm not finished asking questions about the egg **or** the giants.*

"First things first, my boy," came her telepathic answer. *"The dragon is on its way. Until then, we wait."*

R oulic followed Jax upstairs to the Circle Room. *I thought I knew the witches. But now I'm not so sure. I thought I had a pretty good idea about human nature. But these people aren't average humans. They're witches.*

Changing all the time.

"And this," Jax instructed, "is how you move the mouse. So, if you want to go back to the page we were just on, you would click the mouse like this..." Jillian was right. The computer astounded him. Jax showed him Amazon, eBay, and authority sites like Ask Jeeves. They searched and visited websites chronicling the Wright brothers and the Apollo missions. They discussed the plight of Native Americans. And the modern world, pulling up videos about the Second World War, fast cars, and the latest inventions. After drinking two cans of Murphy's Irish Stout, Roulic got emotional surfing a vintage pipe site.

"Staring into the computer feels like gazing into a crystal ball. Whatever happened? How can people be so creative and yet so destructive?"

"Same people, different time and place," Jax said. "'*Chain, keep us together...,*'" he hummed Fleetwood Mac. "Here it is," he said, "her personal webpage. Millions of people have these. It's a way to introduce yourself to the world with a picture or two and a few words. Pretty nice, don't you think?"

"She's lovely," he said. "Who is she?"

"Aeryun Porter. She's going to be your guide in Doth. She knows Grand Pekoes better than anyone," Jax said, savoring the surprised look on Roulic's face. "Oh, I'm sorry! Jillian forgot to tell you. Arthur won't be back in time to guide you in Doth. He told us the next passenger plane won't arrive until tomorrow. Something about 'overbooking and reservations.'"

"Why can't he portal back?" Roulic scratched his head. Jax opened a new tab in the browser, showing Roulic a map of the rugged island.

"Too far to hike and make it back here by tonight. The portal is on the opposite side of the island. And Arthur's on foot with no shuttle service. He's already walked twenty miles from the portal to the Port of Avalon. He's okay now, resting at the Hotel Mac Rae until his plane lands tomorrow."

"Aren't there any boats coming and going?"

"That's where it gets into strange-Arthur territory. You see, my uncle refuses to step on a boat. Years ago, he suffered a dreadful incident at sea and has avoided traveling by water ever since." Roulic nodded. "The elders had no choice but to ask Aeryun. She's the only other person alive who can get you up that mountain. And she will."

"I don't think I'll mind her company," Roulic said. He did a double take of her pixels on the computer screen.

"You'd be a fool if you did," Jax said. "C'mon, enough of this digital reality; I've got something I want to show you. Something you can use."

R ounding the third floor staircase, Roulic stopped. Through Jessamine's hexagonal window, Agnes, Madelyn, and Lilith sprawled in the grass. Cross-legged, with their eyes closed. Agnes's face pointed up to the sky, Madelyn's head to the earth. Lilith leaned behind them with her left arm held to the sky, her right elbow out and down. Lilith's head tilted back and her eyes and mouth were open.

Jax ignored them, saying, "I know my sisters seem a little weird, but their normal once you get to know them. Come on."

"What about Demeter and Gram, and that Natric?"

"To be sure, they can be a tad of a mystery. The day Jillian brought me home from the Hurling Gal, Auntie and Gram were at Black Shadows Beach, waiting for me. My sisters asked them what they were going to do to the pirates. They answered by whispering the oddest of things in my ear. Things my sisters understood and I didn't. But I do now. Cryptic things," Jax said, "like, 'Ye wolves trip at sea' and 'Sins already sent.' I found out later they meant 'We've pirates to slay' and 'Salty's end is near.'"

They passed the kitchen and Glassy Hall, taking a turn at the foyer to Jax's room. "Never underestimate a witch's power," he said, rummaging through an 18th-century walnut armoire. "I know I stashed it here somewhere...," he went about the room, ransacking until he found *it* at the bottom of an old trunk. "Here it is! I haven't seen this in ninety years. I set it in warm wax to preserve it. Here, open it; it's yours."

Jax passed a knife and a bundle of blue wrapping paper. Roulic unwrapped the paper, then dug into the paraffin-covered oblong. Chunks broke apart, revealing the gift. It was his beloved old pipe. Eyes popped and blinked hard at the letter R inscribed around the bowl. He teared looking at the pipe Meyrick had given him after he rescued Ravenna.

"This was in my pocket when I fell into the waterfall at Mayem's Edge," Roulic said in disbelief, sniffing the pipe.

"I know, right? We thought we lost you. And then one day I was sitting on the beach and it fell out of the sky. Never forget what *that* means," Jax said.

"That the gods are toying with us?"

"A sign that we are all connected," the witch corrected.

"Maybe it was a sign," Roulic said, "I don't know, I'm not a witch. I can't see signs or augur the future. All I can see are the ones I love. The ones I want back."

"Then take this pipe as a sign. Its past may bring you into a better future. Get back to the ones you love and make things right, so none of this happens again."

"I will, my friend, I will."

"That's not the only surprise we've got for you," Jax said.

"There's more?" Roulic clutched his pipe.

"Demeter and Gram are waiting for you in Glassy Hall. They only come at night, but are making a special visit today, just for you. Are you ready?"

"If I were, I wouldn't know," Roulic said.

"C'mon, old friend, you can do this," Jax said, moving through the hall. "Sometimes good things come in twos."

Chapter 8

Close as a Ghost

Jax lay on the chambered hallway's plush bench. Roulic waited at the other end, staring across at the big black mirror.

"How do you know when they're coming?"

"Telepathy. Sometimes, they give us a sign or a signal in a dream. Or they'll light up all our cell phones. We rush here in the dark. They're a lot of fun," Jax said. "They're on the other side, so whatever works."

"How often do they come around?"

"Not often enough, but lately, a lot more. Before Marlee got the mirror, they'd show themselves in the water. They've turned up in that big birdbath in the courtyard and even in sheets of rain pouring over the side of the house...and here they are now. I give thee the elder witches of Doth." A wispy fog swept across the dark sea of glass. The gray matter mesmerized Roulic. His breath rolled out and evaporated, yet he didn't notice the dropping temperature. The elders, unseen in the chilling hall, spoke as clearly as if they were there. And indeed, they were. Gram cut through the vapor first.

> Waves did parade below our sheep beneath the clouds
>   that glum

A second rain cast no disdain but left us mud to plumb.
Then, Demeter, in soft, high-pitched overtones.
"Three times that day our kettle sang to cards laid warm
     with thanks
For nevermore we curse ashore the glum on wooly
     banks.

The mirror went black, the hallway silent. Jax and the cool air were gone. Roulic startled when the mirror hummed, fanning an image of a passion flower. The purple-petaled vine spun in front of the mirror blowing fragrant kisses. A rainbow expelled from the scented perianth, invoking Ravenna, with her titian scarf, to cross his mind. Titian plumes drifted, turning yellow and emerald green. Then to sky blue into light indigo, becoming violet. He waved an arm at the lingering color, sending hues about the hall.

The magic plant's corona released a red and yellow prism that chased the hues. A hungry orb swallowed every hue, growing after each color eaten, until they were all gone. The prism went black, flashing rays of each shade. They shot out, puncturing the dark hallway like a fireworks show. The prism spun faster and faster, lighting Glassy Hall in a brilliant finale that made his eyes close. When he opened them, the light and prism were gone. He was alone in the dark.

The apparitions crouched in the mirror. They smiled, then turned serious, realizing they could be seen. Demeter wore a sharp-looking black vest and Gram a maroon shawl. Roulic could hear Demeter's bracelet, jangling on her spotted wrist. At first, the mirror revealed their considerable age; however, when they spoke, the light in their eyes sparkled, presenting regressed images of their zesty heydays.

"Sit, Roulic," Gram said. "You're making me dizzy."

Demeter took over their introduction. "What she's trying to say, dear Roulic, is to forgive us the grand entrance, if not, odd spectacle. But never mind the medium, as our message is all that matters. Although our form has changed, we, like you, are still enrolled in the school of life. If that implies any measure of our ignorance, then so be it."

"Get on with it sister, our window narrows," Gram said.

"Very well," Demeter said. "As you know, in every egg there lies eternity's desire: to carry on through life, death, and rebirth. Every person plays a role in the limitless creation, whether they know it or not. And, amidst time's ever-changing veils, opportunities appear for those receptive to change."

"Changing the world was never my intention," Roulic said, not sure what the witches were getting at. Demeter shifted. Gram turned her head.

"Even so, you will," Gram said.

"Thus," Demeter continued, "it is up to you to know the difference between taking a jump and making a change. Our relentless opponent cares not about the difference between the two. He will abuse both portal and key through countless timelines. But portals don't change the world. People do. A portal's function is pure; its purpose is to ease passage."

"You must be clear on this," Gram warned. "Your mission in old Everlan is to be a singular act of change. Deviations there could lead to unfortunate outcomes for everyone."

"I understand," Roulic said, getting their point. "About these countless timelines, how will I know if I'm on the right one?"

"That's an intricate matter," Gram said. "But, never fear, the gods calibrated our brother's internal compass. And yes, despite Lilith's objections, he is sending Aeryun with you. She'll guide you up that hellacious peak better than he could. Once the dragon's egg is secure, Arthur will retrieve you from the delicate depths."

"He'll be a heartbeat away. Just whistle," Demeter said.

"Shush, sister. Roulic, are you clear on this?"

"Aeryun and Arthur," he nodded. "Killing Mayem—would it not alter the world?"

"Yes, it will. But you needn't worry about that today. Tonight, you're going back to the times of Grace. When a dragon snatched her and left her atop Grand Pekoes Mountain."

"*Before* Mayem finds her there..." Demeter said.

"It's crucial to nestle the dragon egg prominently in the lair. Ensuring that Grace discovers her gift intact is essential," Gram cautioned. "Aeryun will see that you and the egg arrive on time and in one piece. Stay close to Aeryun. Bear in mind that any time lost fiddling around in the past could harm you as well as haunt you. Also, Dyad and Brac are ever on the lookout for their little sister. So, if you see a blue or pink dragon—hide. And don't think that if you see a red dragon that it's not one of her siblings. It very well could be," Gram warned.

"These dragons are known to change their color," Demeter said. "We don't need to remind you how deadly dragons can be."

"I heard that Dyad and Brac perished in the Endless Pit at the Bridge of Belief. They were fighting over the Pearlytok," Roulic said.

"Rumors never cease to fly around them and that bridge. You yourself passed through the Endless Pit," Demeter reminded.

"And, on a horse," Gram's eyes sparkled. "Those dragons have a greater impact on your past, present, and future than you know. After you fell from the Edge, Ravenna connected with Dyad and Brac through the mind of Baby. She also convoked the swarm of dragons to Dandling Oars. They gutted the island, putting fire to the ships and pirates before bringing her home to Everlan."

"She rode on the back of Baby. Callian and your father, on Dyad and Brac," Demeter said.

Roulic's face lit up, speechless.

"The girls begged to tell you earlier, but we wanted to tell you ourselves. Godspeed, Roulic." Demeter's image disappeared in the gray fog covering the glass.

Gram's face turned watery. "Everyone has a protector, Roulic. We'll see you on the other side of this." She, too, dissolved into the murky matter. Her voice cracked, echoing in the hallway.

"Don't drop that egg!"

With Lilith, Jax, and the older sisters out of sight, Roulic passed the day on the roof with Agnes and Madelyn. They giggled a lot and made him laugh by telling him childish jokes, like:

'Why didn't the skeleton cross the road? — Because he didn't have the guts!'

And, 'Why didn't the ghost cross the road? — Because it had no body to go with it!'

The inseparable siblings had come a long way since the seventeenth century. They had lived for four centuries in mortal years. Suffered and survived the devastating shock of losing their parents. Early on, they conjoined to cross that abyss, bonding in their own private world. And along the way, learned to avoid the weight of it all, with harmless shenanigans that came out more and more. This new normal behavior became quite infectious, lifting spirits daily. But as Marlee's serious temperament was too grave for "the youngers," they often shut her out. One day she blew up at them, calling them, "The Deific Frolly & Folic." Yet they were proud the name. So, they mimicked themselves, chanting "Frolly & Folic" until Marlee laughed about it.

By 1999, they were happy-go-lucky witches in their thirties. The duo shared in everything. From work in the family's craft to the young men they brought home to Jessamine on full moon nights. Roulic found their playful antics amusing, though they could be quite eccentric. By late afternoon, after hours on the roof, he was visibly anxious for the egg to arrive so he could leave for Doth as soon as possible.

"When do you think it will get here?" He swayed around the roof.

"Don't worry, it'll be here soon," Agnes said.

"Well, I hope so. What about my guide, Aeryun?"

"Oh, her," the sisters smiled. "Lilith wants to take you," Agnes said.

"What happened to Aeryun?"

"Aeryun can't take you to Doth because she's already in Doth. Waiting for you, silly," Agnes said. "She'll find you when Lilith gets you there."

"I'm not sure this is a good idea," he said, his brow furrowed in worry. "Has Lilith ever done this on her own? She's a mortal, you know."

"More than mortal. You should know that, especially after what she told you last night in the library." Agnes stared at her feet.

"Jessamine's walls have ears," Madelyn taunted, enjoying his apprehension. "Don't worry, Lilith's got your back," she snickered.

"Don't worry, Roulic, you'll be fine," Agnes reassured. "You'll be back here before you know it. We're not done with you yet. And remember, we're always watching you." Madelyn's lambent locks missed his face as they strutted off the roof, giving each other high fives.

Chapter 9

Charming Boots

Jessamine's roof served an ample view of the sun's legacy: messy pink and orange streaks in the sky over Catalina. Messy enough to remind him that life was messy and that no man could live unhindered in his pursuits. *Perhaps in God's eyes, our lives become messy for meaningful reasons,* he thought. Given his solitude, reflecting on God seemed to help distract him while waiting for the egg. But when the doorbell rang, he left the roof, running down all four flights like a kid on Christmas morning.

"I've got a special delivery for Marlee Black." The lightsome carrier held a brown box.

"Thank you, I'll get her. I'll be right back," he said, closing the door before she could speak. Jax wasn't in his room. He sped through the hallway and up the stairs, knocking on doors on the second and third floors. None opened. Jessamine was silent. He ran back to the delivery person with panicked eyes, panting, "Marlee isn't home!"

"That's no problem. You can sign for her," she smiled and handed him a pen, eager to finish her deliveries.

"Ooh. All right." He laughed to himself, signing the receipt, *Callian Ronse.* "Thanks!" She handed him a receipt, then jogged and jumped, driving off in a white box van. He hustled through Glassy Hall, completing the delivery. Putting the package on the mahogany kitchen table, he let out a deep sigh of relief.

It's here! I'll be leaving soon. Home! But Gram's grandfather clock reverberating in the library made his stomach sink. *Where is everyone? It's seven o'clock!* He waited in the dining room, staring out the patio slider until he heard the stairs creak.

"Is it here?" Marlee's eyes got as big as eggs. "I can't wait to see it." She went to the kitchen counter and pulled a steak knife from its block. Rushing in, Roulic stepped back, giving her space.

"Where were you all afternoon? Where did Jax go? The portal's window is closing soon," he barked.

"You realize this is dangerous for us, too, right?" Marlee halted the knife in midair, quelling his attitude. "I'm sorry if you felt lost and alone. We've kept our distance today because whatever happens to you, or around you, could affect us all. So, please, Roulic, be gentle with our little baby."

Roulic nodded. "Don't worry, I won't drop it," he said.

"Ya better not," she said, removing the cushy padding before lifting the egg from the box. She set it on the tablecloth. "It's beautiful, even with this little sliver of a crack. See it? That isn't too bad," she rolled it over. The light green casing glowed, turning bright yellow. "They can do that, ya know."

"Gram warned me they could be chameleonic..." he said.

"This means she's alive in there. Despite the outer defect, her pod can endure the elements for centuries. "She's a delicate miracle," Marlee said, dipping into a pocket and handing him twin red BIC lighters. "Here, take these with you in case you need a quick fire to keep her warm."

"How could any fetus survive for so long?"

"A normal one couldn't. But dragons of Doth transcend time and space," she said, "as will their genetic makeup." She rolled it again, scrutinizing the 350-year-old shell. "Although its shell looks brand new, this egg will hatch a dragon created to help the world overcome fear."

"Dragons have always scared me," Roulic said.

"I'm more afraid of the mortals running around out there. The dragons have earned my respect. I suppose I fear them, too, but without fear in the world, how'd we ever learn to master our own?" The shell turned light green again when older sisters trickled in. They took turns feeling the beating heart. Each sister released an "Aah" as thin, peach streaks pulsed across the shell. Jax came into the kitchen carrying a black pouch.

"Wear this," he handed Roulic the satchel. "Wrap this fanny pack around your waist. Keep your cargo close to your stomach."

"And whatever you do, don't drop it," Lilith interrupted, putting the witches off-kilter.

"Everyone's telling me that. Charming boots, by the way," Roulic said. Lilith turned in a circle, showing off her new knee-high boots, midnight purple leather vest and pointy black hat.

"I wore them for you. Are you ready to go?" she said, eyeing the embryo.

"Glad you could make it," Marlee snapped, "Roulic has been waiting all day for you."

"I've been preparing to send him off. It's not every day one flies off with a dragon. My, that is a colorful duck. Any word of Arthur?" she circled the sisters. "I bet *his* boots are off."

"Thanks for your concern," Marlee stroked the egg.

"Come, dear, we mustn't keep the past waiting any longer." Lilith held her arm out.

"Must it be this way?" Roulic whispered, knowing Lilith could hear.

"I'm afraid so," Marlee said. "You hold the key, but only Arthur and Lilith know where the gate to the dragon's lair is, and she's not telling."

"Can't you ask Arthur? You could take me," he pleaded. Feigning to be dejected, Lilith left through the hallway.

Marlee shook her head. "Too risky for any one of us to try to find it in the dark. And Jessamine's portal won't get you any closer to the dragon's lair than the outskirts of Everlan. We know. We've tried. And we can't have you wandering this timeline looking for the gate because you don't trust Lilith. The sun must set, and we've run out of time. You must go with her."

"So be it, then," he relented.

The witches smiled, hugged, and whispered bits of wisdom. Jax put teabags in the fanny pack. Marlee squeezed his hand, "May your heart, and all you carry in it, be ever blessed. Keep this egg as close to your heart as you do to them."

L ilith called a Yellow Cab before Roulic made it out to Jessamine's front porch. Dusk came without a word between them until the cab arrived. Driving through downtown, she sighed in the winding twilight of Laguna Canyon Road. But her silence didn't bother him. He still couldn't believe the woman sitting next to him had once owned his heart. *That woman is gone. Behind that pretty face is someone I don't recognize and don't understand.* He felt sorry for her as she stared out the window. Until he reviewed her assertion that the witches were after the Pearlytok.

I can't forget that she drank her oath of her own accord and that I mourned her death for seven years after burying her. No matter what she says she did for them, I won't be misled by her beguiling theories about the witches. I'm on my way home to Ravenna.

Intersection lights flashed, splashing colored shadows on passing boulders shouldering the canyon road. The cab driver rolled up his window, looking at Lilith through the rearview mirror. "There's a turn coming up. Should I take it?"

"Keep going," Lilith said, "I'll tell you when to stop."

"All-righty then," the cabbie said, driving until she had him cross the lane into an unpaved turnout. "Are you sure this is where you want to go? There's nothing out here," he said with spooked eyes in the mirror.

"Yes." After Lilith paid the fare, the cab driver spat gravel, turning back onto Laguna Canyon Road.

"How is it that you know of this place, this portal?" He checked the egg holstered around his waist.

"Arthur," she said, ready to speak to him. "He's shown me many things. He always felt bad about what his sisters did to me. I was living in a monastery when he found me, of all places." He couldn't see her face, tenebrous in the clouded moon.

"Is that why they're afraid of you? Because of you and Arthur..."

"Yes. That and because I know the truth about them. But they can't get rid of me until their lusty brother dies. And they don't dare say a word about me because they know he'll stand up for me. Arthur's always protected me. How I've protected you."

He didn't respond, following her along a two-foot-wide trail around a tower of boulders. He waited until the sight and sound of the canyon road and cars were gone. "In what way have you protected me?" He dodged groping cactus tentacles in the dark.

"*Year after year you thanked me for whispering unto your ear,*" she said, rounding a boulder. Stopping in the weeds behind the mass of boulders blocking the road, she said, "'*She's the one with a name you've not heard.*' Do you remember referring to me as '*the one who's as close as a ghost; most would have left her well behind.*' I'll never forget the day you said that. That was the day I knew you wouldn't give up on me, *your* Destiny. From that moment on, I've held hope in any actions that brought us back together. And here tonight."

Roulic stopped. His journey with Destiny was unknown to anyone. He kept his conversations with Destiny private, in mind and heart. *How dare she claim to be what she could never be: my Destiny!*

"I've never shared those words with anyone. And I'm not falling for whatever mind trick you're trying to pull. Getting me to the portal is all that matters." They approached another collection of canyon rock.

"You know what matters now? Climbing this ledge to get to it. Can you give me a boost?" She lifted her left boot, waiting for his clasped hands, smiling like a fox. Jumping off his palms onto the slender ledge, she waved. "It's not far. It's on the other side of these boulders."

He climbed the ledge, catching the sun defy night. Pressing against him, she kissed his ear, "For every breath of secrecy I kept, my beating heart wept 'neath your dancing waves. For I was slain in mystery. And in all your bewitching dreams becoming quotients, 'twas *I* the lightning in your wounded sky, the one whispering in your ear, year after year."

"No, I don't believe you," he rebuked. "This is some sort of foul betrayal," he growled into sunset's last kiss. Opposing gusts rose up over the tight ledge, pinning their bodies together. She turned and climbed to the ledge's noble table.

"I can never betray you," she said, pacing the dark slab. "I never have and never would. In fact, my pact with the witches was forged in love. I can *only* ever love you. Loving anyone *except* you was sacrificed the night I drank the Forever Spell. Obviously, it didn't take. I never got the chance to spend my life with you except as your loving 'Destiny.' Now, after all this time, the great wheel of time has granted a moment to rekindle our fate." Lilith turned, the wind curling her auburn hair. Crawling up the ledge, Roulic chased her on the rock. He spun her waist and got slapped with hair. She clung to his hips, digging her nails in.

"True love doesn't need to be rekindled," he shouted in the wind. "It can't be bought or sold. Or harnessed, or hurried. True love can never die..." Behind her, a small pool of water rippled in the moonlight. He left her, leaning over the bubbling spring.

"Farewell, my love," she said. "But know this: We *will* meet again. I will always love you with a love that is neither here nor there, but everywhere! Go now, find your heart's desire. And if you ever need me, I'll always be there for you—in the dark!" Lilith's long boot heel came like an iced thunderbolt, rattling his lower back into the portal. He fell into the pool, swept in cold circles by the frenzy of love's scathing broom.

Chapter 10

Arthur's Whistle

Do I deserve this? His question, to God and Lilith, plummeted unanswered. So did his weightless body, circling the spring. Lilith's torment washed-out, still kicking. Its fleeting sting, cleansed in the lacuna. All his doubts and agonies evaporated like tiny bubbles swirling the moonlit pool. A vision of his mother, Ren, wearing her maternal halo, came to him, comforting his psyche. But that blithesome moment between mother and son ended abruptly. The tempestuous door met its end, shook his skeleton, and rearranged him two feet off the ground. The hatch plopped him on a field of cattle. The sacred haven's holy water dripped from his back, leaving a puddle in the grass. He let out a gutsy "Aargh." The small bovine community remained oblivious. His tumbling appearance impressed none, except one, the startled cow he nearly landed on. That one trotted away, mooing.

Inhaling a whiff of damp dung, he muttered, "Some things never change." After checking to make sure the egg was intact, he walked from the field to a wide barn built by the edge of a forest. Two saddled horses tied to a small corral beside the barn, carried loaded saddlebags.

This must be it. There's nothing else around. Those must be our horses.

One of the barn's large breezeway doors was open. He entered, finding the building quiet and clean. Beside a workbench, a young woman dozed on a pile of hay: *Aeryun*. He didn't want to wake her so he shared the midday sun, coming through the barn's clerestory windows, covering her body like a warm blanket. She found him standing over her when she awoke.

"I must have dozed off," she said, easing up. She stretched her arms out over her head, shaking bits of hay from her smoky black hair. "Are you Roulic?"

"Yes. I was hoping I'd find you in here."

"Aeryun Porter," she said politely. "So, how was your jump? Where's Arthur?"

"He got delayed leaving Catalina Island—Lilith got me here."

"Lilith?" Aeryun frowned. "She's no portalist. Is she here?"

"She didn't come. She gave me the boot."

She looked at him funny. "I'm sorry about that. If Arthur..."

"I'm fine. Lilith did what she needed to. I'm better off without her, anyway. Please tell me I've made it to Old Everlan and that you know where you're taking me. I'll be your humble companion."

"The dragon's lair is a far stretch — we'll have to pass through the Valley of Princesses and the Serpens River to reach it. The river wraps around the entire mountain. But nothing two fine mustangs can't handle. Arthur made sure they were here for us."

"How long have you been here?"

"A few days. Long enough to confirm the year—1649—and get familiar with the forest behind the farm." She took an item from her backpack: a finger-length silver whistle on a braided leather necklace. An infant dragon talon, the size of a thumbnail, hung attached at the bottom of the whistle.

"What am I to do with this?" He smelled strawberries in her hair.

"In case you get lost and need help," she said. He looked worried.

"Don't worry, you won't need it. You're in good hands," she said, giving him a taste of her dark blue eyes. She put it around his neck.

"I can see that." *Now I know what Demeter meant when she said, "Just whistle."*

They rode into the dusky forest behind the barn on a path that led to a fork. "Stay to your left!" she hollered, picking up speed. "Turn right!" she waved when another fork appeared. And another, and another, until he felt like they were going in circles. He rode close behind until the path became obscured by dead branches, bark, and leaves. They dismounted, forging a trail through the dark forest, leading their horses on foot.

"We're in the thick of it now. Won't be long," she said. He ignored the low branch scratching his wrist, reminding himself they'd be setting up camp soon.

"I hope I don't need to use this." He tugged on the whistle around his neck. "We should have packed lanterns," he hollered, lagging behind.

"You won't need one as long as you keep up. C'mon, we're almost there." She led him through the last dense growth to where the mountainside had dropped off. Fresh air and pink twilight met a panorama featuring the highest alp in Upper Doth. The prominent peak dwelt unrivaled in the far company of the mountains chained around it.

"There she is," Aeryun smiled. "Grand Pekoes has never failed to blow my mind." Roulic fancied the peculiar expression, equating it to the many-colored colloquialisms of mortalkin.

"It's late in the day, so we'll stay on the mountainside tonight. If we're lucky, we should make it to the valley by noon tomorrow and reach the summit the day after."

A star appeared, glittering in the sheen of the vanishing day. "Mr. Nagnee showed me this alp yesterday."

"I heard. ...Arthur conveyed that to me... that he took you to the southern side."

"Where are we exactly?"

"On the northern side. North of Soaring Hills. Nowhere in Doth is more beautiful," she said with a sentimental tone.

"I've never been past the Soaring Hills."

"No need. Unless you're looking for dragons." She checked her mustang's bit.

"Or looking to put one back," he said.

Aeryun led them down the mountainside until they reached a level spot to stay the horses. They made camp for the night. She took their bedrolls out of the saddlebags while he set up a ring of stones and collected wood for the fire. She made a branch bridge and hung a pot over the ring before he lit the flame.

"Why are you doing this? You're not a witch from Doth." He filled the pot with water from his canteen.

"No, I'm not," Ashe said. "I'm just a typical human being. But, you know what? I've always felt different. All my life, I've felt drawn to the wisdom of witches and the ways of nature."

"All good things, but especially untypical," he said. "How'd you meet the Blacks?"

She tread on the back side of the fire. "I was lucky enough to meet Raine at a yard sale in Laguna Beach after I lost my job, then my apartment, then my car. I was staying at a homeless shelter and getting back on my feet seemed impossible. I was starting to think about doing myself in. I thank God every day for meeting Raine. She reminded me that life is worth living, worth fighting for. She took me in. Fed me. Healed me. And I never left. They still keep a room for me at Jessamine," she said fondly. "And then one day, Arthur took me on a jump and declared me a natural. I haven't stopped jumping since."

"How long ago was that?"

"Gosh, 1988? But I've never tired of it. We've portaled to countless places, making friends and helping the family," she said.

"Helping?"

"We do certain things at certain times. Like, right now."

He nodded, rethinking the veracity of Lilith's plight. "Do you ever miss your old life?" One of Jax's tea bags got dropped in a tin cup that she brought for him.

"You mean struggling to pay bills and taxes? Nope. Between the two of us, our knack for getting around lets us come and go as we please. What we miss, we go back for, but we don't disturb the past. We've attended historical events. But we prefer weddings and birthday parties for the people we care about." She dropped a teabag in her cup, setting both cups near the pot of water on the fire. "Because we can."

"What about Lilith? Does she ever get in the way?" He bit his lip, regretting ever mentioning Lilith.

"She means nothing to Arthur. Nothing at all. Besides the fact that he's been holding her hand until he could get her to you. He's more of an absent father figure, enduring her tantrums with pinches of patience. But he stopped looking at Lilith when Raine brought me home," she said proudly about the rivalry. They sipped their tea. He got caught studying her appealing features. She silently acknowledged the pleasantness in his.

"Lilith's been living at Jessamine for decades now. She's driven the witches crazy with threats of what will happen when you arrive," she said in a blink of glamour.

"And when I did, she kicked me out," he said.

"In all fairness, that's just Lilith. She could have been a lot worse. I've seen her dark side," Aeryun cooled.

"For someone who says they love you, she sure has an odd way of showing it." He stretched his back, still unnerved by the heel of Lilith's boot.

Across the fire, Aeryun warmed, reminding herself that Lilith was once a mortal. She took off her fleece jacket. "Lilith never got the chance to show her pain. To grieve you. I don't think her insecurity was born out of possessiveness. I think it came from having no end in sight to the pain of losing her true love. No matter how many centuries got crisscrossed, her feelings for you never died. You'd become a demon too if you suffered, as she has, for that long."

"She might be an angel in the making," he conceded. "Who's to say the road less traveled isn't paved by those running hence? I'm inclined to think it is the will of women and witches that created this world."

"Why wouldn't you? It certainly wasn't born in the minds of men like Mayem," she said.

"No, it wasn't." He took the egg from his pouch and held it. "Why is death so important to him when living is all that matters?"

"Maybe he lost all sight of life, so he chose to chase death. But isn't that what we're doing? Think about it. Without Mayem, where would we be?" They laughed, but Roulic had a bitter aftertaste. He wanted to be with Ravenna instead of having to return the egg.

"I can think of better places. I'm not even sure why I'm here at all. That the fate of Doth lies inside this egg eludes me."

"Don't think on it too hard. You'll end up becoming your own worst enemy." Aeryun untied her brown navy Nike Air trail hiking boots and slid into her bedroll. Roulic searched his effects for his pipe but couldn't find it.

"Damn, I left it at Jessamine..." he said. Their eyes bonded through the fire. A comfortable connection formed; a cozy calm they both relished after riding hard all day.

"Tell me a campfire story, Roulic...I'm sure you've got plenty of tales to tell," she said.

Her friendly request he felt eager to oblige. *It suits the night,* he thought. *The atmosphere of our mission.*

"I do, I do indeed. How about a long-forgotten dithyramb last heard in my youth?"

"A what?"

"A tale of an epic battle pitting a young warrior against a savage specter."

"Sounds exciting. Ready when you are, humble companion," she said, getting comfortable.

"All I have to do is recall it. It was the most popular story of my childhood. 800 years ago," he winked.

Shutting his eyes, he called for the yarn but it wouldn't come. Details skipped the sea of his mind like a children's book blurred in a damp, whipping wind. He sighed and opened his eyes. One finger extended, tapping the egg, while another touched his head. And with an Ancient's strain he hummed, without a care in the world, at the moon and to the cotillion inside the flames by their feet. Word by word, the legend found mooring, its sails intact, homebound in his narrative.

With flame-filled eyes, Aeryun received his recital in a low voice and hammy fashion.

> It was in the days of Lod, in the far land of Frayaaw,
>   where a satyric demigod named Angra stole the
>   king's eldest daughter, Sabina.
> Angra hid Sabina deep in the den of the Emerald
>   Dragon, hoping his forbidden lust for the beautiful
>   mortal might go unseen by the gods.
> Upon hearing of Sabina's kidnapping, the king's
>   youngest nephew, the royal guard, Alvanti, hurried
>   to his uncle, pledging to rescue Sabina if allowed to
>   court the maiden upon her safe return. The

distraught king readily approved of the noble soldier, knowing both of Alvanti's bravery and the mutual affection of his smitten daughter.

Angra became furious, immediately dispatching his most wicked agent to frustrate Alvanti's troth. The phantom assassin sped into a cave above the Emerald Dragon's den, waiting and watching for Alvanti's approaching winged charger, Gadara.

Circling the cindery cone, the duo flew cautiously until Mercy quelled the pit with ample rain, allowing horse and rider rapid descent.

The specter flew out of the cave, instantly attaching itself to Alvanti's mighty shoulder. Eyes glowed red as it spat a foul kindling, sparking fire upon the warrior's flesh. Alvanti sweated as he desperately shook to shed the spook, who viciously mimicked his cry, "Gods be with me now!" Horror came over Alvanti's face, bringing cackles of delight from the tenacious ghost.

This nefarious deed ignited an indignant intervention from the old dragon gods, whose united whispers fired burning blades at the phantom that also scorched Gadara's silver armor. And one chance blow that so knocked Gadara that it cast Alvanti off the horse and down into the smoking lair.

The malicious specter slipped off Alvanti's shoulder and flew up to follow Gadara out of the volcano. But the vile creature couldn't catch the rising steed and vanished, vaporized in the lick of a fleeting flame.

When Gadara flew back down into the pit to retrieve Alvanti, the gods sent a magical mist that filled the volcano, momentarily blinding the horse and choking the dragon below.

But, through the smoke of gods, Alvanti rebounded on the back of the Emerald Dragon, with Princess Sabina by his side. The couple rose valorously,

dodging fragments burning in the mist, ascending
by the holy dragon to the feet of the gallant Gadara,
waiting on a nearby mountaintop.

Aeryun's snug approval of his campfire story came through half-open eyes and a sleepy smile. "That was a good story. Good night, Roulic. I'm glad I got to take you." She rolled over.

He propped up his little pillow. "Night, Aeryun."

Not an hour later, he woke, hearing: "I would kill to be reborn," she moaned in her sleep to the midnight sky. Half asleep himself, he soon forgot Aeryun's enigmatic words. He never caught more than the rumbling of her throat or the soft winds humming over the mountainside. He fell asleep, guarding the egg. He dreamed of a family with Ravenna and of his mother's joy at meeting her grandchildren.

If only I could go back in time and begin again with her at the Bridge of Belief. I'd never leave her side.

Chapter 11

Titan Dreams

It was on day two when Mayem had his epiphany. Although this new land fed his killing addiction, his survival remained uncertain. Especially not knowing the whereabouts of Roulic and the Black family. He knew the witches escaped the Realms using a portal. *But were they here?* He wondered. He could never go near them. They'd kill him on the spot. But he also knew that witches and wizards dwelled here, there, and everywhere, in all times and places.

He has the power of witches on his side. Why shouldn't I?

A like-minded witch could get me out of here. I'll be on my way back to Dandling Oars and he can stay here forever, pining for his precious Ravenna. Faugh!

The painter's pillaged beach house receded into his whilom memory. He'd left, forging the future, walking suburbia as if led by some guiding crosswind. A wind zigzagging side streets, dodging down alleys, and pressing past crossing boulevards. Thousands of people of every size and shape moved about the hub of Long Beach. More mortals than he'd ever seen in one place. They bustled in and around schools and shops. They shuffled on miles of sidewalk lining miles of streets crowded with automobiles. Massage parlors did business alongside laser eye clinics, surf, skate, and auto shops. And a hundred other kinds, all trying to survive in the modern world.

A biker parked out front of a tattoo parlor approached Mayem, "You lookin' to buy any 'speed'?" In Mayem's time, the word speed meant either 'rate of quickness' or 'good fortune'. Had he known what the drug crystal methamphetamine was and could do to a person, he might have stopped. But, fearing the unknown, he ignored the gent and crossed the street, mulling over the odd question. Coming upon a seedy corner motel delighted him, if for nothing else, to find a place to rest his nagging heel. The dilapidated building seemed suited to the folk he was looking for: the lost and lonely. *I will find my witch living among the downtrodden mortalkin. The wayward down-and-outers yearning to mend their broken dreams,* he thought.

A marred door and faint broken bell announced his entrance to a shabby, micro-lobby. Six feet in, a newspaper's front and back pages hid its reader behind a smoke-filled glass partition. The clerk folded his newspaper in half. He was unshaven and dangled a Marlboro from his lower lip.

"No. You can't have one. I'm tired of you guys coming in here, bumming smokes off me," he whined. "Did Maximón send you in here?"

Mayem's heel itched, considering killing the man with his hands. "No. I don't know anyone named 'Maximón.'"

The clerk set the newspaper down. "Welcome to Titan Dreams," he said. "We have rooms, but we only take cash."

"I don't need a room. I need a witch," Mayem said, testing the water. *If this fool proves to be a problem, I will enjoy hurting him.*

"Ah, you mean Nina, the tarot card reader. Why didn't you say so? She's upstairs. Room 208. Knock once, then twice. She'll know you're cool. But no funny business. Don't make me call the cops." The clerk threatened, pointing to a dim hallway. "The stairs are that way."

H e knocked once, then twice. Nothing. He was ready to leave when a childlike face peered between Room 208's door jamb and chain lock. The type of face Mayem felt comfortable with. Grey eyes flickered, then hid, leaving him a telling remnant of her soul's remorse. His dragon keeper, Nagendra, carried a similar look of doom in his eyes, fearing the Masters' wrath.

"Are you Nina?"

"Yeah, hon, that's me. Whatcha need?"

"I'm looking for a portal. A way to my past. And a witch who can deliver me something dark. Can you do that?"

Nina sensed a potency in the stranger's confidence. A man of power. She released the door's chain lock, let him in, then relocked it. A smokestack loomed through a dusty picture window in need of washing. Mayem appraised the cluttered room's view, wasting no words on the mortal until he knew more about her.

"I knew you were coming," she said, admiring his riding boots and démodé cloak, "even though I'm not clear who sent you or why. Sorry about the messy place. I've been rebelling against my daily existence," she laughed. "It's not every day someone like you visits me, ya know. Please, have a seat."

He accepted her black coffee, sitting at an IKEA kitchenette table. Tainted arms picked up wine glasses, beer bottles, and emptied out ashtrays. He followed her painted limbs as they buzzed about, servicing the apartment. But it wasn't only her colored tattoos or snug outfit that pleased him. The girl in a tank top, jean shorts, and pink tennis shoes wore an inverted pentagram in her black velvet choker. Mayem liked what he saw, thinking, *She could be my bad witch.* His fascination, she felt all over her body, making her throat get tight. She tidied up, catching his eyes, waiting for him to speak. But he didn't. His beady eyes never left her.

"I can't deliver a 'time and place portal.' I'm still trying to work that one out. But dark? I can do dark. How dark are you willing to go? There's dark and then there's r-e-a-l-l-y dark. I'm thinking you want to bring about something unspeakably black."

"You thought right," he said.

"That, I can deliver. But it will cost you...more than a high price," she looked him over. "Are you sure you want to do this?" Mayem produced a stack of hundred-dollar bills from the coat he had taken from the old man. He fanned the bills at her and set the wad on the table.

"That'll do," she said, eyeing the cash that would get her as far as possible from the Titan Dreams motel. *And the quiet stranger.*

"Now you'll need to agree with, and do exactly what I say during the ritual. Calling forth a spirit always carries some uncertainty. But calling forth the spirit of a Dark One to do your bidding requires what I call a spiritual token. At some point, the entity will make you abandon something good in your life. It could be anything. Anything at all. And then it will be gone forever, taken regardless of whether you realize it or not. Consider it the cost of services rendered. It's up to the entity," she said, pausing to let him decide. "Do you agree?"

"Yes. I've no good left in my life." The renegade Ancient confirmed a millennium of grudge and spleen.

She chirped, scooping the cash into her jeans pocket. Dashing into the bedroom, she returned carrying a bronze vase. It featured feminine, arm-like handles that bent and rested on its shapely waist. Grace flashed through Mayem's mind, the night he found her on the mountain. Nina motioned for him to help lift it into a copper stand she had set on the kitchenette table.

"What's this?" he grunted.

"This is my magical vase. It's from ancient Sumer. It's been in my family for ages."

"How many 'ages'?" He looked deep into her eyes.

"It's 3000 years old, more or less." She averted her eyes to consider his stressed face. She couldn't know his temples, rife with a horde of crow's feet, were twice as old as the vase. "All the women in my family have the witchy vibe. We see and hear things most people can't."

Mayem bored before the four-foot vessel, delivering a "Hmm" when she closed the drapes. Stick matches brought to life two rectangular black candles, each home to six wicks. She slid the twelve flames beneath the legs of the copper stand. Five white candles, lit in silver holders, circled the antediluvian vase.

"Why not black?"

"White candles represent your true intention. This we need behind the incantation. They also help to impart a veracious spirit—so you won't need an exorcism when this is over."

He nodded as if to say, "That won't be necessary."

"Bear in mind, it's what goes inside the container that will engage the intelligence you're looking for. Getting spirit to take physical form," she fanned the candles, "could take some doing. We'll have to wait and see."

He leaned to get a better look at the classical scythe and Saturnian rings etched around the base. His heartbeat slowed. The intricate hoops jogged him so much that he fell into a familiar vision of his virtuous brother. And Ravenna. She was always standing by Meyrick. *Why must I always see Ravenna? Why can't I see the face of her mother? Grace belonged to me!* He churned in his chair at scenes of the plague he brought to Soaring Hills by poisoning Meyrick's wheat fields.

Above the rings, strings of astrological glyphs danced to the flickering flames below. He turned from their rhythm, looking into the drear of the drapes, until Meyrick's face left his mind. Challenging the macabre receptacle, he looked back at it. The heavenly symbols transformed into a long key wiggling in the candlelight. The key turned into a snake that wrapped itself up and around the vase's neck. He became transfixed by the illusion. The snake's destination was a spiraling keyhole. Mayem's blood simmered when the snake enter the keyhole. He boiled at the thought of Roulic returning the Pearlytok to Doth.

"Get on with it!" he shrilled, pounding his fist on the little table. Two of the five white candles rolled over and went out.

Nina kept her composure, relighting the toppled wicks. "Like I said, this could take some doing. An offering of a personal item might help. Dark Ones often bond through objects that hold a strong connection to the living."

Mayem unclasped a chain beneath his black shirt. "Use this. It comes from my homeland." He held a magnificent dragon-talon necklace over the mouth of the vase. The thick, braided silver chain held three small talons, each clutched by a golden clasp.

Nina quivered. *He's the one in my dream! The dark one who chases dragons through time is at my table! He who will sit beside the Darkest*

One for removing hope from a dragon's heart. The one whose hex changes my world. But how? On weak knees, she said,

"Now, place it in the vase, declaring aloud your intention."

"The Pearlytok shall be mine to do with as I please!" Mayem commanded, dropping the necklace into the vase.

She endured his impatient, "How long do we wait for it to appear?"

"When the vase smolders, the heat of your intention will draw forth the being." She sprinkled circles of salt and herbs into the receptacle. "Why don't you put your watch in there? It might help," she said.

"Might it?" Mayem scoffed, after giving up his mighty necklace. He took the old man's wristwatch and tossed it in. "Since we're getting colorful, let's add this to the pot." He pulled out the dirty paintbrush he had pocketed during last night's .

She lit three matches, dropping them one by one into the vase. The pungency of burning herbs and leather permeated the room.

"He has the egg," Nina declared. Mayem froze. She put her hands on the table. "He holds the egg and plans to return it to the mountain."

"How do you know this?" Mayem bristled.

"I'm being told, as we speak. By Ozrar. Three are coming forward. Bliniloth will appear first, then Smutch, followed by Ozrar. They are the ghosts of Onan." Mayem's eyes locked on Nina in disbelief. She stared back, trembling. Neither had ever heard of the ghosts of Onan. Nor had either conjured a spirit into humanhood.

"Wait... now they're telling me that 'you're to prevent hope from dwelling in a dragon's heart'." She cupped her arms and elbows, brushing goosebumps.

"I've already seen to that. I raised that dragon myself," Mayem argued.

Byzantium fumes gushed from the vase, releasing a figure dislimned by the smoky mass.

"You'll have to raise it again," the low tone emanated over their heads. Mayem and Nina paled beneath phrases of aureate smoke.

"Can you name the Bringer of the egg?" Mayem queried of the hovering voice.

"I cannot," Bliniloth boomed from the Tyrian purple haze. He sprang, illuminated, his spleen that of some hadal ogre dragged from abyssal depths. Mayem rose from the table in awe. Light passed through the ghost's torso in sporadic passages. Yet his features and high cheekbones gave off a bluish sheen, like a gaunt frown dabbed with wet talc. A powdered ponytail swung behind a deep blue tricorn hat. His clothes, long since au courant, were dirty and ragged, befitting the body they hung upon. Wrists wrapped in gold bracelets accentuated maroon trousers tucked into high black boots. Flaring rings played up an unbuttoned coat over a frilly gray shirt. Bliniloth's hard eyes, lined in black, fixed on Mayem, his lips crisscrossed in broken stitches.

Mayem studied the ghost's squinty eyes and long mustache. "Do I know you?"

"Never forget a face, eh? Ever seen a face this happy to see you?" Bliniloth nicked his blue cheek with a long fingernail, trickling a bead of blood. "Listen up, mate. I've been around for a long, long year. But for now—with the likes of you—a short while me hopes, but it'll be *me's* the one asking questions and arranging our oath. Understood?"

"Fine, then. Fire away, Captain!" Mayem imagined *cutting off his head, ghost or no ghost.*

"This dragon egg you're after... on its way back to Doth... who holds it?" Bliniloth drilled.

"A young Ancient called Roulic. He also carries the Pearlytok, a key of mine," Mayem lied about the key, but Bliniloth knew better.

"Hmmm, all right. The egg and your key. Take a moment to consider the face of this Roulic figure. Capture him in your mind's eye so that we may form an impression of him, hmmm?" The ghost's low hum agitated Mayem's heel.

Mayem closed his eyes and visualized Roulic waving the Pearlytok. Then he pictured them falling over The Edge. He seethed knowing Roulic held both the Pearlytok and the dragon egg. That's all it took for Bliniloth to see Roulic's aura, and locate him within a physical plane.

"Now that you've invited me here, do you agree, in exchange for my services, to give me something in return?"

"Like I told *her*, I've no good in my life. So, go ahead. Search my soul, take what you find."

"A fine accord! I'll go now and return the egg and your key," Bliniloth assured.

"I'm coming with you!"

"You weren't included in the invitation, mate. I can't use you. You'd slow us down."

Mayem riled. "How dare you..."

"How dare I?" laughed the ghost. "I'll dare turn tides and spoil the hearts of kings! I feed on infernal wolves like you, lulling lost frogs to crickets in the dark. And when my penance is paid, I'll do it no more," Bliniloth spouted with the pageantry of a veteran thespian.

"You could use my kind of darkness," Mayem negotiated. "This Roulic has a way of slipping through fingers."

"That's where Ozrar comes in. You'll see. You're not the only one dying to become a shadow of the Darkest One," he purred.

"Shadow?"

"Shadow or Light, mate. Them's the choices." Poof! Bliniloth disappeared, swirling in his own smoke.

Chapter 12

Dangerous Dolls

The gust of Raine's stair flight blew out Marlee's candle. And it blew Jillian's reading, spreading tarot cards across the table and all over the floor. Jillian swooped to pick up her fallen forecast.

"Mayem issued a kill order to the Ghosts of Onan. He knows Roulic has the egg!" Raine gushed.

"We know," Marlee said, relighting her candle. "They'll chase him in the forests of old Everlan."

"How did you know?" Raine's left eyebrow went up, admitting the mess she made.

Marlee grinned, tipping her head to the cards on the floor. "...and you?"

"I had a dream," Raine said. "Until a giant water snake appeared. It wound around a great mountain, washing its color away."

"Serpens!" Jillian and Marlee rang in unison.

"They're headed there now, to the Serpens River," Marlee said. "But first they'll pass through the Valley of Princesses. That's where the ghosts will attack them first," she predicted."

"What can we do?" Raine fretted, rocking her petite frame.

"Remember that game we played when Gram took us to the Valley?" Marlee gathered the cards.

"Alison called it 'Dangerous Dolls,'" Raine said.

"That's the one. Good," Marlee said, "Now, Raine, go get candles. White ones. We'll need eight of them, and Jillie, one each of red, brown, silver, and blue. And, of course, Gram's Goldie." They hastened for the candles while Marlee boxed her tarot deck to find long matches.

B y mid-morning, Aeryun and Roulic entered the Valley of Princesses. Walls of boulders, along miles of fine sand, transitioned into a plain of silken shrubs and random palm clusters. The mustangs drank from a rubicund stream meandering across the desert on its way to the river.

"Why is it so ruddy?" he yanked his horse from the scarlet water.

"Cinnabar," she said, "it comes out of the mountain. But no worries, they won't drink enough to hurt them. We'll keep moving. I know a safe place with clean water a couple of hours from here. It's just past the Dolls." He lifted the brim of his hat to wipe sweat. "Statues of princesses," she explained, "from the golden age of dragons. Stone monuments to the daughters of the old king's godsons who ruled during the dragon's reign." He nodded, preferring to daydream of his own flesh-and-blood goddess. They didn't speak again until noon, when an ominous figure appeared dead ahead. Roulic hollered, breaking their silence.

"What's that!?" he yelled, "A red giant? Take cover!" He stopped his horse. The eerie being loomed over a cluster of desert flowers, stretching its arms out to either side.

"It's a Doll," Aeryun said, "come and see." He approached the monument with careful steps, marveling at the cinnabar goddess.

He read to her its carved inscription:

"Gaia Dragonna, first daughter of dragons and keeper of valleys, welcomes you. By the Most High, she rose to ignite the faith of falling stars."

"She was the first," she sipped from her canteen, winking at his blank face. "You didn't think Ravenna was the only one to receive the dragon's gift, did you?"

"I just assumed Grace was the first," he said.

"Oh, no, the daughters of dragons ruled long before Grace. Dragonna served during the period of Great Antiquity. It was because of this valley that historians of Doth gave the dragons their own 'Age'.

"Why isn't this place inhabited by curators and tourists?"

"Too dangerous. Too remote. During the Golden Age, people got mercury poisoning from mining cinnabar. Enough to make the valley taboo; they labeled it a health risk, so it became a forgotten place. Nobody has settled here since olden times. Touching the Dolls can be deadly." He leaped from the statue.

"Come on, then," she said, "we'll make camp by sundown at the Doll's Pool."

They left Gaia Dragonna riding at a brisk pace until they came to a fertile oasis. Dozens of stone effigies guarded the refuge of keeled palms, ironwood, and plum trees.

"What's behind those Dolls beside a pool of water?"

"Nothing but a lot of shade for birds and beasts," she said.

"I could use some shade."

"So can the mustangs." She led the horses along the ring of statues to a gap where a trail led to the poolside campsite in the clearing. "But first things first. Water for the mustangs, and a bath for me."

"I'm right behind you," he said, "after I make a ring and gather some wood." Aeryun liked his playful smile and boyish ardor.

"Don't take too long..." she teased, letting the parched horses guzzle from the pool. Its genesis: the Serpens River.

The three sisters labored in the craft room, making dolls from memory. They sanded ritual wood into torsos, heads, and limbs. They sewed and fitted colored gowns with a regal flair, then detailed heads and hands made of baked clay. Marlee surrendered strands of her and Raine's black and Jillian's sandy hair, styling each figure's head.

"Hurry up, sister," Marlee snapped at Raine, finishing with the coarse and fine hair.

"I'm almost done. I want her to be just as I remember her," Raine said, recalling their childhood visit to the Valley of Princesses.

"You'd better finish her soon. Twilight's near," Marlee decreed. Marlee and Jillian had already finished their Dolls: Melaina and Drita.

"There. Isn't she beautiful?" Raine held up her finished doll. "Talitha Siring, 29th Daughter of Dragons, Keeper of Springs."

"We remember," Jillian said. "She looks lovely. Such a girlish titan."

"Quite the resemblance for a five-hundred-year-old memory. Remember what Gram told us?" Marlee stood, stretching.

"*'Never forget these goddesses. There might come a day when you need one's help.'*" Jillian beat Raine to the answer.

"That's right," Marlee said, circling the table and chairs in chalk. She lit eight white candles around the three dolls set in the center of the table. Raine lit Gram's 'Goldie' candle behind the dolls. Jillian lit the red, brown, silver, and blue candles, positioning them in front of the dolls. A cup of cinnamon was placed by Gram's 'Goldie.' A fragrant bowl of fresh-cut blue verbena and white horehound, put beside it.

"Are we ready, then?" Raine and Jillian bowed their heads. Marlee led her sisters.

When all that was and ever is
stops to charm tomorrow,
there shoots a changeling
out dancing doors to endless shores;
starlight's never ending
For the will of we, calm
amid ireful storms,
coax the odd and wheedle the norm
from head to eye to heart to horn

Where taken, lent, even borrowed
time's memory retreats,
marching tomorrow
on her way to remembering
if not for us old souls,
but for the good of Doth,
whose true kingdom
lies in ancient dragons who birth

air to water, fire to earth

Shall it Be!

Marlee chanted, beckoning Raine and Jillian to hold their dolls in their laps. They chanted together.

O daughters of Doth
heed our call
The hope of a dragon
will carry us all

Less than a minute into the mantra, Raine became entranced and separated from her body. Transcending the floors of Jessamine, her sisters' chanting echoed in her head. A protective pellucid bubble brought her to a small aperture in the sky. It was rectangular, with coruscating balls of light dancing in the evening air. She entered the ethereal chamber, waiting for the light, but it never came. Jillian and Marlee's chanting faded. Carried in darkness, the silent cell let loose, dropping her on the oasis's backside.

She landed at the feet of the favorite statue she had chosen as a young witch: Talitha Sirling. Her siblings' low chanting resumed. She looked up in awe at the moonlit stone princess. *Marlee was right,* she thought; *Talitha does have that 'girlish titan' look.*

Ears of rock turned to flesh. Stone skin restored from red to tan. Garments of fine linen covered the maidenly body. A golden band held back rolling black hair over chiseled shoulders. Tinkling bracelets and charms adorned her arms, wrists, and ankles. The cinnabar goddess towered over Raine like a pillar leaning in the dark.

"I hear you have an interest in the hope of a dragon." Talitha's eyes shone on Raine like white fire. "Where is your army?"

"I have no army," Raine said uneasily. "But I have six sisters, a brother, a grandmother, and her sister and brother. All fighting for the good of Doth. There is great trouble coming here tonight…"

"Where is your good family? I only see a brave woman, alone in my valley. Now tell me about this great trouble."

. . .

"What took you so long?" Aeryun said when Roulic approached the spring. She turned around when he undressed before getting in.

"There are more scraps than branches around here," he said, admiring her wet hair.

"Scraps will do. It's going to get cold tonight," she said.

"We could sleep in this pool," he smiled, flinging drops of warm water.

"We may have to if you didn't gather enough scraps," she splashed him back. They laughed and talked, soaking in the hot springs while the sun melted yellow into pink.

"After this is over, do you think you'll ever settle down?"

"Maybe, maybe not. Life has been good to me so far," she gazed at the fading daylight in the oasis. "I don't know, Roulic!" She splashed him again and grabbed her clothes from the spring's edge. He looked away, but turned to glimpse her stepping out of the water.

Jillian and Marlee stopped chanting when Talitha spoke. But their ritual continued. They held their dolls over their heads and danced in jerky movements around the table. When the sun set, Gram's 'Goldie' candle was lit, releasing sparks that popped when either witch got near it. Flaming candles in the Craft Room's window mirrored the dancing witches and dolls.

"It's getting cold. I'm going to get more scraps," Aeryun said, walking past the horses, then out of the oasis.

Roulic savored Jax's tea. *What magic might the witches be performing at Jessamine House? I can't imagine them sitting around doing nothing.*

"Do you think the witches know what they're missing?" He didn't hear her rustling for scraps. Other than the crackling fire, the camp was quiet as a graveyard.

Conor Jest

"Aeryun?" She didn't respond. "Aeryun?!!"

Chapter 13

Ten Doves Coming

Roulic's tin cup spilled when he jumped, calling, "Aeryun!" He threw on his satchel and reached into the pit, grabbing a flaming branch.

"You can't hurt me with that," a treble voice said. Roulic spun his back to the fire.

"Show yourself!"

"I'm right behind you." The voice laughed like a heckling boy. Roulic turned again, squinting over the flames. The other side of the camp was still. The horses didn't move or make a sound.

"Come out where I can see you. I know you're in there," Roulic challenged.

"If you want to find me, search the inferno," sniggered the foe, his head bobbing in the flames. It was the noggin of Smutch, his charred neck and shoulders merging with the base of the fire. The obese apparition had oily features, forever burning, yet unscathed and unmelted.

"Where's Aeryun?" Roulic shouted at the wight in the fire.

"She's in...fine condition," he sizzled. Smutch's hair and scalp glowed in a spectral fire, but it never burned.

"Tell me where she is or I'll put out," Roulic pointed to the kettle.

"You'll do no such thing." Bliniloth materialized across the fire.

Roulic jumped back instinctively, aghast at the sight of the bluish grotesquerie.

"If you want the wench, you'll do as *I* say," said the head ghost. "Now, give me the dragon egg and hand over that wretched key."

"I don't have it," Roulic opened his satchel, "see?" All he had was a drawstring bag of tobacco and the two lighters that Marlee gave him.

"What!? We'll see about that," he puffed. "Smutch!" The burning, bobbing head leaped from the flames and rolled to the feet of his master, winding up. Smutch delivered a rapid fireball. It ignited their blankets, sending embers across the campsite.

"I'm telling you! I dropped it yesterday coming off the mountain. The egg is no more."

Roulic flinched when the combusting campsite spread fire to the oasis. He ran to the mustangs, so Bliniloth signaled Smutch to throw a fastball at the horses. It ripped like a gazelle, but the horses were faster. They bolted, escaping into the desert, the grinning ghosts cornering him by the fire, moving in.

"Wait! I have the key. Bring me to the girl and I'll give it to you once I see that she's alive."

"She's not who or what we're after. But with no steed or tack, she'll never make it out alive in this sea of sand. So don't get any ideas about hoisting sails. S-m-u-t-c-h!" the rogue commander shouted, then clapped twice.

Roulic found himself steaming on the cold desert floor outside the burning oasis. He jittered, patting his smoking clothing. Unbound yet fully arrested, Aeryun bathed in moonlight by a saguaro cactus. He ran to her and the ghosts.

"What's wrong with her? Why isn't she moving?"

"She's frozen, frozen in time. But she's oh, oh so fine," Bliniloth sang perversely. "This mourning bird won't abandon love with ten doves coming." Smutch besmirched, grinning at his keeper.

"Make her unfrozen. You can have the key," Roulic said.

"You can bet I'll have that key. ...NOW!" Bliniloth roared, doubling in height to over twelve feet.

Bursting boots stomped in wide circles, sending sand seven feet in the air. In less than a second, Roulic produced and dangled the Pearlytok. Bliniloth's swollen palm dipped to the key and opened wide. Gaudy rings on fattened fingers made Roulic's hand holding the Pearlytok seem dwarfish. He gave the Pearlytok one last look and let go of that which he had held so close for so long.

Aeryun's life is worth more than any key. God help us now.

The instant the Pearlytok touched Bliniloth's palm, Aeryun came out of her trance. She ran beside Roulic. The ghosts kept devilish eyes fixed on the coveted key as silver bolts signaled above, in the arch of the sky. Wild gusts wrangled the key. Up and up and up, it tossed and turned until its golden sheen waned against the backdrop of the candescent moon. Aeryun cringed. Roulic reached for his stomach.

Bliniloth turned to Roulic. "That's one down. Now about that egg. Don't think I swallowed your little 'I dropped it' ploy to buy yourself time. Smutch! Go back and find that egg. It has to be lying around there somewhere."

Smutch moved like a meteor. In the light of the palms burning around their camp, Aeryun could see the Doll's sad faces. She tried to hold back her tears but couldn't.

"I'm sorry, Aeryun," Roulic said. "I am beyond sorry." His mind rushed, thinking how they could flee in the dark on foot, but Bliniloth was too big and too fast. *Without horses, we don't have a chance.*

Aeryun's chin lifted. "It's okay, Roulic. I knew what I was getting into. The witches warned me they would come for the egg and the key." He reached for her hand. "I just didn't know they would be an ugly ghost and a fat man on fire." Her face angled with a slight grin despite their despair at knowing they were out of time.

Smutch returned to report. "Well?" Bliniloth said. Smutch shook his head.

"I blazed the place. There's nothing but ash on the ground."

"Hmm," Bliniloth purred, "'Nothing on the ground,' you say," he glared at Roulic. "You know, Smutch, if I were running around the desert carrying a holy dragon egg, I would bury it somewhere in the sand."

"I could *make* them tell you where it is," Smutch said, wiggling flames from his fingers.

"You've left me no choice, Ancient. Smutch!!" The sky grew bright, a white light surrounding the ghosts.

Talitha flashed like lightning, blindsiding Bliniloth. Her attack knocked him over, issuing stomps to his head with her stone feet. Smutch's strategy entailed fleeing the area. He detached his arms and legs from his body, then ignited surrounding brush and cacti. Bliniloth covered his head enough to recover, rise, and lunge at Talitha. But Jillian and Marlee's Dolls from the oasis charged him from behind. After kicking the air out of and through his body, they subdued his wiggling wrists. Each Doll cuffed a joint and knuckle. Then they attacked his formidable arms, taking errant pleasure in his newfound quietus. With rock-hard grips, they swung him in circles, generating a whirlwind.

"Dump him in the Dunes, girls," Talitha said. Melaina and Drita whirled Bliniloth toward the setting moon, laughing like rapacious whelps. He wriggled to break free from their relentless clench until his arms gave out. Following a violent desert tempest, they carried him 20 miles south of the oasis. They dropped his vanquished body in the valley's most brutal area: the Desolate Dunes.

Predawn erased stars over the Valley of Dolls and the smoldering oasis. Raine created a minor downpour, overseeing Smutch's downfall. Green gas came weeping up over his burnt silhouette.

"He's not dead. They'll both be back," Marlee warned when Raine descended from the air.

"I know," Raine said. "But I'm glad they didn't have time to—"

"Your timing was theatrical," Aeryun said. "I'm still in shock."

"A little too close for me, too." Roulic hugged Aeryun and the witches.

"Our favorite Dolls, Melaina and Drita, as you may recall," Jillian said, "were the keepers of Light and..."

"Dark!" Marlee cheered.

"You mean *are*," Raine said. "Blessings be to all our sisters, in light and dark." The witches came together, then stepped back, raising their hands. "In light and dark!" Their moment of joy lessened, though, when Aeryun brought up the dragon egg.

"That fire monster must have annihilated it when he burned up the camp. And now, without the key, we have no way to jump back. Can you get us back?"

Roulic turned to Aeryun and the witches. "We're not going back."

Chapter 14

A Dragon's Hope

The Dolls returned to their posts around the oasis. But Jillian and Marlee's gratitude and well-wishes soon turned bittersweet. They cried when Melaina and Drita petrified at dawn. Talitha Sirling stood at her post, animate, as the direct sunlight did not affect her for the time being.

"I can't thank you enough for what you and the Daughters have done for us," Raine said, looking up to the stone goddess.

"It is for the good of Doth. And the hope of dragons," Talitha said. "How will you and your sisters return home?"

"We are in a witch's dream, riding the astral plane until we awaken at home. My sisters and I are returning to our bodies when Roulic and Aeryun leave."

"Your family has served the dragons well, Raine."

"Could I come back and sit with you here for a while? We could share stories and secrets, like sisters," Raine said.

"That would be nice, little sister," Talitha smiled. "But hurry back soon, for when the sun sets tonight, I too will return to stone."

"I'll be right back, I promise," Raine ran to her sisters.

Roulic spotted the mustangs nibbling on desert marigold. Whistling a high piercing sound, he waited, sighing when their heads popped up. Signaling again, they resumed foraging, moving toward the oasis. He warmed Aeryun, leading her back to the camp. She was still numb from the shock of her near-death trance. They salvaged smoldered silverware, saddles and packs, cups, a kettle, a pot, and plates. But it was the blackened blankets and pillows, scorched to bits of blown ash, that most upset Roulic.

"It's going to be a rough night," he said. Aeryun nodded, stoically.

"Roulic...," she said.

"Yes, about what I said. Follow me." He pointed to the back of the clearing. "To the pool."

Her expression lifted. She followed him around the spring to the spot where he hid the egg. "I buried it under this stone," he said, winking at the witches, "after our bath." They watched him unearth the egg, happy with how heedful he was in putting it in his satchel. "I'll regret to my last day, failing the gnomes," he said. "In Mayem's hand, the Pearlytok will be lost."

"Not lost," Marlee consoled. "Do you remember when Eeo held the Pearlytok?" They took their boots off by the pool.

"He found the key in Gadbanti's cave. Why?"

"He hid it in his jacket pocket."

"Yes, then he gave it to me."

"Not quite." Marlee came clean, dipping her feet in the pool. "You see, days before the Pearlytok theft at the schnaball game, Demeter gave Eeo a replica key. He then passed it to you outside of the caves. Eeo gave you a fake key. After you and the gnomes outran the giants, you went to Demeter's cottage where Eeo slipped her the real key. Three days later she brought Eeo and the Pearlytok to King Vim at Trumbleton Wells. So you see, the actual key's not lost. It's not lost at all. The fae used Demeter's replica to get their land back from Captain Salty. You've carried the replica for quite some time."

"I've been carrying around a fake?" Roulic shook his head, feeling duped. "But why? And what about Mr. Nagnee? He used the key to jump me from your house. I saw Ravenna with my own eyes. Didn't I?"

"You most certainly did," she swished her feet in the pool. "But Forby didn't deceive as much as distract. He simply got you to think you were using the protection of the Pearlytok. In fact, he used our little old well. It's an extraordinarily safe portal — and was the deciding factor in choosing Jessamine. We were going to tell you about the replica when you arrived, but we decided to wait until Mayem got it. Belief holds great power."

"And to think I seldom questioned you before Lilith. Maybe I should have believed in what she had to say."

"I wouldn't believe what comes out of Lilith's mouth. We never needed the key. Ever. We needed you to need the key so we could get you closer to Mayem. We've been more than forthright with you, Roulic. Yes, we've hidden a few details along the way. But hidden for good reason, considering the weaving nature of your passage."

"Was Eeo in on the theft of the Pearlytok in the schnaball fields? I've long wondered about that."

"Yes. He and another gnome. They made sure Gadbanti was waiting below the field on the day of the game. Gadbanti's grudge goes back generations with Mayem," Marlee said.

"Is that why the giants sealed Mayem's cave?"

"Yep. But now, Gadbanti's vendetta includes you, as your team of gnomes killed his brother, Kubba. His sons, Jabdu and Innick, will carry on the vendetta, so stay alert and, if you can, never again cross a giant. They don't soon forget their enemies."

"Why'd Eeo do it? For silver?" Roulic removed his feet from the spring.

"Eeo's always had criminal tendencies, but he didn't steal it for money. When Mayem hunted creatures for sport, the Inner folk rose against him, Eeo included. He knew Gadbanti could and would use the key to hurt Mayem."

"But there is some good news in all this," Marlee said, lacing her knee-high leathers. "When the ghosts of Onan deliver the key, Mayem will be content for a while. This will buy you time to get up the mountain."

"Any final advice for two weary travelers? We'll be heading out after we water the broncs," Roulic said, getting up.

The witches, cleansing their feet in the pool, concurred, "Don't drop the egg!"

They all laughed, and for a moment Roulic felt at ease, like he was back home with Ravenna. And when his gladsome moment returned to reality, Marlee said, "Don't worry, Roulic, we'll be with you every step of the way."

Mayem took over Nina's place at the Titan Dreams motel. She didn't object to his staying there, realizing she had no choice. He allowed her to let people in while waiting for Bliniloth. Some she knew, some she didn't, but they were all strangely familiar to Mayem. He considered these "darker-soul mortalkin" more to his liking than the mortals of Doth.

She stayed in the bedroom when Bliniloth and Smutch showed up. Using the vase to do Mayem's bidding was one thing. But escorting him on his black path no longer served her intention. So, she listened, sitting on her bed before her Tarot de Marseille deck. Her left hand card faced her, her right hand anxious to reveal the final card's front. Before it was too late. *Before this gets out of control,* she thought. *It's bad enough he's had his way with me as much as he has. And that I like it as much as I do. This has got to stop.* She flipped the Death card, fearing not Mayem as much as what her transformation might entail.

"I appreciate your work." Mayem lacked eye contact due to staring at the counterfeit key in his hand. "But I must have that egg. A dragon's hope, you see, is what stands in my way. When that hope dies, I will cleanse Doth of all its dragons. And giants, and so on. Mortalkin will come to obey me, praise me for ridding the land of those pesky creature folk. But I've got to have that egg. And now that we've arranged oaths, I expect you to honor yours as I shall mine." He paced, putting the key in his pocket; his hand kept on the key.

"Understood." Diabolic eyes tested Mayem from across the room. Mayem's arrogance ruffled Bliniloth. Enough for him to entertain *annihilating the infuriating mortal. He's treading curtains, this one is.*

"And where is the third ghost of Onan, this Ozrar? He might have brought the egg back had he been there," Mayem rattled, itching at his heel.

. . .

"He's on his way; don't you worry, mate," Bliniloth said, sick of listening to Mayem's demands.

"He'd better be," Mayem snarled, sick of looking at Bliniloth and Smutch.

The singed oasis behind them, a sea of sand and rolling dunes lay ahead. Skinny vultures circled the mustangs, watching for anything bigger than a finger that moved. Roulic rode up beside Aeryun.

"How far is it to the river?"

"Not too far. Just past the cliffs," she pointed.

He didn't see any cliffs. All he could see was sand. He shook his canteen, debating a swig, then bathed his parched throat in a last gulp of spring water. It wasn't long before he nodded off with his hands holding the reins wrapped around his saddle horn. Thunderbolts couldn't have stirred his desert languor.

His head jounced, coming to rest chin-to-chest, dreaming. Beyond a field, he could see a little bridge made of stone. Its princely arch keeping watch over a pond that occupied both sides of a road. To him, it held only one similarity to the treacherous rope-and-plank bridge of Belief: it was there. A bridge. And she upon it. His heart raced watching her lean over its arch. She mused at a creature in the water below; a determined, humbled duckling. She cheered as it waddled up the sloping grass beside the roadway, shaking its tail. He ran through the field, waving his arms, shouting, "Ravenna! Ravenna!" but she didn't hear him. Two wandering monarchs accompanied him before disappearing underneath the belly of the bridge. He stopped on the grassy bank below the bridge. Their eyes met.

"It's a fine day for bridges," he said to the silhouette shrouded in sunlight.

"And butterflies, too," she leaned out over the bridge. A passing cloud blocked the sun, allowing him to see her radiant eyes.

She's more alive than all of creation.

With the darkened sky came an odd torrent that drenched the land but avoided the bridge. Soaked, he slipped, running up the grass to greet her. The warm rain dragged him beneath the bridge. His knees locked. Arms flailed, shoes stuck to the sandy bottom. He wondered how he could breathe while submerged. Until the slithering Ozrar violated his mind. A horripilating monotone, uttered neither fast nor slow. Its steady cadence was smooth and calculating. It cut, enunciating syllables rhythmically, the pulse lulling him.

"Be still, Roulic. All your troubles will diminish when you let go of the egg. To your eternal credit will come a well-deserved glory. Return the egg to its rightful owner. To the master whose magnificent hearth it was made to warm, and you will not go unrewarded. Praising the sacred beast in holy ceremony is something mortalkin will long remember. And not to boast of the fire-breathing treasure, but to honor its exalted seat as the reborn symbol of Doth. It will become the One Realm's ever-lasting mascot; a living emblem of the people. It is a gift from the gods, bestowed by the Masters from on High. It holds the greatest prestige among any of its kind ever made. Doth will forever be in your debt, bowing in gratitude for your selfless deed."

"No!" Roulic gasped, taking water into his lungs. "I'll never give you the egg. It's not for you or for Mayem or for anyone. That dragon will be born again among its family as the Masters intended. It's not for your 'beast'. And never will be." He woke in Aeryun's shadow, rolling in gravel at the edge of the Serpens River. She slid off her saddle, holding his shoulders while he expelled water from his lungs.

"I fell asleep," he sputtered. "I dreamt of evil. Coming for the egg. We must get the egg to the mountain before Destiny changes her mind."

Jax sat at Alison's feet on the wide hearthstone in her bedroom. He took apart handfuls of Oreo cookies, eating them until she finished painting her toenails.

"They match the wagon," he said.

"I know."

"They also match your hair," he said.

"I know."

"What do you call that color?"

"Metallic Burgundy."

"Your feet look nice."

"I know."

She reached for a hooked needle that Gram gave her as a child. Within minutes, a series of looped stitches, steadily appeared, meticulously thread in green yarn.

"We've got to do something about them—and soon," he said, breaking his silent stare into the tiny fire.

"I know we do, little brother," she swayed in her ash ladder-back rocker. "That's why I asked Auntie and Gram to meet us at midnight tonight."

"Where?"

"Where else?" Alison tossed her head. "Glassy Hall."

Chapter 15

All Sun Faery

The Blacks' gathering in Glassy Hall was brief. And more a family affair than strategic discourse about Mayem's perennial curse. That Mayem had overshadowed the family for as long as they could remember was a given. That their parents' violent end blocked contact from the other side only caused more pain. So they always met any communication from the elders with loving hearts. But they never knew what to expect from Gram and Auntie.

Vintage images rippled across the enchanted glass, enrapturing the witches. The faces of Frane and Damira, and a young Arthur holding his infant nieces, brought oohs and ahs from the ladies. One in particular, an early visage of Demeter and Sionann, especially thrilled the progeny wedged in the plush purple pew.

"They were so beautiful in their day," Aurora said.

"Famously beautiful," Jillian said.

"They were a beautiful infamy," Alison said.

Arthur appeared at the end of the pew, standing by Jax. His profuse apology about Catalina received nods and lyrical drivel from the witches. Their complete trust in Aeryun Porter to guide Roulic to the dragon's lair made up for his late arrival. However, had she been unavailable, he would have sensed their contempt forever.

Gram's whisper to Demeter slipped through a dark wave of dissipating vapor. "His delay *might* have been a disaster, but it wasn't, so let's not agitate their poetry-ran-rue."

"Good evening, my darlings," Demeter announced her authority. "I hope by now you can all accept the inevitable: that the mysterious ebb and flow of Change. It will erupt, weave like a serpent, and alter course with no notice. Your great uncle most certainly lives with this acceptance. He has no other choice. But the lessons of Time, for better or worse, have made him adaptable. Might I remind you, it was Arthur who restored Gadbanti's family bones, and Arthur who found the lost egg. Now, moving on to address our current development, I give you Lady Sionann."

Gram pointed at her grandchildren. "Oh, but let us remember that whenever one window closes, another one opens. Aeryun is a part of us, and we have faith she will lead Roulic to the peak. We hope she can. She's always been an all-sun faery; undaunted on paths lacking illumination."

"But we see no harm in aiding her in this complicated calculation," Demeter interrupted.

"And that's why we've propositioned the hidden hand of Leaf Nelson," Gram said, "as a backup of sorts."

"Beware the fallen ones..." Agnes murmured to Madelyn.

Marlee shushed the duo. "Yes. He fell with the others, but that was ages ago. I'm sure he's seeking redemption with this gesture and other deeds, too. And no, that's not his true name. His true name is unspeakable."

"Why contact *him*? Mayem's akin to that dark ilk." Aurora stood, booming at the mirror.

"Because sometimes one must fight fire with fire." Gram's said, dropping an octave, putting Aurora's tush back on the pew. "Unless you've got another notion to safeguard and remedy the ebb and flow of unseen events." Demeter quavered at Gram's method of discipline.

Alison supported Aurora's objection to connecting with a fallen one. She stared into the eyes of Gram and Demeter. "When and where will you find him?"

"We already have, child. During the last new moon. We don't know if he'll show. But we've opened a door for him, just the same. Aeryun and Roulic need all the help they can get. The ghosts of Onan may be wayward, but they are relentless in pursuit. They carry their own motives — dark motives, I might add. For now, we hold our breath for Roulic and the dragon. Our hearts and hope are with you."

She rambled some old tune, holding up a long yellow candle.

> "It's seven minutes to the witching hour. Lock your
> windows, lock your doors."

Then, blowing the family a kiss that blew out the candle, she dulled, as did Demeter, after sending out a big hug. The mirror went black. The elders were gone.

"Well, that story didn't take long, but we got to see some pretty pictures," Madelyn joked. Agnes laughed.

Jax turned on the hall light. "There's always such a great buzz in this house when they stop by, no matter how long or how short."

"Undoubtedly," Arthur said, "a great telling weaves within their convexity. But I fear this 'buzz' may ring in our ears for a while." Agnes and Madelyn followed him to the kitchen for scoops of Häagen-Dazs sorbet.

Dusk faded like a thief running. "Keep up, will ya? You don't know how lucky you are. You're lucky you didn't fall off a cliff before we reached the river," Aeryun laughed, fording the Serpens River.

"My horse back home wouldn't have let that happen," Roulic said.

"We'll leave the mustangs here," she said, reaching the bank. "They'll roam around, but they'll be waiting for us when we get back."

"Might they meet predators?" He unsaddled his horse.

"Maybe. But they could outrun them. There are miles of this rocky beach around the base of the mountain for them to explore. No need to worry about the fire-breathers down here, though. Let's get moving. We've still got enough light to climb some of the mountain and look for a cave. We'll reach the summit, and return the egg, tomorrow."

"And it won't be too soon," he said. They found no caves, so at dusk, they crawled between a cracked boulder, using its crevice as a wind block. Aeryun kept close to him before the temperature fell. Wrapping her body around his back, she burrowed her hands, keeping them warm in his jacket pockets.

At sunrise, they drank the last of their water, hoping to reach the summit by dark. By sundown, they'd only stopped twice to collect water caught in the crotches of tree limbs and porous rocks.

"Grand Pekoes could well be Mt. Nocturne's big brother. Have you ever been to Top of the World?"

"Arthur took me there once. It was beautiful. I'd like to go back someday," she said, giving him a brooding look. They refreshed their dry throats, ready to ascend the summit.

"To Grand Pekoes," Roulic raised his canteen.

"And to Mt. Nocturne," Aeryun proffered.

"To Mt. Nocturne." Their canteens met with a hearty clink. As they drank, an unusual darkness overshadowed their toast.

"Take cover. It's a dragon!" They dropped to their feet, scrambling to hide behind the closest boulder. They peeked out from the stone. It was Brac, circling the mountain. Roulic recognized the emerald green half-moon birthmark underneath his wing. The massive, dirty pink body sailed by like an Athenian trireme. Tan wing tips cut through the air not a hundred yards above them, landing the dragon on its perch. The fire-breathing Brac sounded desolate moans, silencing all creatures on the mountain.

"He's yowling for his baby sister," Aeryun's whisper invoked a memory of his little sister, Kolleen. "His brother's even bigger," she said in awe of the forlorn dragon. "We've no protection here from dragon fire, so be ready to move." Roulic didn't dare move from behind the boulder.

"Wait. We've got time. If he sees us, we'll be in a worse way." A mountain hare stopped to study them, crouched behind the boulder. Its curiosity made him think of his little brother, lost in the caves of Black Shadows Beach. But a skinny wolf cornered the creature between two stones, making him wince. Rooting for the hare, he remembered Fere's dragon encounter and final survival.

Aeryun tapped his shoulder. "I've spotted a place for us to hide. Get ready to get across that shale. There's better protection on the other side of it, this side of the trees. Do you see it? That house of boulders? We can crawl in there through that door. Do you see the opening?"

He spotted the mound of huge rocks and the cave opening. His eyes went back to the hare. "It's too far. The dragon could see us before we get there. Let's wait to see where it goes."

The wolf pawed, backed up, hungry, and pawed again. At the lair, Brac heard the echoes of the whining below. His wings flapped, scaring the wolf. When it ran, Brac lunged from the perch, landing a dragon's step from the fleeing hare. The dragon's weight sent a ponderous wave of earth and shale careening over a jagged ledge on the mountain. A second wave slid, sending a black sheet of dust that shot back high into the air over the ledge.

"Now's our chance! C'mon, we can make it," she said, jumping from the boulder.

"No. Wait, Aeryun!" Roulic screamed, but it was too late. She ran towards the brittle sheet of loose debris to reach the cave. The wolf ran again, huddling behind rocks surrounded by shrubs. Brac's mighty jaw lowered, baring scores of sharp teeth. A single flame flew out from his throat and scorched the brush. The wolf fled to the tree line. Brac pursued, his leap pushing edgy debris and deadwood that collided with Aeryun as she ran for the cave. Roulic shuddered when she fell. She tried to get up, but the rolling wave of moving shale dragged her down and over the cliff.

"No! Aeryun!" He ran from the boulder to where the shale had taken her and crouched, looking over the drop-off. A sheet of dust shot up over the ledge, forcing him to scoot back and wait for the dust to settle. Crawling back to the edge, he surveyed the heap of earth and rock. But Aeryun was gone. Buried in a tomb laden with mountain runoff.

Brac circled the summit, spinning wind over Roulic's head. He ran, quivering behind a tree, hiding until the dragon flew into the setting sun. When he lost sight of the body of the beast, he hiked to the dragon's lair. They had carried and nudged boulders, creating a ring around their lair. Heaps of strewn feathers and pine needles blew about the open den. Gathering plenty of cushioning, he fashioned a shelter inside a hollowed log. Then he knelt, putting the egg onto the soft bed.

"May the hope in your heart grow as big as this mountain." The dragon egg vibrated, then glowed a light green. Each time it vibrated, it rolled to either side of the crib. So he kept the cup of his hands ready to prevent it from rolling over and off the feathered bed. That didn't work as it rolled too far too fast and slipped past the reach of his hand. But before it could fall off the bed, it rolled back to the middle. This made him sigh, then let out a laugh and then a cry. A cry that shed tears that wet the pregnant shell.

"That was for my friend, Aeryun." He stayed with the dragon egg until it was warm and stopped moving.

"By the god who made and took Aeryun, I will see Mayem's end," he declared from the lair, into the day's last light.

Chapter 16

The Dragons, the Heart

He shivered, staring at the lonesome campfire he built between two trees. "Oh, Aeryun, how I miss you. As will all at Jessamine. You lived in peace, my friend, and now peace has brought you home. I pray someday we will meet again in peace. God bless your soul."

At daybreak, he left the southern side of Grand Pekoes facing the Soaring Hills. His final words to the daunting mountain: "You've taken Aeryun, but I'll not let you take me. My kismet is with Ravenna, so be it, evermore." He filled his canteen from a pool of water trapped in a bowl-shaped rock. It was tough descending the mountain without Aeryun to guide him, but he moved fast, focusing on each step in front of him.

I may not have to worry about carrying the egg, but I've still got to keep an eye out for wolves and dragons.

It wasn't long before his heart came back to his short time together with Ravenna. *How raggedly beautiful she looked when she came off the Bridge of Belief. And how ravishing she was at the castle. How gentle she was, saving that man's dying wife in the wagon. How fearless she became, squashing that traitor, Bandy Ambage. While I was safe at Top of the World, she was in Dandoorthose, battling the face of villainy behind enemy lines. Her letter helped Callian win the war. Oh, I hope to forego war. Maybe I'll never return to 1999. Why should I? Maybe I'll stay here and wait for her. I might find her riding Arrow on one of her lone rides near the bridge. We'll build our new life together, here and now.*

I'll hide here in old Everlan and wait to end Mayem. Before he gets to her... and why not? The Pearlytok is safe. Finding Ravenna before Mayem means her not getting tied to the bridge. I can finally ambush him and break the curse. Before he utters it.

He obsessed over Mayem, working his way down the lonely mountain.

How did he learn to cast curses? He couldn't have done it on his own. He cursed the witches. And my family. He's been attacking Meyrick since birth. I hope I can stop him before he harms more people. Fere won't get attacked by a dragon, and Kolleen and Ren won't know what it is to be enslaved. Alastar can come back to our family... damn that Mayem! I'd be with Ravenna and my family if it weren't for him.

Eventually, his mind receded to Rubina, the gnomes, and the mortals of Doth.

Callian and Jensen were great friends. People that feel like family. And the witches, whom I've grown to love and trust as my own. Oh Destiny, I've refrained from thinking of you, but thank you just the same. I've never felt so loved as I have since meeting Ravenna on that old bridge. That crazy old bridge. For so long, the world has been my home, causing me to forget the meaning of family. Family is home. Who was the herder on Mt. Nocturne? Alexander. Ah, yes, Alexander Chase. She called him Sasha...

He slipped, then slid several feet on his butt when Dyad and Brac flew over. Their massive wings drove a current of chilled air over the slope that felled him.

They were in a hurry — in fight or flight. But did they see me? And let me live?

"Good God!" Roulic got to his feet, taking cover behind a fallen trunk. He lay beside it, clinging to its damp skin. *They could make another pass any second. Better stay here for now.* Rolling closer, he smelled the dank wet bark. Not yet rotten. Water dribbled out of the trunk like a sponge, soaking his back. The decaying tree lay leaking over a sinkhole.

Planting his hands on either side of the opening got him sliding down on his back. Six feet into the hole, his boots met the half-foot-deep pond of sludge. Bracing on the wet walls of earth, he stepped side to side, wiggling his way back up. Mud oozed over his head and body, but through the opening, he could see the slope.

I don't see any sign of them. I'd better get out of this hole now.

A chunky root serving as a ladder rung dropped into the sludge. Water splashed around the bottom of the sinkhole, causing the recess to start caving in on itself. Straining against the buckling walls, he kicked his legs out like a trapeze artist. Rolling over onto his stomach, he pushed up and out until his torso, then head, followed. Reaching solid ground, the sinkhole collapsed.

"Phew!" He jumped up, panting after evading suffocation and a muddy burial.

God, get me off this dragon's mountain.

After hastening for an hour through unforgiving boulders and brush, he stopped. At the altar of an efficacious evergreen, sacrificed branches scraped off encrusted mud. His canteen served its last cup. *Thank the gods I've such a light load. No pack, no egg to slow me down.* Forsaking the glorious shade, he descended to the nearest tree, then the next, and so on. At last, he found his bounty: deliverance on the floor of Grand Pekoe's southern side.

From the mountain's base, he hiked along the Serpens shore, never expecting to find the mustangs. They were well-acclimated to mountainous terrain, but prone to going off on their own.

..yet they are able, able as any, and will survive. They would have found a ford to cross and be halfway over the dunes by now. And I've not got the physical strength, nor the will, to keep searching for them. But when he found them idle along the riverbank, he jumped for joy. The curious duo came trotting when he whistled, as happy to see him as he was to see them.

He rode bareback along the bank at a slow trot so as not to exhaust the hungry horses. He soaked his feet and bloated himself on fresh water as did the horses to get their fill. They were ravenous, with no choice except to keep on keeping on.

He crossed the river through a beaver's dam on Aeryun's horse. The other horse followed, and soon they were back in the thick of the trees. *But that much closer to Everlan and with no dunes to tread.*

S pirits soared when the trio came upon an unoccupied cabin. His mouth watered at the sight of six chickens in a coop and then barrels of grain set alongside a hay barn. The lot held a trough, an outhouse, a one-horse corral, and cut logs stacked alongside the old cruck house.

With the mustangs inhaling hay, he enclosed them in the barn and got a fire going. Matching rocking chairs faced the cabin's modest hearth. The opposite corner held a cowhide-cushioned pine sofa and a brass-hinged cedar chest serving as a low table.

I'll open that later.

Further inspection revealed a bedroom furnished with an empty dresser and end table. Clean sheepskin throws covered the bed and pillows.

I'll sleep warm tonight.

Along the hearth's wall, a corner kitchen held an empty pantry. A cupboard held cups, plates, and bowls. Drawers held sacks of skin bags, cloth, linen, bits of paper, and various household articles. Frying pans hung on nails over a butter churn. A second set of drawers held an inkhorn and quill among utensils and aged silverware. Sacks of corn-meal, sugar, flour, pouches of cinnamon, spices, pepper, and a salt pig filled a large bread box.

Okay, now that cedar chest.

Lifting the lid, he found a note on top of two folded wool blankets. Scrawled in nutgall ink on the back of an Everlan advertisement for *The Dragon's Market*, it read:

> Gone to town. Feed the chickens. Milk in the river. Mind ye my house, Robert.

I'll eat well tonight. But did he know I was coming? This is strange. Is someone else the way?

The want of fresh milk found him rushing to find the river. He darted from the cabin into the forest, finding a trail leading to a soft bank and the sound of clear running water. *Thank the gods!* A staff knotted with ropes tied to several skin bags held the precious milk. He warmed his belly drinking half a bag then and there. Back at the cabin, he scrambled a four-egg feast with a side of fire-baked cast-iron cornbread. Gazing at the fire after dinner, a heavy sleep took over his weary body, rocked by the hearth.

Waking to a bed of embers, he hankered for his pipe. *I should be with my Ravenna. My family. Home.*

Rummaging through the cabin by a flickering oil lamp, he found no tobacco, only flint and steel. Outside, on a cold porch rocker, he sipped coffee in the chill of dawn.

Need warmth. Blankets are in the chest. He dashed back into the cabin. *Ah, the smell of cedar.* Out came a blanket. And an item that knocked; the humblest of reliquaries, put beneath the colored wool throw. A handsome house made of brass and silver, identical to the cabin. Its centerpiece, a row of five stones set on its A-frame roof. Opening the oblong ceiling revealed an inner box made of cedar and similar in design to that of the cedar chest. Lifting its lid, the chamber held dozens of coins from faraway counties and countries. He went to the cabin's one window, admiring the gem's opalescence in the morning light. Turning the house over, written in script on the bottom, a bold hallmark read *Atlas Boxes*. But as it tipped, the inner box of coins fell out, revealing the larger compartment's floor. It held a dozen or more envelopes. Letters of gratitude from people who sheltered at the haven after finding it uninhabited.

It wasn't until reading the seventh letter that his head spun.

What is this place? Blood withdrew from his face. The hair on his arms stood up as he read the seventh letter, written in his handwriting.

It is by your kindness that I survived the night from two dragons, the hearts of whom I was born to serve. I thank the god of good fortune for the light on my path of wandering that came in no small measure from your goodwill.

Please accept this fancy jasper; it is all that I have.
Roulic

"I've been here before," he uttered, dropping the letter. Then he spied on the floor what he couldn't comprehend. Among the fallen coins was the stone Agnes had given him on his first night at Jessamine House. His face contorted from the mind-boggled flux. *I've not touched it since Jessamine!* He dug into his pocket for the stone. *What! It has to be here!* It wasn't. He searched his satchel on the porch. It wasn't there. He went back in and checked his jacket. Nothing.

I'm not staying here a moment longer. After doing a clean sweep of the cabin, he stopped. *Should I take both the letter and stone?* He didn't know what to do. So he left both the letter and the stone, his uncertainty rearing its head as he readied the horses.

There's so much I don't understand about timelines and portals. I may never know. But I need to leave here. And fast.

He left the empty skin bags tied to their post by the stream. "We've got to drink while we can," he said to the mustangs, filling his canteen as they lapped in good spirits. Hunger returned by late morning, bringing him to swallow the juice of chewed pine needles. *Not too bad. Not as good as a drink from the Harking Toad, but better than nothing.*

He rode Aeryun's horse, switching to the other at noon. When the forest got too thick to trot, he walked them through the maze of fallen trunks and snapped branches. They stopped when shafts of sunshine fell on their heads. Under the needles and cones, a path lay at their feet.

Why is it so wide? And why would it end here? Or start here? Who uses this?

They followed the path finding pockets of white clumps weaved from tree to trees. Bush-entangled trunks coated in stringy thread. Whole thickets blanketed in the yarn, like silken snowdrifts, walled the web on either side of the road. The mustangs responded by moving erratically, speeding up and slowing down.

A massive communal spider's nest. I've never seen the likes of this. What lies ahead? A den of giants or...

The ground shook, and all the trees swayed. Swaths of leaves fell from the trees on panicking rats. He squeezed the reins when the horses flinched and whinnied. *Go!* They accelerated, galloping for cover. *Nothing but spiderwebs!* He kept them running until a patch of light revealed the path's dead end: a cave, surrounded by trees. Built of mud and stone, its opening was high enough to clear the horses. *And a giant! But I've got no choice...I'm not exploring it. We'll stay put right here.* Reluctant to enter the cave, the mustangs did so only after another thunderous thud.

That felt like a dragon landing in a nearby field. It could be both of them. And so close! Gotta stay here. Roulic's heart sped, reining the mustangs into the cavern. He turned them around, keeping them close to the opening to view through the forest.

More dragon thuds ensued. Thrashing about and shouting over great squashing footsteps. *I know those voices. The ghosts of Onan! Going after Dyad and Brac. He must be huge! He's looking for the egg!*

With each ground-shaking dragon stomp, he stepped farther into the cave. The mustangs shrieked and broke away. "No!" he screamed when they bolted, his echo slapping the depths of the cave. *God help me in this cave. Gotta stay near the opening, ready to run.*

"You got him! Throw that boulder on him!" Smutch spun out from the trees. Dyad's furious screech preceded a long blast, catching fire to the forest. Bliniloth threw another boulder and yelled at the grounded beast. "Almost got me with that one!" Roulic heard wings flapping and the sound of boulders cracking. *Good for you. Fly over them.*

"Can't burn me. But I can burn you," Smutch jeered.

There must be a clearing. Don't hear trees breaking. Roulic looked out of the cave for another path—anywhere to run. *I'll run back the way we came. Gotta get out of this cave.*

"Forth, Roulic, always forth. Isn't that what the man said?" Ozrar's derision bounced off the walls, parching the cave. Roulic spun around.

"Stay away, demon! I'll have nothing to do with you."

"Oh, yes you will. We want the egg and you have it. And don't tell me you crawled up the mountain and put it back for the dragons."

"I did! And almost died. My guide gave her life saving that egg." His hand found his knife handle after Ozrar's eyes turned red in the dark. *Ozrar's showing himself!*

"Dare ye raise your voice? Your mind, your metal? You're in no position to resist!" The truculent devil spewed violent emotion across Roulic's mind. "We went to the lair and found nothing!" The cave got muggy and dripped with the sentiment of friable trees dying outside.

"And now the dragons are after *you*," Roulic yelled back. "And they won't give up chasing you until you dwell in perdition, where, Lord knows, you belong." Ozrar's eyes expelled all the red into darkness. Roulic sighed in solitude, then peeked out through the flaming forest. He witnessed Dyad and Brac swoop over Bliniloth and Smutch. They whisked and whirred, sending a barrage of brotherly fire over the warring ghosts. Touching the reignition taking place at the back of his head, Smutch screamed, "Blow me down!"

"Turn around. There's someone I want you to meet," Ozrar's sinewy whisper returned, seeping through Roulic's ear. He turned around, agitated at first, then fearful, shaking his head, trying to get the demon out of his head.

"You know this isn't my grotto," Ozrar hissed, blowing embers inside the perspiring cave. "I borrowed it from this unholy fellow." Roulic faced the indeterminate form concealed in the shadows behind Ozrar. He shuddered in his own trepidation, anticipating what dread germinated within the darkness. All the while, Ozrar fed his mind with fear wrapped in words promising solicitude.

"All you have to do is give me the egg and I'll tell my friend here to fly away." Squinting amid the embers wafting about the cave, Roulic couldn't make out the anomaly. It looked like a man covered in pasty-grey fur. Blurred in darkness, the figure moved. Long, spindly arms and legs swung and extended. Its bat-like head tilted below the ceiling. Behind it, another form moved to and fro. Flapping. The being took three steps toward Roulic. Then he saw Ozrar's freakish 'fellow'.

Its body was burly for that of a nocturnal omnivore, its hair matted over malformed features. Buried in its beard, he made out two long, sharp fangs, resembling walrus tusks. He'd seen unusual creatures in the Inner before, but none with eyes as protuberant or as bright red. He looked into the eyes unhinging him. Eyes of utter futility. They pierced his, testing his courage. But when the creature fanned its fingered wings, Roulic prepared to defend. Then flee as fast as possible. He called upon the innervation of his four favorite victors: *Alastar! Callian! Janson! Rubina!* In that moment, Ozrar's mind-grip slipped. The chiropteran creature also released its unrighteous glare.

The gods have given me a chance! Get! Out! Now!

Chapter 17

Leaf Nelson

The colossal cadre of Leaf Nelson, twice as tall as the exaggerated Bliniloth, struck the top of the cave. With walloping feet, he trapped the hairy-winged 'fellow' in a crevice of the cave. Roulic fled the fallen one's fury; earth and rock crumbled, tumbling behind him.

"Good gods! Bolts and all!" he screamed, running from the towering menace, the living skeleton. *The fury of an eternal carcass!*

No one in Leaf Nelson's path evaded punishment unless decreed by the gods. In ferocious form, Leaf pounced, aiming to land on Smutch. But the dodgy fire-starter performed a quicksilver move, missing the crushing bony digits. In retaliation, Smutch fireballed the feet of the bounding corpse.

Roulic ran like a wild dog from the trampled timberline. Past the woeful webs. Back to where light shone through the forest. He cut through the trees to the forest's edge. Sprinting through the field, he veered from Dyad blasting fire against Bliniloth's back. He passed the cadaverous Leaf Nelson morphing into a slick black bull. His horrifying horns were wide enough to pick up a tree. Leaf scooped up a fallen pine, rushing, ripping sharp branches at Bliniloth. This punctured the ghost's ethereality, deflating more than his prior expansion.

With both eyes closed, Roulic ran from death. Yet, the silhouette of the dying winged creature in the cave, like an enemy target, superimposed his mind. It stood for everything in the world he hated, everything he fought against. So, instead of running from the image, he tapped his pure anger. His original anger. His first true fit, his earliest angst. A time when he felt abandoned and lonely without love. In absolute terror, he ran at the red ghost, expelling 700 years of pent-up rage. The winged demon was powerless against the angered aura. With eyes still closed, he ran straight through the devil, shattering it into a thousand pieces. Taken apart by the Ancient's willpower, the trapped cave creature disintegrated and was no more.

"He may be gone from your mind, but I'm only a whisper away..." Ozrar laughed. Roulic plugged his ears with his fingers, but didn't dare open his eyes in the inner cave of his mind. Over ideological rocks and murky water, he ran toward life. *I rebuke thee!* Mindful elbows scraped cerebral walls until the gush of sunlight warmed his face. Cool wind cleansed his ears. When he did open his eyes, he was running through a field and couldn't stop. His speed prevented him from slowing down in time. He tried to shut down his limbs, but they kept moving.

"No!!" he wailed, flying over sharp bits of broken boulders pebbling a sparse shore. Ten feet of pond water broke his fall as he ran over the cliff. The soggy bottom knocked the air out of his lungs. Up, gasping and swiveling, he looked for dragons and the ghosts of Onan.

"Roulic is fine, ladies. He fell into a pool on the mountain, but he's okay. Leaf Nelson is keeping the ghosts at bay for now," Gram said, speaking through Marlee.

"Thanks to Dyad and Brac," Aurora said.

"And Leaf Nelson," Agnes and Madelyn chimed. The seven sisters occupied the roof's pentacle holding hands, raising an energy circle. Conjoined, they created a psychic circuit connecting to Gram. As a conduit, Gram then reported back what was happening to Roulic. Jax leaned on the roof railing, listening to Gram's gravelly voice coming out of Marlee's mouth.

"He's in old Everlan, on his way to Soaring Hills," she said, "and if he keeps up with this mindset, he may never come back. Seeking Ravenna, he could reach the Brambles of Belief in a day or two."

"Oh, no. What can we do, Gram?" the witches fussed and murmured.

"No need to get in a swivet. We haven't come this far without bagging a few tricks along the way," Gram reassured, fading from Marlee's mouth. "—We'll keep you posted. Keep the faith." When the witches' hands separated, Marlee's link to Gram disconnected.

R oulic aimed to put as much ground as possible between himself and the ghosts of Onan. *And whatever that winged abomination was. No steed, no food. I've got to find a safe place where they can't find me.* He tromped through a maze of fields, his sun-dried clothes stiff and smelling fusty.

Ozrar said there was no egg at the lair. How can this be? Unless Mayem took it right after I put it there. Maybe he came back for it after bringing Grace down the mountain? There was that epic storm hitting the desert side of Pekoes three nights ago. Grace must have stayed the night in the lair before the storm hit. And a second night on the mountain before descending with Mayem. The egg had to have been there before the storm three nights ago. Yet I placed it there two days ago! I was camping with Aeryun three days ago. This is impossible.

The thought of the egg missing, or worse, stolen or destroyed, filled him with anxiety. So much so that he reached a point of overload, unable to think straight. Only able to move on, he trudged forward, farther from his past.

What's the point of this? I've run after a fake key. I've carried an egg that isn't there. And the ghosts of Onan...getting closer and closer. And Mayem. He'll never stop hunting me. The woods could hide me until Ravenna reaches the Bridge of Belief. But that's 250 years from now. What if I found her sooner, before all of that?

An odd feeling came over him as he crossed a scenic pasture. His anxiety was gone. *I know this field. I've been here before. It feels so familiar. Why can't memory serve me one way or the other? No,* he changed his mind; *I've never been here before. I would remember this place; it's so idyllic. Besides, I don't recall going this far north of Top of the World.*

Across the meadow, he spotted a family of four picnicking by a stream. He crouched in the low grass.

Should I intrude? My appearance might scare them. He may have a weapon. Oh, they're packing up their carriage. They'll be gone before I even get there. Oh, well. At least I've reached civilization with a road to follow.

He waited until the mortals carriage was gone. Within minutes, he was on the bank of the winding stream where their picnic blankets had been. Stepping stones crossed the stream to an inviting forest. An old spruce table and chair graced the shade a few feet from the water's edge. Blue jays picked at a loaf of bread sitting on the table. Roulic hopped across the stream to the table. He tore into the sweet dough, savoring the last bite as the jays squawked and jeered, "jay-jay."

This is the locals' 'offering table.' Kind of them. He slid his hand across the grain. Bits of melted wax and carved initials surrounded the bread. *This table has seen its share of winters. Perhaps that family left bread for me. They might have seen me, thinking me a hungry wanderer in the woods. Either way, I thank them.*

Sets of humid breezes careened, rolling over the field like Poseidon's children. Wind spit over the stream and through the woods, splashing his face with loose grass. Crumbs blew off the table. The forest floor swelled, rustling in spurts until the aberrant drafts subsided. The trees fell silent.

"Ah, there you are." It was Arthur, calling out from the heart of the woods. "I've been looking for you." His entrance was identical to his rooftop appearance at Jessamine House. He came out of the shadows with a jaunty stroll, looking sharp; his black suit, brown cane, and fur hat, all intact.

"Did you come on the wind to whisk me away? I'm not sure I want to leave this time. There's nothing for me in 1999. I've got a good mind to stay here forever."

Arthur shuffled over the woodsy mulch. He stopped a foot from the old table, looking for Aeryun. Roulic's stomach seized in a compunction of conscience. It settled only after dismissing his self-blame and accepting Aeryun's death for what it was. An accident.

"I'm sorry, Arthur... she's gone. The dragons were over our heads when the land slid. The mountain took her." Arthur's head fell. The unexpected blow to his heart brought tears trickling over his nose and off his cheeks. He turned, aiming an intent look into the forest for what seemed, to both men, an eternal moment.

"I can think of no better reason to stay here in this majestic place. To be with the woman you love." Arthur laid his cane across the table and warmed in the chair, calm and composed. "But I'm afraid that is unacceptable." His eyes wandered over the stream. Beyond the meadow, young evergreens dotted the base of the looming mountain.

"It is imperative that you come forth immediately," Arthur said. "If you stay here, you risk rewriting not only your past but the past of Ravenna as well. She has many experiences to go through before she'll be ready for you."

"Isn't that why I'm here? To rewrite the past? I've done what you wanted." Roulic rambled, pacing in front of the table. "I rescued Ravenna. The Divine of Doth. I put my life in peril for the Pearlytok. Ghosts are after me. What more do they expect from me? I put the dragon egg back where it belongs. Baby will be born as destined. Even though now, one of Mayem's devils said it went missing again. All I know is the woman I love is near, and she needs me. And I need her."

"Not so fast, son," Arthur stopped him. "When did you return the egg?"

"Two days ago, after surviving the dragon's breath."

"When exactly did the demon mention that the egg was missing?"

"A few hours ago. He comes and goes in my head." Roulic stopped pacing in front of Arthur's cane.

"I see," Arthur nodded. "Time to leave," he said, standing and donning his beaver hat. "If the demon isn't lying, then it means two things. One, Mayem *did* bring Grace off the mountain the day before you got there. And two, he's returned and already taken the egg you just put there. He might still be in the area. I can't risk him confronting you here. We must leave at once."

"That can't be!" Roulic said, bewildered. "Grace slept with the egg. She kept it warm before Mayem found her."

"She did," Arthur stated. "But the egg you put back isn't the egg you think it is. There were *two* eggs in the nest when Mayem rescued Grace. He only managed to purse one of them when the dragon returned to the lair during the storm. He got Grace off the mountain and returned three days later — today — for the second egg."

"Good gods!" Roulic said.

"And now as we speak, Gadbanti the giant has stolen the Pearlytok. He's going to use it to jump with Mayem to Catalina Island and then he'll bury that egg. Then he'll return to the cave where you and Eeo found the Pearlytok."

"Now I know why your nieces were so interested in those bones," the Ancient said. "Why did Gadbanti bury the egg on Catalina?"

"His distant relatives are buried there," Arthur said, catching Roulic's curiosity. "It's a long story," he said, waving his cane toward the heart of the forest. "I'll tell you on the way." They hurried through the trees, looking out for Mayem.

"We don't know what portal they took to get there, but we know they landed by the excavation sites. Gadbanti and his crew of three giants remained there on the uninhabited side of the island. Mayem went off exploring and found the town of Avalon. He returned excited to discuss conquering the new world using the baby dragon. You see, Catalina's portal is whopping, large enough to bear the passage of a dragon. Mayem always wanted to use the Pearlytok to locate a dragon-sized portal in Doth. Luckily, he's never found one. Yet. You can thank the gods he made a huge mistake with the giants while on the island. --A bad joke about Gadbanti's family and the excavated bones. An argument ensued, leaving Gadbanti and his crew less than thrilled with Mayem's plan. Gadbanti took the egg from Mayem and buried it on the far end of the island. The giants decided to jump back to Doth with or without Mayem. Of course, Mayem returned with them, seething all the way about his stolen dragon egg. Which, in turn, brought about the unfortunate incident of their return." Arthur's cane swept aside a series of low boughs.

"What happened on their return?" Roulic kept close behind the old witch, swatting the pesky branches.

"Mayem's energy was so negative it disrupted both the key and portal. His disturbance caused a return to the Inner Realm instead of the Outer. Villagers reported that Mayem assaulted one of the giants with a knife when the group landed in Doth."

"That explains Gadbanti's nasty scar."

"Yes. And how Mayem returned to the Outer. He was still in the portal when it closed. Gadbanti escaped, with his cut. The other three giants were less lucky. A mob of mortalkin in a cow town called Laughters, attacked and killed them."

A light came over Roulic's face. "I know. I was in Laughters when it happened, searching for my family. That was my last entry into the Inner before getting involved with your nieces. Another resurfaced memory, thanks to you and yours, Arthur. I won't soon forget your aid."

"Nor will Gadbanti." They reached the portal through an opening circled by thorny thickets. "Two centuries after he buries the egg on Catalina Island, he'll steal the Pearlytok with Eeo. So mind your back. For now, the ghosts of Onan are our only worry." Arthur extended his hand. "Get ready. Jessamine is a jump away."

Eyes rolled. "A hot meal and bath? Count me in." Their hands clasped within the womb of the forest. In a blinding flash, the Ancient and Witch transcended time and space.

Chapter 18

Aspired Mountain

Upon his return to Jessamine House, Roulic didn't take long, after going upstairs for a nap, to fume in the kitchen at Alison.

"You knew all along about the second egg, didn't you? Of course you did! It's clear to me now that I've been an unknowing pawn in your clever little game of chess with Time and Death. But now Aeryun's dead." He paced beside the breakfast table that had seen his goodwill and high hopes.

"Now you wait one minute, Roulic," Alison said, swiping her burgundy bangs. She centered the faucet over an old French watering can in the kitchen's fireclay sink. "Things changed pretty fast for us, too. We didn't see it coming any more than you did."

"Her final circumstance should have come later. A *lot* later. But I guess she didn't matter as much as that egg you're after." The aggressive outburst surprised him more than it did Alison. It wasn't only the grief of losing Aeryun. It was the witches making him feel like a wandering puppet.

"Her death crushed us," Alison fended, filling the watering can. "To us, she was akin to a little sister. If she hadn't saved 'that egg', she might have lived as a grand dame. But karmic law rules us all. Aeryun's fall was bound to occur. But from her tragedy, a dragon born will save countless lives. And it'll be Aeryun they should thank and remember for getting you across the valley and to the dragon's den." She placed the watering can over a cabinet drawer, pulling out a pink apron.

"Tis true," he agreed, watching her put it on, "without her, I wouldn't be here. We were growing warm in our friendship. But I put her in harm's way. Could be my disdain isn't towards you or your family, but towards myself. Wherever I go, whatever I do, those closest to me always seem to get hurt. I'm afraid I may hurt Ravenna, and that I must never let happen." Alison's tender glance soothed his misguided guilt.

"You mustn't ever stop living your life, fearing you'll hurt another. When I was a child, I ran into the woods at dark and got lost. My sisters searched for hours but couldn't find me. I spent the night listening to the forest's wonderful world of unseen creatures. Making my way home at sunrise, I felt enlightened with a newfound sense of self. I brought home flowers, herbs, and pockets full of berries for my little sisters. But those all got discarded. My sisters were furious at me for enjoying myself while lost. They called me 'the self-centered sister' for a fortnight. And then Gram told me a thing I never forgot. She said, 'Never let a fearful mind confuse a yearning heart.' She was telling me it was okay. That it was okay to search, to find myself, to look my own truth in the face."

"I've been searching all my life, but I'd comb the wildest of woods if I believed I could find her," he said.

"Oh, you will. Perhaps sooner than you think," Alison said, perking him up, "you're going back tomorrow. To Aspired Mountain, to kill Mayem, yearning heart and all... for the good of Doth." She picked up the watering can, leaving him with, "And I've got plants to water."

Mayem lay on Nina's sofa wearing a wide-brimmed black hat and smoking a long cigar. "This one isn't bad. It isn't good, either. What's taking them so long?" he said.

"These things take time," Nina said, knowing he was ready to blow.

"That's not helping. Bliniloth better report to me soon," Mayem sulked.

"Or what? They're ghosts. Spirits unchained. There's nothing you can do except wait. You might as well eat lunch and forget about them for now," Nina said. Mayem respected her boldness. But he carried on, fidgeting with something in the back quarter-shaft of his boot.

"I can't wait!" he smoldered, "And I won't forget about them. I want that egg. It's mine. I have plans for that portal. Big plans. Roulic and Ravenna think they've outsmarted me. Well, they've got quite a surprise coming. Without that humorless giant in my way, your realm will become a vastly different world. A world ruled by me and my dragons instead of these mindless mortals running around in circles."

She didn't attempt talking him down, let alone consider asking about the *'giant in his way.'* That would only bring more magnetic chaos. *Or violence,* she worried. *I'll get my chance to run once he gets the egg. Who knows? He might leave before then.* So, she made him lunch.

Up in the Circle Room, Agnes and Madelyn engaged in a medieval card game called *Pagan: Fate of Roanoke.* They played both witch and witch hunter, getting heated at times into the late evening. He observed from a pillowed chair, curious about their competition.

"One of these villagers is a little too witchy-poo for my liking and I shall root out...*who?*" Madelyn said, drawing a card from the deck and waving it with a confident grin. She was bluffing, of course, and Agnes wasn't falling for her ruse.

"Investigate as you please. And when your three dead villagers *still* don't bring her to justice, don't blame me," Agnes pushed back. He listened to the sisters squabble, telling himself he wouldn't dwell on tomorrow's jump, but how could he not? Only days ago he'd reunited with Ravenna, if only from a distance.

And despite the deadly circumstances—fighting with Mayem over the key and falling over a waterfall... She's worth fighting for, worth dying for.

"Is there a chance that I will see her tomorrow, do you think?" The siblings stopped playing and stared at each other. They turned to him — on him, as he took it, hearing the duo answer in unnerving unison:

"A part of you will," they said with blank faces. The hair on the back of his neck tingled. Agnes and Madelyn resumed their game as if he had never asked. Faking a yawn, he left the Circle Room, his exit unacknowledged. Light glowed in all the cracks of all the bedroom doors. *A hint, perhaps, of the promise of an everlasting light. Even when hidden, healing happens. Through thought, word, and action,* he thought, working his way downstairs.

The witches retired right after dinner, yet they're all still awake. What are they doing? And where is Lilith? Her room is alight, too. She would have come to visit me. Not one of them mentioned her all night.

The biggest challenge of his life became clear: to eradicate Mayem from the world. He decided he wouldn't mull over his mission at Aspired Mountain. Or rethink every exhausting moment since getting kicked by Lilith's boot. Or worse, since leaving Callian's farm. His head hit the pillow, focused on his future with Ravenna.

Will she still feel the same? Will we raise a family? I won't need to rush from the castle chasing after Mayem if he's dead. There's relief in that idea! But if I ambush him as planned, what will happen to the old me? Will the witches take me back to my old life among mortalkin? With him dead, there'll still be work to do in crushing his allies. And what of the Pearlytok? Will Gadbanti steal it with Eeo? I don't think so. With Mayem dead and gone, the whole world will change for the better. All I know is I'm going to see Ravenna soon.

While Roulic dreamed of Ravenna, a sinister form crept through his bedroom window. The airy black mass oozed meandering strands of cold smoke in front of his nostrils. It was the vaporous Ozrar, slipping into his subconscious mind while he slept.

"You cannot avoid us forever," Ozrar said, his whisper cutting like a surgical intern's first incision. But his rigor grew, aiming for and piercing the heart of the matter. "Don't think for a minute we won't get that dragon egg," he purred, "You've already given up the key. Why not the egg? If you give in to us now, we won't go after Ravenna. It's only a matter of time before the Divine of..."

Ozrar's proposal seeped into Roulic's deepest interior. It poked at his most tender clefts. Hollows never intended to receive, let alone entertain, a phantom's syllable. The Ancient's angst gushed. It purged from the pit of his soul, cutting short Ozrar's operation, all while the Ancient slept. The mental eruption burst out in shrill cries, benumbing the fiend.

"Who do you think you are!? You have no power or place in my mind or dreams. How dare you tread where you are not wanted? I am a child of God, of all gods of love and light. My being lacks a space for your void of darkness! Prey elsewhere, demon, before I squash you with the might of my mind backed by a thousand souls who dwell in heaven. Souls stronger than you. I pity thee, weak and sniveling to your master of dark deeds. Go to him now; he calls you out!!" He lay in his ire, spitting the last of his fury. "I said, demon, get out!!" with Ozrar retreating through the window.

Roulic's spirit floated to the ceiling. He checked around the open window for Ozrar, not realizing his disembodied state. Looking for the intruder, he found himself sleeping in the bed below. The initial sight shook his core. *Have I died!?* The question mattered less when the Black family began to gather around his body below. Some murmured when Lilith took her place beside Arthur. Then Aeryun entered, the bedroom becoming sacrosanct. She locked her bedroom door with a brass key that glowed, radiating a familiar warmth up to the ceiling. He felt it to be her essence. She put the key on the bedside table and joined the others. After a few moments of silent prayer, they all dematerialized. And Roulic's spirit found his body below.

Back in the four-poster bed, he woke, electrified. *Ozrar's gone!* He rolled over, turning on the bedside table lamp. Aeryun's brass door key was still warm, lying at the base of the lamp. He touched it, getting goosebumps. Jumping out of bed, he closed the window. When he couldn't fall back to sleep, he picked up the paperback novel he had found under his pillow. Flipping to the inside cover, he read the words he'd missed before:

This book belongs to Aeryun Porter.

Chapter 19

Face to Face

Motives of the vicious Ozrar came up during the sisters' morning discussion. Half decided Roulic's mind-ghost was nothing more than a wanton soul conjured by Mayem to do his dirty work. The other half suspected the attacks to be of a more personal nature.

"That he strikes from realm to realm, wherever Roulic goes, is especially personal. Frightening," Raine said, sitting around after breakfast.

"Well, yeah, he is a ghost. Worldly laws of physics need not apply," Jillian said, reheating her tea in the microwave.

"Isn't it strange, though," Raine said, "you'd think Ozrar would know that Mayem was the one who retrieved the second egg."

"You'd think. But who are we dealing with here? Just because they're demonic entities doesn't mean they're exempt from acts of idiocy. Yes, they can wield a lot of power. But these three don't exactly fall into the adept category."

"That's good for us," Aurora added.

"Which leads me to think they're newer to the ghost spectrum, especially Bliniloth and Smutch. Ozrar, I'm so sure about. I'm still trying to pin him down," Marlee spoke as if she were the embodiment of logic and reason.

"They're well into old Everlan by now," Raine said. "You'd better pin him down soon because we have little time."

"Whaddaya mean, time? We've got all the time in the world," Marlee said.

"You mean Uncle Arthur has all the time in the world," Raine said.

"Are you sure about that!?" Aurora glowered, leaving them confounded. She got up and left. Agnes and Madelyn remained quiet.

A rthur and Roulic portaled from Jessamine after breakfast, landing without mishap by a thin creek separating a plowed field from a wall of woods. Roulic immediately scanned for signs of life: farmers or fishermen. Anyone. Arthur picked up his hat and tapped his gold pocket watch.

"Are we where we need to be?" Roulic wondered.

"A precise jump depends on one's intent," Arthur said, studying the forest. "Portals are living things and much more forgiving when carrying a true heart. Knowing you, I assume it's safe to say we have reached Everlan."

"Right before Mayem curses Ravenna at the bridge?"

"Give or take a few days. I'm confident we've arrived when and where you need to be, finding Ravenna a young woman, and hopefully, coming to realize the power of dragons." His voice quavered.

"You don't sound so sure."

"I'm not." Arthur tapped his watch again. Roulic frowned.

"What's that riddle about?" he pointed to the witch's watch.

"I was hoping to stay until I could determine exactly where we are."

Roulic gulped, worried that Arthur had fallen short—or past the Spring of 1649. He also worried about the place of their landing, despite Arthur's assumption.

Is the old witch's skill waning? Or, is he under psychic attack from Mayem? He did lose Aeryun. His heavy heart might be taking a toll on his jumping. He'll soon return to Aeryun; this I know.

"It's not only about her." Arthur's telepathy made itself known. "It's this old watch. It's acting up again."

"How so?"

"Whenever the hands move backward, I can expect difficulty with my next jump."

"When did it last go backward?"

"During breakfast," Arthur stated. "Which means I must go now, before it becomes too late." Roulic's head tilted like a dog. "I've jumped so many times that I'd swear the portals have united in discouraging my passage. One day they'll keep me put. Forever. When that day comes, I plan to be at the right time and place." He stepped forward, bidding farewell.

"Have a safe journey, Arthur," Roulic said with a nervous smile, "and tell her hello from me."

Arthur nodded, twinkling an eye. "She knows you tried to protect her," he echoed over the creek. He walked along the sandy edge of the rivulet, pointing his cane across the water to an opening in the trees. "Find Aspired Mountain before it finds you." The dapper traveler and his trusty cane slipped into time's fine line.

"In the blink of an eye!" Roulic exclaimed.

W alking a stuck log, he crossed the stream into the woods where Arthur had pointed his cane. He followed a well-preserved path that ran along the flowery banks of the stream. His spirit lifted, toying with an Ancient melody in baroque fashion. But then he twisted it, humming it scratchy until the tune was lifeless. The trail had taken him nowhere. It zigzagged back from the banks into the woods, a good quarter mile. Sharp turns forging the forest floor like a hedge maze. *It's wasting precious time weaving beside itself! This is more a redundant scenic trail—or drunkard's downfall—than an actual road.* And then, it ended. He cautioned, feeling ill, finding the puzzle's prize: an ill-boding dwelling made of upright tree trunks.

Chunky branches protruded from its bark walls, displaying lanterns, hats, and colored kerchiefs. Belts of all sizes hung alongside a wealth of glittering necklaces rattling in the breeze. A funky chimney, made of bits of broken boulders, buttressed the right end of the cabin. Bluish smoke ascended from it, lingering at the treetops, tainting a hidden sky. A large, bored-out knot by a hingeless front door served as the peculiar structure's front window.

Someone's definitely living here. Little light ever kisses this dark heart of the forest. Why live in darkness unless you're in hiding? Or doing deeds you shouldn't?

He crept toward the door of the minatory shack, stoking his suspicion. Vapor fled from an ominous black cauldron on the porch. Its hot mist wet the trunks and seeped into the house through the makeshift window. He peeked into the kettle's departing steam.

Bones. Human bones! The femurs of poor mortalkin, murdered in these woods!

"Good gods!" he shrieked, jumping back from the boiling pot, tripping on a child's doll. He could hear heavy footsteps scurrying about the timber hut. A pair of dichroic eyes popped through the hollowed knot. A cat-face foe with monstrous eyes, big as teacups. He froze where he fell. Chills rolled over his body as the glaring amber and green eyeballs sent fury to his pupils. He couldn't move. Long, gray whiskers violated the knot as the uncouth cat cocked its cranium, trying to back its head out of the hole. It was stuck. This severed their eye contact, breaking the stuck cat's gaze of power over him. He ran from the house, but halted where the path met the property. He could see it, still trapped, the freakish feline wrestling and wriggling to break free from the crude window. With clenched fists, he walked back to the porch and kicked the cauldron over. Boiling water steamed up into the knot, scalding the creatures face and burning its whiskers off. He kicked the door in, finding a stack of skulls. *More atrocities against mortalkin.* He wrapped a blanket around a branch and lit it in the fireplace. After spreading the torch, he left the big cat and cabin to burn.

He didn't stop running until he collapsed, winded on the wicked path.

"I'm tired these mazes; do you hear me?" he panted defiantly to the vacuous trees. *I won't stop until I find her!* He got up and walked toward bits of light seeping through the trees. Running water gurgled. He ran toward it, finding himself back at the same spot where Arthur had left him.

Damn that cat-face foe. Putting the evil eye over me. And damn

Mayem and his evil... damn them all! They can't stop us from being together. I will find her.

Moving in the opposite direction, he crossed the river log and the field, glad to get out of the woods alive. A lone utility road offered an untended wagon, but was missing a wheel. Beside the bare axle leaned a grain shovel, its shaft fractured at the socket. He kicked it in frustration, freeing a scrap of paper from under the spade. He picked it up:

Everlan Bread & Honey
Award-winning Barley, Rye, Oats, and Wheat
Everlan Grain Council
Best Beekeeper Award

He jumped, clutching the unweathered label. *I'm getting closer to Aspired Mountain. And Ravenna.* He sprinted over the utility road to a highway bridging the stream. The highway ascended a hill that dropped into farmlands bearing signs of a thriving populace.

The idea of reuniting with Ravenna put a strut in his step, but it didn't cloud his head. *I've got to steer clear of towns full of people. What if I encounter someone I know? I'll stick to this road until I meet someone traveling by themselves.*

The highway was empty until late afternoon when a farmer driving a two-horse cart came along and gave him a ride.

"I'm going to Apis. Get in," the farmer said. Roulic hopped in. He said, "Thank you," then kept silent. The farmer talked at length about how well his wheat fields were doing this year and the coming harvest.

"Do you recall the last year Everlan Bread & Honey won an award?" Roulic finally spoke, fishing for which year it was.

"There's never been a year they didn't," the farmer squinted into sun. "You're not from around here. What brings you to Apis? A job? A friend of mine's lookin' for hands."

"I'm going to Everlan," Roulic said.

"Well, yer *in* Everlan, son! The heart of her, anyway. Where about's ya comin' from?"

He hesitated, remembering his disastrous conversation at the cigar shop in Laguna Beach. "I'm meeting someone at the Bridge of Belief."

The farmer carried on. "Hmm. Not much left in Old Town 'cept a tavern and an empty mill. The mill got moved to Apis. But New Town's got shops and fancy hotels for the tourists goin' to the pools. You might want to meet your friend there."

"I know. I've been to Belief. It's close to the old bridge."

"Yep." Roulic turned white when the farmer mentioned a fire in the woods today. The farmer didn't seem to notice; he kept chatting about farm life until he dropped him off in downtown Apis. "I've got to make it to the feed barn before dusk. Keep going south; you'll run right into Belief." The Ancient hurried through town. Main Street led to the lattice of old Everlan—miles of crisscrossed cropland.

I'll travel by night as far as I can and lie low during the day. Until I make the bridge.

By late evening, far from Apis but still north of Belief, he passed through Everlan's High Hills. The area didn't boast any high hills, but it did offer many slopes. The name came from a pre-war Dwarven colony famous for its rolling vineyards. He strode the wee slopes by moonlight, and by eleven o'clock, he stumbled into the Brambles of Belief. Local Everlanians harvested berries there, selling to regional merchants at the 22-acre grove. Before getting past the farm's barn and market, he'd felt his fill of dewberries and loganberries. Still, he took plenty of raspberries and blackberries for the road. At the far end of the grove, he entered a former plantation of pines. The untended woods were warmer than the breezy farm, so, he chose a broad trunk and fell asleep, exhausted.

Nestled in a ball, he dreamed of lying with Ravenna. They were together when a gentle rain fell, sprinkling the trees and his slumber. It broke her image, but not her words. "Come back to me, come back to Everlan," her soft voice beaded in the drops, kissing his brow. Damp and drowsy, he found a drier tree to cover himself for the night.

. . .

A delicate dew permeated his bed of tepid needles. But by midmorning, the sun's adhering rays had warmed his face and dried his clothes. The mighty pines had dwindled. He was in good spirits when coming to a sparse line of arpeggiated shrubs and saplings that triggered a tug in his heart. This stretch of forest caught his attention. He recognized it, knew it, and even loved it. For it was in this place that he would discover his cave. He just didn't know it yet.

Carved into a steep hill, a man-made grotto faced the woods from fifty feet. The cave setting looked and felt so familiar that, for a moment, he feared it.

Odd, he thought, getting goosebumps, *I know I've never been this way before, or have I?*

It was quiet inside the earth and rock hollow. Outside, the absence of fluttery birds that usually shadowed him amplified his nervousness. So, he stopped, hesitating in hot strands of sun illuminating the cavern's airy doorway. The floor was flat and held imprints of boot heels in the dirt. Stepping back, his hand readied over his sheath, waiting until he felt ready to enter. When nothing happened, he went in and found meager bedding at the cave's far end: A farmhouse throw blanket folded over a stratum of pine needles. Over a protruding rock hung a brown jacket. His brown jacket. Identical to the one on his back. He panicked and lunged at it. Searching in the ebbing light revealed all but one pocket to be empty. He pulled out his old pipe with the letter R on it and smelled the cherished bowl. "God, I've missed you... Too bad you'll end up in the pools of Everlan." He put the pipe back, dusted off the coat, then slung it on the jutting rock.

It's mine, all right. But in what year? How much longer will it stay trapped here, waiting to be with her? The garment dispelled any doubt he had about the reality of his former self. He credited Ravenna. *She was right—we don't believe in coincidence. Still...* "I should have asked that farmer what year it is," he muttered in regret. *But I couldn't risk him thinking me dangerous or crazy, and reporting me to the Apis police. I might never see her again because of some little thing like that.*

Bits of ripped paper stirred along the cave wall below the coat. He squatted, connecting the torn paper, knowing what it was despite the cave's obscurity.

My map of Doth. How can this be? I left Janson's farm in the year 1649. I won't get the map at the Harking Toad for another 50 years.

He checked the jacket he was wearing for the map he had when he landed on the sand in Laguna Beach. But it wasn't there.

"You can't keep running me in circles," he shouted, his echoes ringing the cave. "This is madness. All to kill that wretched Mayem! I hope you can hear me!" Footsteps crescendoed, stopping outside the cave. He froze, putting a hand over his mouth. Blocking the sun, a shadow filled the center of the cave.

That's not either of the ghosts. I would feel Smutch's heat and Bliniloth's wider than that. Could it be me—or — Mayem?

His recoil before standing in defense came with the territory. The idea of Mayem entering the cave threw him into fight-or-flight mode. He had no time to consider any other option besides battle. Drawing a hastened breath, he lunged from the cave, crashing into his adversary.

He pulled back, blinded by sunlight, his assailant down. A body lay lifeless in the dirt. The head didn't move. Drops of blood trickled down the small rock it landed on. The gusting wind ceased. Roulic stared, hyper-aware, at the body, his mirror image, lying in the dirt.

"I've killed myself!" he cried, crestfallen.

"Oh God,... what have I done?" he sobbed, brooding over his former self. Kneeling, he wept, then lifted the head, getting blood-soaked hands. He dragged the body into the cave and laid it on the bedding, then paced the cave in disbelief.

"Why did you do that to me?" a voice pleaded from the languishing body. His voice.

Roulic fell, offering water from his canteen. "I thought you were someone else...I thought you were Mayem."

Solemn eyes united, neither pair realizing their part. The canteen dropped. "Mayem..." he whispered, his wounded head finding the blanket.

"I'm going to get you help," Roulic said, picking up the canteen. "Drink this. I'll be back as soon as I can." He stood, but an arm stopped him, pulling at his pant leg.

"Wait."

"There's no time. You're hurt and ..." Roulic resisted the arm.

"There's something I must tell you. Before it's too late..."

Roulic knelt again by his former self. "Tell me."

The fallen Roulic lifted his head and whispered, tilting to his future self. "I knew this would happen... A witch told me it would... I didn't believe it and put it out of my mind. By the time I met Ravenna, I had all but forgotten... you must go to her. Take my place. She'll be waiting for you at the Bridge of Belief..." He squeezed Roulic's hand, fighting to keep his eyes open.

Roulic's head spun. "I'm going to get you help. You can go to her then, I promise. But I need you to stay awake. I'll be back as soon as I can. Hold on!" he said, rushing from the cave.

Chapter 20

Darned Night of the Soul

"I'm not waiting around here forever for my dragon egg," Mayem rankled, waving the key around Nina's apartment. "I'll look everywhere until I find a portal to go back and finish this myself."

"You don't need to look everywhere," Nina said. "—just in the right places. I've got a friend who found a magical place on a hiking trail in Laguna Beach. She calls it a 'gravity hill.' There might be a portal near there. Somewhere. Who knows? It's worth a shot. But you'll need a car and driver.

"Call your friend. She can drive. And she'd better be here soon." Mayem's parasitic glare wormed through Nina like a terminal flu. A malady she'd regretted letting in and whose complaint wouldn't end soon enough. Within the space of a few days, the condition of his distemper had scared off her walk-in clients. His constant chaos complicated her insomnia. And her disjointed apartment became a haunt for energies far darker than she had beckoned before.

She was on the verge of seeking salvation. Or suicide. But she didn't show it and wouldn't talk about it with anyone. Keeping it in, she hoped Mayem would give her up and be gone, telling herself to *Hold on. You'll be home free soon. So he was in my dream. It might not come to pass.* But she knew better: the prophecy warranted more than fear.

. . .

Marlee spent most of the day upstairs with shades drawn and candles burning. Looking. Seeing. Watching. And she didn't find out Roulic's condition or whereabouts using a crystal plate or obsidian bowl like Gram taught her. She worked with a pencil and paper, remote viewing at a table in her room or lying on her bed in quiet contemplation. But she didn't have to concentrate behind closed doors. Her sessions could take place anywhere suitable to form and pinpoint impressions.

In the kitchen, a pot of cawl soup simmered. Madelyn kicked a Hacky Sack to Agnes, across the hall to the living room. "Do you think he'll beat the ghosts of Onan this time?"

"I suppose so. He has before," Agnes missed the footbag. Marlee appeared, followed by Alison, Raine, and Jillian.

"Have you two seen Aurora?" Marlee and the others gathered at the kitchen table.

"Nope," Agnes and Madelyn chirped.

"Well, here's what's going on with our willowy friend," Marlee said. "He's mortified thinking he's killed his former self, and now he's run off looking for help."

"What if he decides to pick up the path of his former self?" Jillian speculated, advising, "In that case, he'll rush to Ravenna. Either way, it's getting complicated. We think it's time to call Arthur before it worsens."

"Agreed," Marlee said. "We can't have Roulic running about Everlan disrupting the past. He's returned the egg. Now it's time to bring him back. I'll alert Arthur to find a new window near Aspired Mountain."

"So, we're going to make it rain on him again?" Bored, Madelyn and Agnes resumed their game of Hacky Sack.

"Yes, we are," Marlee said. "If my information rings true, I've located a portal in the woods close to the cave. All we have to do is remove him from public scrutiny and back into that cave."

"Think of all the running around you could have saved, Roulic," Agnes sparred with a silken tongue.

Marlee played back, always on guard with the terrible twosome. "Sister! And rob Uncle of his only joy?"

"Wasn't Lilith his... I mean Aeryun...," Madelyn frothed, entering the ring.

Marlee cleared her throat, silencing Madelyn's jab. "Now, about the Water Element..."

"A flight soon thundered," Agnes confirmed. "Oh, so that's why you were looking for..." Madelyn said. Jessamine's front door opened and closed. Tapping high heels announced her passage through the foyer. No one spoke until she walked past Glassy Hall, making a sharp turn into the kitchen. Then the name, "Aurora!" was uttered by all.

"What's going on?" She clutched a small Macy's shopping bag. "What? So I went to the mall..."

"We need your help, sister. With an art you're roaringly good at." Marlee's dark eyes washed over Aurora.

"You want me to conjure a storm," Aurora presumed. Her siblings nodded. Jillian clapped twice.

"Nothing too devastating, mind you, but it must be..." Marlee searched for the right word. "*Menacing. Completely compelling*—enough of a wet menace to push Roulic back into his little cave. Arthur will meet him there and usher him back here."

Aurora eyed her Macy's bag as if saying goodbye to it. "This can be done. Sure, I'll do it," she said, setting the bag on the counter. Marlee waved her over. The sisters scooted around, "charging" her by conducting the air with their long hair and nails.

"Okay, we're all going to become one in this," Marlee directed. "We all need to see Roulic running from the cave, then running back to it. That's the visual. And Aurora will call down a torrent so magnificent he'll run for that cave as if Ravenna's in there waiting for him." She adjourned from the kitchen table, "Let's do this, then. To the Circle Room."

"The roof has the sky over it..." Aurora recommended.

"I stand corrected," Marlee bowed. "Ladies—to the fifth dimension..."

. . .

M oist beads fell from the ceiling of the cave, one droplet landing on his right eye. His puffy lid opened, scanning the cave while he questioned the quagmire. He tried to sit up but couldn't.

If I'd only come into the cave whistling, he would have heard me. Oh, how my head hurts. Dizzy. It won't be long before he brings someone back with him. And then what? By witnessing the two of us together, that person will forever change the future. This must not happen. I've got to get out of here before he returns...

After an aching ascent, he managed to stand, only to sway and fall, hitting his head so hard he fell unconscious. The ensuing brain injury would remain in effect for many years. But his blackout was short-lived, for the witches of Doth immediately met him in the realm of Thot. Dressed in orchid-colored robes, they carried green candles and bouquets of daffodils.

"Where am I?"

"You are in the Heart of Thot, the heart's space in the realm of dreams," Alison said.

"Am I dead?" The atmosphere around the witches lightened. The witches convened in his mind, the council uniting in a unique timbre he couldn't recognize as their collective voice.

"No, Roulic, you're not dead. You're alive and in the hearts of many. We've come, bringing hope to you and Ravenna. Fear not, it's only a matter of time before you're back on your feet again to live another day."

"I hope I get more than one," he said. "Oh, but my head is in a terrible place. I can't recall a thing."

"Consider these things not lost, mislaid perhaps, but not lost. We'll aid in your recovery wherever you may go. You won't remember this conversation, and your head may hurt for a while, but you *will* wake with a sense that all your dreams are yet to come." The witches raised their daffodils and he slipped from the Heart of Thot, into dreams of Ravenna.

. . .

I'm almost there. Maybe I can find a doctor, if I'm lucky.

Roulic rushed to the brambles under ominous skies. He ran through the empty grove, stopping at the deserted Berry Market Store where sheets of clouds united to dim the sun.

"This doesn't look good," he said. Aurora's lightning fired on trees and berries but didn't strike the store. The witch's thunder made him jump and run, missing a blitz of 'dragon daggers' hurled in succession. "Where did you come from!?" he yelled at the violent sky, covering his ears. Chickens ran amok between the market and barn. They screamed in the rain to an abandoned horse kicking its stall.

There's no one here. They must have seen the storm coming. There's no way I'll make it to Apis and get back in time to help him. I must go back.

He retreated to the brambles, getting hit by biscuit-sized hail. And yet it didn't sink in, the obvious, the most logical of all conclusions, until he reached the cover of the woods.

If my former self dies, so must I. But since I am alive, he has to live! To become me. This revelation, hinted at by the witches, eluded him during the shock of felling his former self.

But what if the witches are wrong? Marlee only said 'peculiar consequences', as if she didn't know. Could he die and I continue to live in another timeline? How could he lose his future to me if I am alive?

Aurora drenched the woods before dropping her final deluge on the hill above the cave. The icy onslaught spilled runoff over the cavern's top, covering the ground with sludge. He shivered, tromping over mud to the cave, rushing inside to the motionless body. He felt the cold wrist, then neck.

No pulse! I've killed him. And now he's gone. What have I done? He sat by the body, sobbing as the rain stopped. *Why have the Masters made this possible? Why have they treated me so? Had Destiny, or was it Lilith, all along who led me to relive my demise? Why must I suffer a plural death? Have I not learned over centuries the universal lessons of mortality?*

He checked the body's pulse again. *He's gone. My old self.*

"No words can express my regret. May God be with you. You're home now," he whispered.

He reached for the brown jacket, more confused than the day he met Aurora at the Pools of Everlan. As he slid the coat over his former face, a shadow covered the hill and cave. He spun, bracing himself in the cold darkness.

"Don't you know we're attracted to thunder and lightning?" Ozrar drawled, goading him to accept defeat. "Mayem is well on his way to eliminating what little hope that young dragon has left. Its heart may be near empty, but I must say she's rather plump, getting fed quite well. That is until she reaches maturity. A voracious hunger is coming upon Doth. Starved and angry, she'll do her master's bidding. And now that Mayem has the key, his hellfire awaits both realms."

"Oh Bliniloth," Ozrar sang luridly.

"...taker of the finer things, you've yet to greet your maker."

"You've swayed a lifetime taking forever, and now you're broke and can't forsake her."

"Oh, Bliniloth, thine heartsick heart frightens an immortal hurling gal."

"I'm not listening to your nonsense, you damned swine! Consider yourself un-minded! And good luck with that key!" For the second time in four days, Roulic fled a cave carrying the tribulation of Ozrar's voice. Raging from the chamber, he aimed for a dry rock, treading the tree line. He caught his breath and moped, faint in the aftermath of killing himself.

What if there are other Mayems coming after me? Even without the Pearlytok, I'm sure he'll find a way to chase me through time.

Will my torn soul ever mend? Will God keep me? Or cast me out? He spilled his heart out on the rock, calling out to the Masters with an unsettling address:

"I know there can be no living without dying! Haven't I died enough for you!? Let me live!" He ran beside the forest, then walked in circles, trying to process the death of his former self.

Maybe I've turned into a ghost wandering the woods. I'd rather be a ghost in her life than not in it at all. I'll go back to the cave and bury the body. Then I'll find Ravenna. By gods, if it kills me again, I will find her. Witches aren't the only ones who can change the mind of time.

Solace found him, outside the cave, at the foot of a pitch pine circled by wildflowers. He smelled the sweet colors drying in the sun. *I'll bring them to her.* He picked the brightest, tucking a handful of blossoms in his jacket's inner pocket.

"Sorry I was late. That Ozrar is one depraved puppy. Indisputably so." The smug cat, Natric, sat on a twisted limb, looking chunkier than Roulic remembered him to be.

"You again! Oh no, I'm not going back there. My future is here, in 16-whatever-it-is, so you can forget about 1999."

"Really, Roulic? You're going to let Mayem live just so you can enjoy a few years with Ravenna before he destroys Doth? How many times must we go through this?" Natric scratched bark.

"But I can kill Mayem here!"

"Not with the ghosts of Onan a hundred yards away. You might want to blow that whistle tied around your neck before they get here. Any second now. They will kill you..." The brambles shook. A wave of wind swayed the pussy's perch. "You've got about one minute before it's too late," Natric warned. Roulic's hand hovered over the silver instrument dangling by his heart.

"Smutch!!" Bliniloth's numbing thuds through the woods panicked Natric onto all fours, tail high.

"Blow the whistle!" Natric yowled. Roulic blew hard and blinked. A translucent image showed up beside the trunk. It was the old witch, Arthur.

"Take my hand, Roulic. Into the heart of dragons, we go." Arthur held out his hand. Natric jumped from the limb onto the magician's shoulder.

Smutch screamed, "They're over here, boss!" The flaming spirit shot a white-hot fireball at the trio by the pitch pine. Roulic put his hand in Arthur's, and they all disappeared before the fireball struck the trunk.

Chapter 21

Merelands

Raine removed the coat from the body's face and hung it on the protruding rock beside the bedding. She touched a shoulder, watching hazel eyes open.

"Where am I?" he said, thirsty with chapped lips.

"You're in a cave. You suffered a blow to your head," she said.

"How long have I been here?" he took in her delicate features, "and who are you?"

"Nobody... just a passerby who happened to find this cave and found you in it. Are you thirsty?"

"Yes." She helped him sit upright and drink from her canteen.

"Do you remember what happened? How you got here? Can you remember your name?"

"I can't remember...anything..." a frightened look came over his face.

"Do you remember Destiny?"

He stared at the cave ceiling. "Oh, I remember Destiny all right," a light returned to his eyes.

"Good. That's a start. Remembering is only half of the experience. All you have to do is wait, and it'll all come back in good time," she said. "You'd better get some rest now."

Some hours later, he woke, but Raine was gone. *Who was that beautiful, crystal blue-eyed woman? My mysterious passerby.* She returned to the cave the following day, and the day after that, bringing him soup and bread and tending to his swollen head. He slept, anticipating her return, and when she didn't, he didn't attempt to leave.

Days went by waiting, surviving in the cave, meditating, recuperating. Headaches persisted, but the painful swelling ceased. And as he knew his mysterious passerby wasn't coming back, his appetite for life returned. Slivered memories crossed his mind, just before sleep, like cometary glass inside a cosmic kaleidoscope. One such shard brought a glimmer of hope,—enough to leave the woods; in his former life, he had worked as a mason. So, he regained his strength, relying on hickory nuts, clover, and berries from the grove.

Who am I? How can I be me if I don't understand who I was? If I worked as a mason, I should seek employment as such. Maybe then my past will come back to me.

He set out. Two construction outfits rejected him in Apis due to no resume or local references. A foreman at the third pointed him to an entry-level position in a three-man candle factory. He hated the work. He slept in a field behind the factory. It only took his first payday before he took to heavy drinking to cope with his disorientation. He knew no one. No one he could love or trust. No one at the factory or the bars cared. And so, he didn't. A verbal dismissal from the candle factory came with a shameful letter stating:

...'your mishandling of beeswax, a blatant negligence of duty and the product of gross intoxication.'

With little memory of his former self, another emerged: the desperate man. An angry young man, headstrong in taking an all-too-common path. That mulish road, paved in denial, frustration, and unexamined grief, could take a man a long way, in circles. And it did. His cycle of inebriation sabotaged job after job until he became a desperate man. Begging in the streets for food became his profession. But he accepted his way of life, his addiction to misfortune, blaming the gods for nine years.

It was during this long period that the oldest of Ancients, Alastar, found him. He lay in a barefoot stupor, curled up in an alley behind Old

Apis Road. Alastar rousted him with a staff. Then he picked up the jabbering sot and threw him into his wagon. When Roulic awoke, he occupied a gilded mahogany bed. A bed at whose ornately carved feet lay clean clothes and a new pair of suede ankle boots.

So it was, in Alastar's care at the mountaintop estate, Merelands, where Roulic found his place and purpose. That first afternoon, Alastar limited his hungover protégé to one drink per day at Merelands. He then gave sober instructions to shave 'the raggedy beard' and display 'a proper head-cut.' After a hearty supper, Alastar lectured on Ancient lineage and gave a brief history of Doth. It came as a shock to Roulic, the startling news that he was an Ancient. But it answered the question of why he didn't age as fast as mortalkin. Of course, staying shaggy and drunk and on the move helped hide his heritage despite not knowing of it. The moment he did, his excited mind began adapting to a new outlook on life.

Within a fortnight, the Ancient's outer transformation was complete. Any semblance of his former demeanor was indistinguishable. The desperate man stumbling through the streets of Apis was no more. The young Ancient humbled himself, thankful to be alive. He walked in self-respect. This, in turn, brought newfound self-reliance. And then self-confidence, measured and tested daily during his alchemic sojourn at Merelands.

Alastar's arduous regimen included intense physical training and multifarious mental and spiritual exercises. Roulic called it the 'mind and heart calendar.' Round-the-clock trials taught him to see more than he had before.

One such technique, practiced by day, triggered vivid forays using lucid dreaming. Roulic's deep sleep became training ground nightly journeys delving into subtle signs and premonitions. After breakfast, these nocturnal omens received review and examination from Alastar.

"I keep seeing a rider wearing a red cape, but I can't ever see her face."

"What does your heart say when you see her?"

"That I'm supposed to pursue her. That I already have."

"Perhaps you have. Listen to your gut feelings. Sometimes a future part of us leads the way for the part of us that hasn't yet found the way."

Months of rehabilitation shone new light on a multitude of mislaid facets. Organic reflections of his regenerated character. Two such qualities became traits Roulic would become known for. Traits he would carry the rest of his days like a well-worn garland. One, the simple joy of laughter. And two, keeping an eye open for the uncanny. True it was that Roulic enjoyed a good, hearty laugh. He laughed most days. And also true, there wasn't a lot he missed. Both gifts were a bounty renewed, bestowed from the wreath of Alastar's extended welcome. The elder's paternal care marked Roulic as a sagacious son. And a dedicated scholar of life, living with a reformed attitude.

In heart and in art, all things are possible.

Alastar mentioned this credo daily at Merelands. Yet, it had always been with Roulic, instilled in him at birth by the Masters. He just didn't know it. And he especially enjoyed their after-dinner discussions. They weren't limited to talk of creatures and kings or dragons and men. Alastar taught him, "Wisdom isn't learned; it is remembered." He ate up Alastar's food for thought digesting discussions about the soul and the concept of eternity. It wasn't long before he acquired a taste for engaging, notional topics. Or, as Alastar put it, 'those of a butterfly's pavilion.'

"If the Masters created us, who created them?"

Alastar stoked his pipe, then took a puff. "Perhaps some stories have no beginning or end, only the tale told between—like a dream within a dream."

It was in dreams at Merelands, where he dreamed of a farm boy named Janson. And where he dreamt of his siblings. Fere and Kolleen's smiles renewed his faith in family and himself. But memories of his mother were enigmatic and those of his father were problematic. Those of his mother were as vague and syncopated as those of his siblings. Yet with all three he felt he shared their love and could remember their bond. But of his inscrutable father, he would leave Alastar's estate as he came to it, with no knowledge of the man. No recollection, or voice or word, or even a name to remember his father by was ever given at Merelands. Not that he didn't inquire. It's just that Alastar didn't tell. But he had his reasons for keeping Roulic from the truth. King Meyrick and his brother, Mayem, were only mentioned in passing. And of Ravenna, no mention other than Roulic's dream about her; the inkling of his 'red-caped rider'.

When a year and a day had passed under the tutelage of the sage elder, Roulic left the mountain life of Merelands. He bid Alastar a teary farewell, setting out to restore his good fortune. Avoiding Apis and city life, he headed for the low woods of Everlan.

"I'll revisit my walk in nature. I'll know when I'm ready for mortalkin," he said, waving goodbye to his mentor.

"You've become a voracious pupil, tempered by the tenets of truth and the merits of compassion. God be with you, my son," Alastar praised him.

A nd all his wandering past began to make sense.
My life's work is to help the creatures and people of the realms of Doth.

And as moons passed, so did he grow in his meditations to respect the unpredictable Destiny. He had no idea the voice he would come to consider godlike had been with him, in one form or another, for centuries.

Who but a god could guide me so? Maybe she is an angel. Whoever she is, she's not of this earth. She must be otherworldly.

At first unsettled by the surreal company, he suspected he might go mad. But he chose not to, hearing the strangely familiar laugh. The granular tone solaced his lonely soul. And assured that people lost could be found and people forgotten, remembered. After warning him of deadly night predators, then of a coming storm, he learned to trust the voice. When it told him to leave the woods to help local Everlanians, he obeyed without question. But only for a time. Her ongoing "missions on behalf of mortalkin" had begun to take a toll on his conscience. Some of those "requests of the gods" led him to question *their* motives. So, he returned to the woods, telling Destiny he needed a break for his own good *and* the good of Doth. He'd been running her errands for thirty years.

He enjoyed his calm in the solitude of the forest for a season until one day, he up and left. Partly out of boredom. But mostly because of Destiny's recent whispering about an important thing for him to do. And an important place to go.

"Tell me again why I must go work on a farm? 'Until the time is right' isn't an answer. Honestly, Destiny, your calls are getting suspicious." In the end, he left because he really did trust her. And, after months of forest living, he felt a change was overdue. He knew most of the low mountain folk, and those few living in the forest, but they weren't what he considered 'people'. They were almost like creatures. Like him. A simple country creature of the wood.

Enjoying a conversation with the mind of someone like Alastar is what I need, the Ancient thought. *I need new experiences. A new day.* And so he left the woods of Everlan, revived in his cause, and Destiny's call, believing both to be for the good of Doth.

She guided him to a farm and family high on Mt. Nocturne where he lived and worked for three years. There were many others, but he never stayed more than three years at any one farm. Crisscrossing the mountain found him working in the valleys below, bordering Dandoorthose, for over three decades. He hated leaving the Ronse family, especially Callian, whom he'd grown to consider as a younger brother. Ditching the idea of lying about a nonexistent school or a faraway job, he decided to leave hotfoot. *It will be best for all,* he thought.

He'll be hurt but soon forget about me, like all the others, and get on with his life. But Callian never did.

"All right Destiny, I hear your call, but I must admit leaving the Ronse farm will be harder than leaving any other. They've treated me like family for over two years, and I've come to love them. And now you demand our separation to climb up a mountain to warn of a war where there is none?" He took two days stalling to ready his leather pack, knowing she'd pester him until he bowed to her prompt. Venturing north, far from Everlan's Southern Valley, he stopped at a rustic tavern in a charming hamlet called Little Town.

"Welcome to Realm's End," said the bartender.

"Excuse me, sir, but I wonder, could you tell me the fastest route to Mt. Nocturne from here?" To Roulic's surprise, the regulars sitting around the bar at the Realm's End Tavern didn't laugh at him. But they did stop talking and stare. The stranger interrupted their debate about a recent dragon sighting. The red-haired bartender tossed his rag behind the bar top. He sang to the Ancient a droll tune that suited his robust voice, face and physique.

"Ah, Everlan, that place lost in time, where hopeful dragons weave and bind...the hearts of young lovers, wizards, witches, and mere mortal minds." Claps and a hoot came from a little bald-headed man wearing green overalls perched on the bar's end.

"What brings you to the foot of old Nocturne? Wine, women, or song?" the jolly proprietor teased, goading the overalled patron.

"Or, perhaps, the dragons of Doth?" squeaked the little man. He began counting empty glasses beside him.

"I've got an urgent message for the folks at Top of the World," Roulic blurted. His words met more than curious faces. They looked concerned.

The tavern grew quiet again, and when the bartender leaned over the bar top, the locals leaned in as well. Roulic didn't say another word. He cautioned in light of unwanted attention. He then broke the parlous silence with a lie.

"The new schoolhouse they are building up there is getting a sizable grant from the governor."

All curiosity waned. The tavern keeper pulled back, exhibiting a prosaic business face. "Well, first off, you've got to pass a place called Giant's Hill. It's not too far from here. Go south a ways. You can't miss it. Follow the road around Giant's Hill and you'll be heading north, passing through the little old town of Dragon Fyre. That's where you'll run into Old Rock Road. It's a rough crawl, but it's the only way on this side of the peak to reach Top of the World. And when you get there, say hello to my little brother, Barrett. He keeps a place up there called The Harking Toad." The others straightened up at their stools and raised their glasses.

"Home of the great mountain ale," the little man celebrated. After a round of "cheers!", the regulars gulped, resuming their great dragon debate. They fast forgot the stranger walking out the door.

Chapter 22

Of One Soul

Roulic couldn't sleep. He'd returned to Jessamine keyed up since surviving Smutch's fireball. He went to the roof, thankful to be alive, and at the same time, sad about losing Aeryun.

"It's after midnight. Why aren't you in bed?" Lilith leaned on his shoulder, scooting to sit beside him.

"I can't sleep. You're not going to kick me off the roof, are you?"

"So...how was Arthur's return? We're worried about him. He's been acting strange lately. Ever since you got here, he's been a little restless. Fidgety."

"How so?"

"His timepiece. He's obsessed with his watch and can't stop looking at it."

"Oh, that. He thinks the portals are uniting against him. He said they're trying to prevent him from crisscrossing time. That, and he's having a hard life without Aeryun."

"Maybe so, but he can always go back in time and relive it with her," she sighed. "Unless he has outlived his welcome among the portals."

"That's funny coming from you. If Arthur can't get through a portal, why would he need the key? You told me the witches wanted the key, right? So they could live forever, riding across time?"

"That's the point. Don't you see? Possessing the key would solve all their problems with portals. With the Pearlytok, anyone can go anywhere, anytime, without aging. It's a free pass. And don't forget, they'd be able to reunite the entire family. I think that's their genuine desire. To rewrite that whole scenario." Her face turned from his disbelieving look. "Forget about it, Roulic. It doesn't matter. I'm just glad you're safe."

"I still think his watch needs to be replaced. He's probably had it forever," he said, avoiding her theories about the witches.

"He has. I should know. I'm the one who gave it to him," she laughed. "When the family moved into Jessamine, I gave him two time-pieces in case he ever lost one. Identical 1905 Waltham pocket watches."

"You always were one to give twice as much as you got," he said, looking for more emotion, finding cynicism.

"That's good of you to say, but that girl has gone and left the building," she said, sparking her Zippo.

What building? he perplexed.

"So, are you having a hard time without your Ravenna?" Lilith blew smoke.

"Every day I don't see her, I feel like I'm dying. I long to hear her voice...I'm sorry, I don't mean to carry on like this..."

"No, it's okay," she touched his hand, "you can talk to me..."

He stared at the moon. "It's just that our time together was so short-lived. It all went by so fast. And now, finding my former self makes it all that much harder." He wanted her sympathy, getting instead, her jaded fashion.

"So, go get her. Undo Mayem's foul noose and go find her. It's not like you don't have time on your side."

"I'm not so sure time is on my side this time...," he said.

"You don't need to be sure. 'Sure' is for people afraid of taking chances," she said.

"Maybe time doesn't want me with her. It keeps bringing me back here."

"To me," she sighed again, snuffing her half-smoked cigarette.

"You don't want me, Lilith. Damnation follows my every step; wherever I go, whatever I do, those close to me get hurt. Yesterday, I nearly killed myself. I can't let that part of me hurt Ravenna any more than I already have."

"Then don't," she huffed. "But for the love of God, stop running away. You'll never walk in peace if you keep running from the ones you love. Have you not come full circle? Face to face with yourself?"

She rose. "I'm going to bed. It's later than you think," she said, kissing him on the forehead, "but never too late to carry on." Lilith left him ruminating beneath the clear night sky. But he wasn't alone on the roof. Jillian's black-rosette Bengal, Laclain, appeared on the landing, purring. He sauntered over. Ignoring the patter of Marlee's fawn-faced Ragamuffin, Jannos, he brushed Roulic's leg. Jannos didn't rub Roulic's leg until circling it twice. On a third pass, he laid into his limb. Roulic laughed, patting the tubby house cat's thick fur sliding against his leg.

"What makes you carry on so, huh?" Laclain and Jannos meowed. "She's right, you know. I guess I'll have to carry on, too." He gave the stars a last look. "Come on, cats, let's carry on together." They followed him to the kitchen, where he filled their bowls with Friskies and warm milk.

"Hey," Charlotte said, humming into Nina's place. She accidentally swiped Mayem's elbow with her shoulder-length red hair.

"What is your name, and where are you taking me?" Mayem gruffed.

Her fair cheeks bloomed, heading to the kitchen. "My name's Charlotte Ruse. I'm taking *us* to a walking trail in Laguna Beach, behind Laguna Canyon. Anything else?"

"How far is that from here?" Mayem eyed the twenty-something, top to bottom. Charlotte's petite physique and style choices were those of a close cousin to Nina.

"Girl, you gotta get some fruit in here. There's nothin' in this house but cold pizza, warm beer, and the smell of weed." Closing the refrigerator door, she didn't intend to make eye contact. But the incensed stranger did.

Mayem attacked her retina, transfixing her equilibrium. She wobbled in the dank void of his heady gaze, landing on a kitchen chair. He flopped on the sofa, haughty with the effects of his control. He repeated his question telepathically, ignoring her swearing, until she responded.

"Not far. Twenty or thirty minutes from here." Even while hypnoidal, she continued to snub, refusing to look him in the eye.

"Tell me about this 'gravity hill' I heard you found," Mayem said. Nina went to Charlotte, bringing her back by clanking her lighter on the kitchen table.

"You didn't tell me this 'new guy' was, like, insanely intense," Charlotte whispered, unchained.

"You wouldn't have come over if I had," Nina whispered back.

"Oh, I'm never coming over again." Thrilled to have her 'little sister' over, Nina hoped Charlotte was teasing. But she wouldn't blame her, or anyone for that matter, for not wanting to be around Mayem. Ever since he set foot in her life, she had seen less of her friends. Only the creeps frequenting the Titan Dreams motel. *I'm never coming back here. Once he gets that egg, I'm outta here,* she thought. *Even so, there's a mystic quality about him. Powerful. He's the darkest man I've ever met. How can I resist that?...Why can't I resist that?*

"So, what's it all about? This gravity hill?" Mayem's insouciant look perturbed Charlotte.

"You know what?" Charlotte blurted at Nina. "I just want to go for a hike with my friend."

Nina's eyes urged, *"Don't piss him off!"*

"It's, ummm, it's kind of like a vortex," Charlotte answered, if only to appease Nina. "When you get near it, it pulls you in. And when you stand in the middle of it, it feels like you're moving on one of those flat elevators at the airport. If you know what I mean."

He didn't. "Come on, let's go, then," he rushed them. Charlotte didn't bother explaining what a conveyor belt was, so Nina changed the subject.

"We'll need to stop and get drinks on the way there."

"Some fun," Charlotte told her as they readied to leave. "And I was just starting to like him."

. . .

Nina didn't mind riding in the tiny back seat of Charlotte's green 1975 Volkswagen Beetle. It was a typical Southern California summer day. Breezes along Coast Highway blew ocean air through her hair, erasing some of Mayem's bad mojo. She spent the drive rethinking her long coquetry with bad boys. And how far she'd go, playing with black magic, the latter mistake always attracting the former. Around Mayem, at least initially, she felt excited by his confidence and raw power. Like she'd found someone who could help her become the "true, dark witch" of the 1990s. She once thought she wanted that. *But now? At what cost? Do I want to go to Hell for this guy? Who am I? I could open a card & candle shop, like all my friends, and do pretty well. If I wasn't so drawn to toxic losers from the dark side. Yeah, that's gotta stop. That's going to stop. And why am I getting so disoriented whenever I think about moving toward the Light in his presence? It must be him. It is him. I know better. I wish I'd never dreamed of him.*

"Don't worry, we're not going past Main Beach. Traffic's a zoo," Charlotte pointed to the long line of cars waiting at the intersection. She'd ignored Mayem all the way from Long Beach to Laguna Beach. He didn't notice. It was his first car ride. Turning on Cliff Drive, she parked the Bug a few blocks up at the base of the old Water Tank Trail. "It's gonna be steep, crazy steep, but once we reach the top, the rest of the trail will be pretty easy." She got out, opening a little red Igloo cooler in the Bug's backseat. She grabbed two Kiwi Strawberry Juicy Juice boxes and two mini tequila bottles.

"We're gonna need these, girl." Charlotte tossed the drinks into her Aspen Trails purple-and-black mini backpack.

"No doubt about that. But I'd rather we were going to the Sawdust Festival," Nina reminisced about their day at Laguna's annual craft fair. She pulled out a tall can and a bottle of water for Mayem from the cooler.

"We'll always have the Sawdust," Charlotte joked, slamming her door shut across from Mayem. Airtight cabin pressure inside the Bug seized his ears. He gave her a look that said, *You'll pay for that.*

He surveyed the cliff, grumbling, "It better be there," and, "Let's go, ladies." Charlotte mocked him, making goofy faces behind his back. *God, I hope she doesn't piss him off,* Nina thought.

Trekking the rigorous incline, the women stopped to catch their breath. The cliff was sandy and rutty and caught the offshore wind. They laughed, looking down at the 'miniature cars' on Pacific Coast Highway. Mayem had already stopped, out of breath. He panted, viewing the coast from Nixon's Point in South San Clemente all the way to Palos Verdes in the north. Charlotte scowled at him when he reached the clifftop, the dirty look speaking for them both. The trio hiked the interior for a good half mile before the trail forked. Charlotte veered left, leading down a winding descent. Wary and breaking a sweat, Mayem surveyed the pass before entering. A slivered stream fed the thin valley's grove of enduring oak trees.

He went for the shade of a giant sycamore, where a piece of plywood hung from the tree's arm. He swatted at flies, attempting to straddle the pint-size swing. The seat's withered rope snapped, crashing him to the ground. Nina and Charlotte laughed so hard they cried. When he got up to dust off his pants they doubled over, giggling. He kicked at the fallen swing until the wood snapped. Then he picked up the rope, he rolled it in his hand, holding it like a coiled whip.

"Keep it up, ladies," he waved the rope at them, adding, "keep moving," while he attached the ring of rope to a clip on his hip.

They followed a neglected trail in silence until Charlotte stopped. "See that weird rock formation up there? It looks like a half circle. That's where it is. That's the spot." She made sure to direct her speech to only Nina, as if Mayem wasn't there. They followed her, tromping through rocky scrub and around cactus. "Look out for poison oak, too; there's a lot of it here," she showed Nina a cluster of fuzzy green leaves. A slight incline led to a chalky plateau of solidified magma. She did a half pirouette on the floor of igneous rock inside the U-shaped wall.

"I give you, 'Gravity Hill'. I don't know if it's what you're looking for, but it's pretty cool. If you stand over here, you'll see what I mean." Again, Charlotte made sure to only look and speak to Nina, as if Mayem were invisible. They took to the slight grade, then the plateau, facing her. "Now, turn around. Look at where you've just walked up from," she said.

"Oh, wow, you're right, that is pretty crazy. That's awesome, girl," Nina said. She swigged from her can of Arizona Iced Tea, then lit a More cigarette. "What do you think, boss?"

Mayem didn't answer.

"That's freaky," Nina said. "I wonder why in this spot?"

"It's an optical illusion, that's all," Charlotte stated. "It looks like it's sloping down, but that's impossible. We just walked up it."

"This area is magnetized," Mayem said, speaking only to Nina.

"Okay, professor," Charlotte mocked him again, this time under her breath. But Mayem heard her, and his face soured, beet red. He turned to study the unusual wall of quartz-veined granite. When he turned to face the women, his face was no longer red. It was cold as a fallow stone. One hand rested on a hip and the other on the coiled rope.

"Nina! Stay here while Charlotte and I have a chat," he said. Charlotte didn't catch Nina's nervous look or notice her fixed stance.

"Yeah, right, professor. You can school me on limestone and magnets and *whatever*," Charlotte said, cockier than ever.

They walked to the trail in silence. Nearing the bend, Charlotte turned and winked at Nina before rounding the corner. She didn't notice that Nina hadn't moved a muscle. Mayem stopped Charlotte at a dry creek by a hundred-year-old oak and sycamore trees.

"Okay, so what's so important that you can't say it to me in front of my best friend?"

"Look at me!" he shook her shoulders. She looked anywhere but into his eyes. She punched and kicked and squirmed, having no effect on him whatsoever. Her spitting defiance failed to evade the strength of his demonian clutch. He covered one of her boots with his, then grabbed her hand, and holding it behind her back, pulled her in. She struggled to break free, biting his other hand, --the hand that got the rope around her neck. Had she screamed, Nina might have come running. But Charlotte didn't scream. That wasn't her way. When Mayem walked back up the grade alone, Nina was on her knees, kneading her stomach.

"Where's Charlotte? What did you do to her?" she bawled, jumping back. He pulled the counterfeit key from his pocket, humming a dissonant string of notes. She stepped a foot back for each of his steps forward. He rapped on the coiled rope, then stopped, his eyes reaching hers like a key slipping into a lock.

"I'm not going to hurt you," he said. "But I need you to go first. I've just one more thing to do here. Wait for me in Doth. I won't be long." His eyes glowed a soft red.

"But..." Nina's throat got icy.

Mayem paced the plateau in a mechanical manner. He held her spellbound, reciting arcane incantations until a paroxysm of blathering laughter consumed him. Syllabic fits contorted his emotionless, fallow face. Nina's spine met the rock wall, ending her getaway from the deadly outlander. The bad boy dragon chaser she had dreamed about weeks ago won. Once his fit calmed, he resumed intoning godless chants, keeping her pinned to the wall.

On the outside, her throat jiggled like Jell-O. On the inside, her vocal cords were frozen, inoperable. So she couldn't muster a desperate, bloodcurdling scream. She would have if she could have. She trembled in vain to massage her throat by inching her hands up to her chest, but they fell short of her jugular notch. Both arms came flopping down, useless. Her legs were locked and her neck couldn't turn more than an inch. All she could do was jitter and jiggle, muttering cries amid a spate of tears wetting her new Utopia Parkway T-shirt.

Only when she seemed lifeless did he stop chanting.

"I will find you in Everlan," he said, "I'm going to need you in 1699." A final shot pulsed from his eyes; an arrow of light that coruscated over her pituitary gland. His arms raised to the sun. The portal opened, enveloping Mayem's entranced captive.

Chapter 23

To An Uncertain Demise

Jax, Agnes, and Madelyn, the 'youngers,' joined Raine and Roulic for mid-morning breakfast. Smells of hot coffee, toast, and bacon permeated the kitchen, streaming in sunlight.

"But what about the map of Doth I found in the cave?" he quizzed Raine.

"Remnants of a prior jump, I suppose," Raine sipped mocha from a Bailey's Winking Yum teacup. "You must have left it there."

"Why would it be ripped up like that?"

"I don't know, maybe you got mad at it. Please pass the butter and jam, dearies." Agnes complied, and Madelyn did so only after spreading gobs of jam on her Pillsbury biscuit.

"You *have* been known to fly off the handle now and again," Jax said. "You sure did with Haggarty," he said, between bites of crisp bacon and Aunt Jemima waffles.

"The old wizard?"

"You slayed him in the woods of Everlan before heading to Mt. Nocturne," Jax said. "Lilith and Raine helped you then, but it the end, it was your deep-seated anger that finally took his ninth life." Madelyn grinned at Roulic, but Jax caught the look and returned her a stone-faced frown.

"I don't recall the event. Nor do I want to. I must have been crazy, out of my mind."

"Lilith always had the best in mind for your former self," Raine said.

"I wouldn't have listened to Destiny all those years had I known she was Lilith."

"One's destiny cannot be unheard," Raine said. Agnes and Madelyn left their plates on the table, walking up the stairs backwards. Nobody noticing their flippant strangeness.

"Well, to my former wife's credit, I would have to say she's taught me a lot. Besides leading me astray for centuries and then giving me the boot."

"Astray? Roulic, you have no idea how many times she has come to aid and protect you. Her power to occupy multiple dimensions—of which she has many times—is just one gift that came with the spell. Her true genius lies in her split-second volition. She can steer things in one direction, then suddenly, she's off, weaving another track. We've witnessed her uncanny magic all our lives, haven't we, Jax?"

Jax went to the teapot, nodding. "She can turn on a dime all right. Some of my earliest memories are of Lilith's steadfast hand." Roulic's brow flashed. *I could never love her again.* Green tea poured into Jax's cup. "When Captain Salty kidnapped me —you were out flying around with the Keeper of Clouds," he laughed. "Anyway, I was as frightened as any boy would be, taken by pirates. Then Lilith came to me. In the flesh. She appeared in my cell. She instructed me to get the pocket knife off a drunken sailor who lay passed out, outside my cell. It was because of her I felt I had a chance, that I could make it off the *Hurling Gal* alive."

He appeared unmoved by the story, concealing his concern about the side effects of the Forever Spell. *Why are Jax and Raine so keen on keeping my blessings for Lilith?* His body shifted, unable to contain what he had bottled up. He argued, holding the idea that some rueful truth haunting her agitated her emotions. But he didn't entertain her claim, as off as he believed it to be, that the witches sought the Pearlytok for themselves.

"Brother, I've got another," Raine rhymed.

"Go ahead," Jax said, getting into the spirit of family memory-telling.

"Okay. Roulic, do you remember the candle lantern you bought the night you found Ravenna tied to the Bridge of Belief?"

"How could I forget that lantern? It led me to Ravenna."

"Do you remember how you came to carry that lantern?"

"I found it in a shop in Belief," he said. "Some call it New Belief."

"But you left the shop before returning to buy the lantern, didn't you?"

"Yes, come to think of it, I did. It so struck me that I went back in and bought it. And like I said, it was a good thing I did."

"Remember, our eyes have been on you since..." Raine stopped herself. "And on Lilith, as well. You may never have gone back to that shop if Destiny hadn't whispered in your ear. And Ally might never have galloped the path to Knowing. Without Destiny guiding Ally, you would have missed the posse. You would never have met Aurora at the pools of Everlan."

"It was Lilith all along," he whispered, admitting to himself so many things on so many levels.

"Our Lilith was your Destiny," Raine said.

"Ahh, but we delivered the rain," Jax gloated, pouring his tea into the sink.

"It's always been a group effort," Raine said. "We've always worked better behind the scenes. Lilith won't admit it, but..."

"What exactly won't I admit?" Lilith startled them, this time taking Madelyn's seat. Her coy look tickled Roulic.

"They were telling me about your modesty and good-natured side," Roulic perked up.

"All my sides are good," she winked at Jax, tucking her reddish-brown mane behind one ear. "It's my bad side you don't want to mess with."

"No, I do not." Jax shook his head. "I've met your evil twins, and I prefer the nice one. Buttermilk?"

"Yes, please. Banana bread, too?" Lilith batted her lashes.

"Coming right up, m'lady." Jax winked back.

"Speaking of evil twins, do either of you have any idea about the current lot of our elusive dragon?" Lilith joked.

"Don't get smart with me." Raine took it the wrong way. "You know Mayem's got Baby on Dandling Oars Island."

"Depending on what year Roulic goes back to," Jax said.

"Oh, he's going back right when and where we want him to. By this time tomorrow, there'll be no more running from ghosts."

"I'll never take this whistle off again," Roulic touched the talon to his chest.

"Third time's the charm, right?" Jax said.

"Fourth, counting Nagnee, but without Arthur and Aeryun, how?"

"By the power of the dragon," Raine whispered. Devouring the aromas of banana bread, waffles, tea, and mocha, a rich petrichor followed the witches into the kitchen. Roulic straightened up. *Something is afoot.* Two occupied barstools and two hopped on countertops. Agnes and Madelyn leaned against the doorless jambs.

"Shall we let this, then, be an end to a curse in time?" Lilith said. Raine approved with a nod.

Lilith focused on Roulic. "Darling, do you believe we are all one? As in, really all one? Because if you don't, this will never work. But if you do, then there's a chance we—you—with the power of dragons, can put a stop to Mayem."

"I believe in *you*," he said to the sisters around the table. "But if you're asking me to believe someone like Mayem could ever be one of my family or a part of yours, then no, I don't believe it. I couldn't and wouldn't want to."

"Could you believe that all things, be they good or evil, are part of one thing?" Jax tendered.

"How about a forest?" Alison said. "If a tree is one thing, then what is a forest, if not many trees existing as one thing?"

"Only one Mayem exists," Roulic countered, "one... whom I believe you'd agree is committed to evil. And as for the power of his dragons, what is it if it isn't burning things?"

"If you can believe that all energy comes from one collective source, then you can believe that collective power, for good or bad, can come to anyone, even if for a moment. *That* is the power of dragons, in a nutshell, my friend," Jax said, "...to believe in your heart that we are all one."

"How do you think Ravenna can harness the power of dragons?" Lilith spun her Zippo on the kitchen table. "Because she holds an instance of pure love. As pure as anyone can be. Grace also received the dragon's gift. In fact, her dying words were, 'We all are one, that's what we are.' And that's all we're asking of you today. To entertain our shared ideal; the positive use of this ageless notion." Her case made, Lilith stepped outside, lit a cigarette, and sat in her high-back rattan chair on the patio. The six sisters adjourned, going to their rooms without declaring further testimony.

"I will certainly think about it," Roulic said. "It's not like I've never contemplated the 'oneness.' I've been around a long time, ya know." Jax and Raine continued their attestation in the quiet kitchen.

"Only those connected to the heart of a dragon can tap the dragon's power," Raine whispered.

"And a love that never gives up comes from the love that always is," Jax whispered.

"Oh, you know I won't ever give up on Ravenna, don't you?" his features angled in puzzlement. "It's just that dragons..."

"Shall it be," the siblings chimed, closing their case.

"Are you two trying to paint pictures in my mind? Because if you are, it's working," he sensed they were enchanting him viva voce.

"Uh-oh, the Ancient's onto your delicate work." Jax turned to Raine. "Do you think he's ready?"

"Is one ever ready when presented with the present?" Raine riddled.

"What present?" Roulic's eyebrows went up.

"You'll see." Marlee peeked at Raine around the hallway wall. "Are you ready? Let's go."

"Come on, Roulic, let's go for a drive. There's a place we want you to see," Raine said.

"Is it a magical place?" he asked, glad not to be discussing the power of dragons.

"It will be when we get there," Marlee said.

Alison, Aurora, and Jillian trickled down dressed head to toe in tight black. They looked like they were going to a goth party. Agnes and Madelyn made everyone wait. They were dressed in black, too. But they wore lustrous red combat boots and carried Chanel brown quilted suede shoulder bags.

"We'll follow you in the 'witchy wagon,'" Raine told Jax.

"Yes, you will," Jax said.

Marlee drove the Black family's 1997 bright burgundy four-wheel-drive American General Hummer H1 wagon. Jax roared through Laguna Canyon Road, passing Marlee like a glib chauffeur. Roulic puffed his pipe, waving at the witches as if he had ridden in fast cars all his life.

"So, what gives, Jax? What is so special about this place?" Roulic hollered, hanging on to his hat. The Jag turned, accelerating.

"You might not need to kill Mayem at Aspired Mountain. He's up there right now, as we speak," Jax hollered back, pointing at the 440-foot cliff looming ahead. "We think he's found a portal..."

"But he doesn't have the key." He stashed his pipe in his vest pocket.

"He's opened portals before, using mind power wizardry. But he's never discovered a portal without the Pearlytok until today. If he gets back to Doth, he'll destroy the Realms. Then he'll return here with an army of dragons led by Baby's twin sister—the egg you put back in the lair on Grand Pekoes."

"Good gods." *Then this is it.* Roulic paled, both scared and excited.

"None of that will happen if you stop him here and now." Jax pulled hard on the Jag's handbrake, parking the car at the base of the Water Tank Trail.

Marlee parked the Hummer too close to Roulic's passenger door, dwarfing the Jaguar. "I'm guessing they're here to back me up?" he waved at Marlee.

"They didn't come along just for the ride," Jax said. "Oh, that reminds me. Gram and Auntie have a message for you," he said, reaching into the Jag's tiny glove compartment.

"Wait, what?" Roulic befuddled. Jax produced a shiny object from the glove box while the witches milled outside the Hummer.

"It's a Panasonic recorder. They whispered in my ear at 4 o'clock this morning, telling me to go to Glassy Hall. So I recorded them on this device while they spoke through the mirror. But they didn't stay long." He pressed a button that emitted Gram's foreboding forewarning through a micro-speaker. The skin on Roulic's arm crawled.

"Now, Roulic, listen closely. And remember this: Only by transcending your past will you receive the gift of a new present. Speaking of the present, Jax, be sure to pass along Ramil's blade. Our dear Ancient may need it if the hand of fate decides to meet the foot of doom. A more timely equation, if there ever was such an occurrence, I have not seen."

When Demeter's sage message came out of the recorder, her words met the air like a caressing mother. "Whole lives come and go by the hopeful swords on that which they rely. But one who wields faith can count on the power of a dragon to end a curse in time. You, and you alone, will decide your future by deciding the future of another. What must be done must be done."

Gram and Demeter repeated in unison: "What must be done, must be done. Shall it be!" The hair on the back of Roulic's neck stiffened.

Jax turned off the recorder. "That's it. That's all they said. I'm still getting used to this thing. Oh, and they wanted me to give you this for good luck." Jax handed him a handsome relic of a blade: a black-handled cross-hilt knife kept in a tan leather sheath.

"It belonged to my great-great-grandfather, Ramil."

He attached the sheath to his belt, following the group around the water tank along a yellowish trail. Like Mayem's group, the witches stopped to catch their breath along the grueling grade. Roulic scanned the 180-degree view, finding an express ferry heading to Catalina.

My fate lies before me. But how can I defeat Mayem with just a knife?

"Busy little ants moving back and forth beside the sea," Madelyn hummed. Agnes followed two kayaks gliding beside the waves below. "What does that make us?"

"B-u-s-y l-i-t-t-l-e b-e-e-s," Madelyn purred.

"Let's hope our Ancient stings him like a scorpion," Agnes said.

"Dead... like an Arabian Deathstalker," Madelyn said.

Jax nudged Madelyn. "Time to press on, ladies. Be wary, be ready. He could be hiding anywhere up there."

He reached the clifftop first. Agnes grabbed Madelyn's hand, following him up. Chest-high sagebrush edged the sandy trailhead amid the kingdom of wildflowers. In the bladderpod and white sage, a colorful, flitting chatter caught his attention.

"Stay on your guard," Roulic told the witches.

They hiked in eerie silence. But when the road descended, winding into tall oak and eucalyptus trees, they halted. The birds stopped conversing.

"Be ready around this corner," Jax said.

"He'd better be ready for us," Madelyn scorned. She joined Alison, who was pulling yellow flowers from a gray shrub. "Right, sister?" Madelyn said.

"That's right, Mad," Alison nodded, tugging the brush until she held a handful of bright yellow petals. She dipped her nose into her palm. "Did you know that sagebrush talks to one another?"

"No, I didn't," Madelyn whispered. Jax and the others huddled around Alison.

"They signal each other by releasing chemicals that convey stress or danger."

"What are they saying?" Roulic stepped closer to Alison. She sniffed her palm again.

"Nothing good. This plant is releasing poisonous toxins."

"It's a defense mechanism," Jax said.

"They've sensed the presence of Mayem and are warning each other," Roulic said.

"That's a lot of warning going on," Raine surveyed the thousands of sage shrubs in their immediate vicinity.

"Let's keep moving," Jax said. "Alison, you and Aurora go with Agnes and Madelyn to the right. Jill and Marlee, you'll come with me and Roulic to the left. Stay in tune. Godspeed!"

Both parties moved toward the fork, looking in either direction. They didn't see or hear a thing except for the trees rustling on the opposite side of the trail. A solemn draft swayed the oak forest.

"That's odd," Jillian said.

"It could be coming up through a ravine," Marlee said.

"Or maybe a canyon. Unless…" Jax stared at the treetops.

"Unless...he's brought them with him," Roulic tensed. "Quick! Everyone, into the trees!" Jillian, Marlee, and Jax darted into the oaks.

"I hope the others are safe," Jillian said, hiding in the trees. "Should we try to find them?"

"No," Jax said, "it's too risky. We don't know what's out there."

"Agreed. Let's follow the trail from within the trees until it's safe," Roulic said. But trudging through the noisy leaves, he changed his mind. "Wait here for me." He ran out onto the trail before the witches could respond. "I'll stay within earshot and see if it's clear up ahead," he said.

Raine looked hopefully to her little brother. "Do you think he will survive this time?"

Chapter 24

Revive God's Soul

The ghosts of Onan hid on a ledge, lodged behind the wall of rock above the portal, waiting for Mayem's signal. Loyal to none, their pledge differed from Ozrar's. Their retribution was redemptive. This played a big part in the plight of their liberation and in the outcome of Roulic and Ravenna's fate. And the fate of the witches and of the realms of Doth.

Smutch sputtered, "To the bitter end, Blini! They're all here, all of them except the grannies."

"That's fine by me. We'll end this in one sweep of the deck," Bliniloth said.

"They might be here, too — their parents, as ghosts, I mean. Like us," Smutch babbled.

"Shut up, you fool!" Bliniloth domineered. "I don't want to hear another word from your burning hole until this is done and over. Understood!?"

"Yes, sir," Smutch's fiery eyes dimmed to that of morning embers.

"This human points like a lead dog on the hunt. He hasn't shied from danger and has proven relentless in his pursuit of love. I would have been, too, had I lived long enough to find the right wench. The question remains: Shall he find his end in the sting of Mayem's whip? Hmm, we will wait and see, we will."

The ghost stood as high as the rock facade he hid behind, squinting at Smutch, letting him know he could speak again. Bliniloth couldn't stand listening to his inferior companion. Yet he couldn't endure waiting in silence any more than he could bear the blunt mind of Smutch. "This Roulic aspires to revive God's soul in the hearts of men, Smutch."

"What are *we* aspiring to revive, sir?" Smutch's eyes sparkled.

"What lad!? What we've long aspired to revive! O! Gold revives us! Always did. Always will. Were it not for the forever fight among the golden and the tarnished, would we be here, hidden behind this rock? I think not."

"Well, there are those witches coming. And that Ancient has always been a thorn..."

"Shut up, Smutch," Bliniloth squatted. "That Ancient will soon suffer our sweet revenge. His calamity's long overdue. He's gone too far, wiled with those witches far too long, to our ethereal thralldom that no human's hex can fix. From the moment he..."

"And *then* we revive the Pearlytok?"

"Yes, Smutch. *Then* we revive the Pearlytok," Bliniloth said.

"Look!" Smutch shouted, his face blazing. "Mayem's got his arm up. That's the signal!"

"Don't lose yer head over it. Wait for his second signal. And look out for them witches," Bliniloth said.

Chapter 25

Sable Hilt

"I've been waiting for this, our moment," a dark voice taunted.

"Show yourself, Evil One!" Roulic spotted a shadow dart behind the portal's jagged veneer. He put his palm over Ramil's knife.

"Don't be so harsh. I'm your lover's uncle. We could have been family, you and I." The sinister voice ricocheted across the floor of granite rocks.

"Never in a million years!" Roulic squinted at the chaotic shadows.

Mayem jumped from the rock façade, holding black-gloved hands over his head. "We meet again," he said with a wicked intimacy. Light shed on the lines crossing his forehead. From his dark eyes shone specks inviting death to the one person he despised more than himself. The rival Ancients gazed, sharing the same thought: *He'll never give up without a fight to the death...*

When Mayem's arms fell, Bliniloth and Smutch appeared, standing guard on either side of Roulic. Inching, he moved from the heat coming off the accursed Smutch.

"There's no point in resisting them. It'll only make it worse for you," Mayem mouthed mercilessly, pacing at the foot of the portal. Then, he bowed, like an arrogant bullfighter displaying callous enmity born of countless kills. From his hip, he produced the coiled rope from the broken swing. Roulic tried to ignore his shaking insides. He wanted to run.

But how do I dodge the ghosts? Where are the witches? Where is Jax?

"J—a—x!!" His holler for help rang through the canyon.

"Go ahead, call them out. They'll sing like nightingales before I'm finished!" Mayem snarled.

"Couldn't you think of anything better than a rope?" Roulic stalled. *This is it. I'm going to die here.*

"J—a—x!!" he yelled louder and longer.

"Care to take the first lash?" Mayem's nonchalant unraveling of the rope for Bliniloth seemed to sicken the ghost.

"You've got the fag end, you do it, mate. We'll take no branch from you," Bliniloth took two steps back. Smutch mimicked the move. Mayem's face sagged.

"Mutineers, eh? I should have known you'd cut and run. Fine, I'll flog them myself. You two were washed up long before I conjured you." He pulled the rope taut over his head, uttering a string of seven indiscernible syllables. Smoke puffed from the rope as it transmuted into a long, silver-jointed whip. Bound within the whip was a ferocious snake. Mayem cracked the whip. Bolts of electricity spurted from the writhing snake's tongue. With each lash, the armored viper grew longer and thicker.

The ghosts of Onan wasted no time in their transformation. Bliniloth ballooned, dwarfing the warring Ancients. His spectral minion's whirring blaze hummed and burned the sand. Mayem responded by unleashing a barrage of lightning from the hissing whip. Roulic jumped frantically onto a wide boulder and slid over its side in time to avoid the strike. Bliniloth dodged the tip of the serpent's tongue by deflating his body while leaping back. Mayem lashed at Smutch, who unexpectedly yielded, letting the creature girdle his flaming frame. The flammable figure seized the silver whip, melting it. Then he severed the serpent using his burning hands. Mayem fell to the ground, letting go of the wriggling whip. His aging face squinched when both halves of the molten switch stopped slithering.

"We've held up our end," Bliniloth jumped, straddling Mayem. "We delivered your key. As for the dragon egg, you know where it is, mate. Go get it yourself. We'll be seeing you," he shouted at the perspiring Ancient. "C'mon, Smutch!"

"Yeah, go get it yourself! We'll be seeing you, mate," Smutch sneered, evaporating behind Bliniloth.

Mayem muttered in disgust, humiliated in the dirt, "Deserters, the both of them. Neither fit to scour an anchor." He scouted the area and quiet trail pass. Roulic was gone. "Oh, Ozrar, I call on thee."

Roulic's heart pounded. He kept his head low behind the boulder, Ramil's knife in hand. *I'm much younger, stronger, and have the power of the dragons on my side. I can do this. With their help, I can kill Mayem. I must kill him. If not, he'll destroy all of Doth and everyone I love. But how?* He looked up at the sky from behind the rock. *Good gods! Oh, that's how.*

Shadows whirred past Mayem's head, shadows that sniffled. He looked up, staring at the heavens in horror. Seven flapping dragons poised above him. The creatures were dusty and pastel, like weathered buildings. Their dragon skin was the pigment of the precious gems ruby and sapphire. Deep orange, yellow, green, blue, indigo, and violet. Among them hovered Dyad and Brac. Their huge wings blew stale canyon air through Mayem's dusty hair. He recognized the dragon brothers and Baby, but not her future sister, Nysa. Her eyes seethed a brilliant blue. He gasped at their conductor. A gigantic eighth beast hovered over the group, almost as large as the seven below combined. The glistening black behemoth launched a giant fireball into the sky. All the dragons flew into it, leaving the dimension. Mayem wiped his wrinkled forehead.

"It's not too late to rid hope from the heart of the youngest, I should think," came Ozrar's icy whisper. "Although from what I've heard, she is the fiercest of the brood." Mayem blenched, looking side to side. He bolted, retreating to the U-shaped wall circling the portal. His back slammed against the rock.

Roulic chased in full sprint, halting on the chalk plateau. He held up Ramil's knife. Their eyes locked again. Mayem laughed, "Let me guess. You wield a magic knife cast by your new friends? Tell me, where are they now?"

"Come a little closer and you'll find out." Roulic wasn't relying on the witches to come rushing to his side. He relied on their magic, stepping forward with blind confidence in the warlock's knife. *They made sure I would carry it today. It must hold some terrific power.*

"Do you really think you can stop me with that?" A seasoned fighter, Mayem believed he could best the young defender in close combat. But he wouldn't take any chances and certainly didn't want to fight boxed in at the portal's door. So, he inched forward, trying to gain ground. Pelting Roulic with small rocks, almost comically so, proved a desperate act. Most got dodged, and some were even thrown back. Then, with just six feet left between them, he stopped and pulled out the counterfeit key. Waving it, he tried to tempt him.

"With one whirl, you could be back in Ravenna's arms. Think of what the two of you could do with the Pearlytok. Neither of you will ever see me again, I swear," Mayem deceived.

"Luring me with lies won't work. Even if you held the actual key, I still wouldn't trust you."

Mayem's beaded brow danced, inspecting his key. "You're bluffing."

"Am I? I carried it around for months, thinking it to be the genuine Pearlytok. That's the thing about witches. They can be real tricky like that. Catching you off guard where you least expect it." Roulic rotated Ramil's knife, reflecting light on Mayem's face. Mayem squinted into the crisscrossing beams. The key dropped. He swooped to pick it up, slyly swiping a hefty pinch of sand into the palm of his glove.

"I never needed this thing," he said, saving the key in his pocket. "It seems I've become a master portalist without it. So, step aside, son, unless you want to relive the fall you took at Dandling Oars."

Roulic's blood boiled. He raised the black-handled blade. "I'm not about to let you leave."

Mayem shrugged, pulling a deadly push dagger from the shaft of his boot. "You'll never leave this place."

Roulic stepped back from the short blade. But then he lunged full force, bashing into fear itself — and the sand thrown at his eyes. His thrust nicked Mayem's ruffled cuff, trickling red over the elder's damaged hand. In crushing retaliation, Mayem's backhand splattered his own blood across Roulic's downed cheek. The fierce felling allowed Mayem to pounce and aim his dagger toward Roulic's heart. Ramil's knife rose, covering Roulic's chest. Mayem's deathly dagger clashed and clinked against Ramil's sable hilt. Vanilla-colored sparks flew from the ebony handle clutched in Roulic's hand. The witches voices shot past his ears, whispering "Searing Son!" as the arc of fire encircled Mayem's blade, turning his hand red-hot. Mayem screamed, dropping the scalding weapon on Roulic.

"Damn your magic!! And damn the witches of Doth!!" He held his burned hand while running to the trees.

Roulic rolled over, shaking off the burning metal. Running, he ran past the incline, waving Ramil's knife and shouting back, "You can't hide forever!" Combing the oaks for Mayem, he found a shallow, twisting stream. *He'd want to cool that hand... stay alert!* He performed a 360° scan, kneeling to splash water on his waist where Mayem's dagger had burned through his shirt. *I'm getting dizzy...* He cupped his hands with cool water and rinsed his face. *Look at me... God help me...*

Gleams of light etched by the wavering oaks animated the stream like flickers on a silver screen. He froze, catching the witches dance on the roof of Jessamine. Seven heads of wild hair flung violently. Fourteen syncopated arms and legs swinging, kicking, sending rhythmic ripples across the gurgling water. Then, two miniature cyclones the size of arms rose from the stream. The first aberrance spouted a coarse whisper from its little gray eye. A whisper he knew well.

"Love never gives up; it lives on in the love that always is."

Lilith's husky breath bubbled out from the faery-sized storm. He turned, but she wasn't there, only the unmistakable sound of her voice in the wind. Then a second message swirled forth from the cyclonic twin. A call embodied in the witches' harmonic accompaniment.

"Embrace the One in your heart."

His tension lessened hearing them despite clutching his waist and scanning for Mayem.

The cyclones fell into the rocky water, revealing Aurora's face on the calming surface. Arthur, Demeter, and Gram were beside her. That nanosecond of peace made him smile. But they didn't smile back. They raised their arms, and with wide eyes and fitful faces, threw nuts at him. An acorn plopped from tree to stream, disrupting the shimmering semblance. Then another, and another, until twelve acorns fell, disturbing the witches' presence.

He was reaching for an acorn when Mayem kicked him in the back. His head got shoved into the water, held down by Mayem's sadistic boot. When he didn't move, Mayem crossed the stream, dancing over his body.

"Miracles are for fools, Roulic. I ask again, where are your witches now?"

Roulic ignored him. He gasped for air, catching the gabble of water and the kibitz of trees. *What was the dragon's power? Jax told me...* it played through his head, tinny, like it was coming from the Panasonic recorder.

"If you can believe that all power comes from one ultimate power, then you can believe that ultimate power, for good or bad, can come to anyone, even if for a moment."

Mayem's boot squished harder, twisting his cheek into the stream. "I can't hear you, Roulic!"

He caught a breath, catching with closed eyes what would change his world forever. The same eight dragons that appeared to Mayem: Dyad, Brac, Baby, and the others, unknown by name.

Time slowed like dripping honey. Each dragon appeared in his mind's eye within the space of one second. Each thought came with the thrust of a flaming sword. Nysa slayed his heart with a riveting pulse of tranquility.

"In the eye of every storm lies the sight of seven heavens."

The second message came from Baby. Her eyes radiated euphoria, unlike her days on Dandling Oars Island.

"To every island, opportunity approaches."

Next, Brac breathed out a ball of fire.

"Every star and atom hath a brother and sister to shoulder its pain, should one ask."

Then Dyad, whose low hum quivered from his surging core.

"From the depths of despair rises the greatest hope."

Dyad's quantum signal made his torso twitch like a live wire dropped in a puddle. The electrified lollop regenerated his body, and then his hope, the former he thought lost. The relay gained its ground, as lightning does to earth. His inner reserve got tapped with enough punch to put his trodden arms back to use. And enough juice for his right hand to grasp the stream's pebbled edge. But with Mayem's hard heel hopping on his fingers, he panicked. *I dare not raise my head... my breath is running out... no time left...*

In a sapphire flash, the unknown dragons sent a crystal vision. It showed three angels in flight, intertwining his fleeting prayer:

I've prayed a thousand little hopes,
heard a thousand little deaths.
Yet in you, found everyone in all things, and all things in everyone.

The miracle taking place reignited Roulic's mind. It commanded his beaten body up and out of the water. One elbow dug into the sand, the other wrapped viselike around Mayem's ankle, tearing him to the ground. A ring of moss-covered stones met the back of Mayem's head. Bloody, Mayem reached for the bedraggled wound. But Roulic grabbed the hand, pinning Mayem with one knee over a shoulder. Roulic's other knee punished Mayem's burned hand. The evil one lay trapped, wriggling like a rabid fox.

"Kill me, then! *You* decide the dragon's future now," he groaned, Ramil's knife held against his throat.

"Who would I become if I killed you?"

"You won't do it, you can't do it, you never could. You're no different from your father," Mayem scorned through his teeth. The ensorcelled blade exacted a thin red line that bubbled, beading across his throat. Roulic pulled the knife back and stood over him, ready to exact fists of fury.

"Get up before the dragons come back for you!" he barked. Mayem's eyes softened, then he sighed, getting up without a fight. But Roulic didn't trust those eyes for a second. He torqued Mayem's right arm high and hard behind his back, an inch from breaking it. With his left hand, he held the spine of Ramil's knife to the rib cage.

"Where are you taking me, then? There's no place that can hold me."

"The gods have a place for you." He shoved Mayem.

"Can I at least drink some water? I've got a terrible thirst." Roulic allowed him to kneel over the stream. Mayem cupped his left hand and took a sip. Then another. Pretending to take a third, he lunged backward. Swinging his right arm, he tried to knock Roulic down by the waist. But Roulic was ready for trickery and spun back, missing the gist of the blow. The movement led Mayem's right heel to catch the tip of Ramil's blade as Roulic spun back and around. Mayem fell, reaching for his heel, then passed out beside the stream.

Mayem came to, late in the day, on buff limestone in the same spot where the portal had taken Nina. His somber jury faced him: the witches of Doth, and hovering over their heads, the dragons of Doth.

"This is interesting. All my favorite friends are here," he mocked, then broke down. "No matter how hard I tried, I never could bring back yesterday, nor change tomorrow. But the changing world never changed me. Go ahead, take my life. I'm not so blind that I can't see the sun is setting on my life today."

"For as much pain and suffering as you've created, you deserve to die here. God knows I've wanted you dead for a long time. But I am not going to kill you. Stand up, Ancient, and take your fate." Mayem got up, his bruised body getting pressed against the granite wall.

Roulic turned to the witches, then to the dragons, proclaiming:

"Mayem, by the God of all gods, you will atone by facing the sorrow of your deeds. If it takes ten thousand years, so be it. May today's consequence mark the end of your stain, your curse in time. Shall it be!"

Roulic kneeled, praying to and for the power in all good things. The witches held hands while the dragons stirred, changing colors one by one. Leaves flew about Mayem and the portal's door opened, washing him in a prism of swirling colors.

"Where is it taking me?" Mayem winced.

"To a place where you'll face those you've injured." The portal swept the chalk floor and rock wall clean until he was no more.

It was 4 a.m. by the time the celebration and long goodbyes at Jessamine House ended. Since falling from the Mayem's Edge, Roulic had spent nine days coming and going in a sphere of the witches' making.

As per the elder's instructions, Jax dropped him off on Pacific Coast Highway. "I'll see you soon, my friend," Jax said, speeding from the empty movie theater. The marquee lit the vacant sidewalk across from Main Beach's boardwalk. He wished the moon over his head was the same moon over Ravenna's after finding the spot on the beach where he'd landed.

"Neither here nor there,—yet," he spoke to a silent sea in the fragile night. *Ah, to hold her again...*

Demeter and Gram appeared on the sand, moonlight streaming through their diaphanous bodies. He startled, then smiled with all his heart.

"Your family will be so happy to see you, Roulic," Demeter smiled.

"And..." his eyes and heart hung on her words.

"You may go to her now with no fear of mishaps."

Roulic's heart pumped so hard that an immediate glow covered his face. *Thank God, the Masters, the Goddess, the Witches. All of them. I'll be with Ravenna soon...* Then he remembered the Pearlytok.

"But I thought King Vim had the key. How can I return to Doth without it?"

Demeter stated, "King Vim is, and will always be, the keeper of the key. However, given the circumstances, he has consented to allow Arthur to hold it. Momentarily. Upon arrival in Doth, you are to return the Pearlytok to Trumbleton Wells. A troop of gnomes will meet you there to deliver the key to the Inner Realm."

"But I thought Arthur was out of commission." Roulic's face flushed. He couldn't stop thinking of holding Ravenna.

"Uncle's still got some juice left in him," Marlee said.

"Witches don't call it a day until the job is done," Aurora said from behind Marlee. The seven sisters formed a circle, breaking it as fast as it had formed. Arthur appeared its center, his palm out, offering Roulic the Pearlytok.

"This ought to get you where and when you want to go," his eyes sparkled.

Chapter 26

Humor Nor Cruelties

Sitting atop a dinky cloud, Smutch pointed at the river's edge and wailed. "Blow me down! He's walking across the water."

"I always hoped he'd survive," Bliniloth whispered. Then, in his usual bluster, he declared, "I do believe, despite possessing no humor nor cruelties, he would have made a good pirate. C'mon lad, our work's done here. We're off to receive our recompense."

"Where will that be, Cap'n?"

"Forever and a day from these fair winds." The ghosts of Onan vanished in a gray vapor above the clouds.

Roulic waded through the tranquil shallows, howling at a chevron of honking geese.

"It's a *f-i-n-e* day to be alive!"

He held the Pearlytok, following the birds toward the lofty stronghold. They cut through the blue sky over grassy banks beside the Soaring River. And when the last goose had flown beyond Meyrick's towering castle, he felt the rush of a newfound peace. An inner peace that lies on every path, every road, and in every journey.

Had it not been for the Master's gift—a gnome's reward for good works, I'd never have understood the true meaning of the Pearlytok.

With happy hands splashing in the river, he hummed, looking for her along the low wall by the bank. When he saw her, he tromped, then strode to her. Ravenna ran into the river, pressing their hearts together.

"I knew you'd come for me," her arms took his torso.

"I hoped you'd wait for me," he leaned back to see her eyes.

"I would have waited forever for you, but I'm glad I didn't have to," she said. Time stood still for the Ancient lovers as they kissed. But when he shivered, she released. "Oh, you poor thing, you're trembling and pale," she said, cupping her hands on his shoulders.

"It's good to be home," he said, looking into her soul.

"Oh, my love, you look like you've just seen a ghost!"

"I'll have to tell you about that sometime," he said.

"You can tell me all about it after you've warmed by a proper fire," she said, escorting him ashore.

"Yes, I'd like that, a proper fire," he said. She wrapped him up in her red cloak. And with the help of Kolleen and Fere, she hurried him across the green to her father's castle, where he slept for two days.

Chapter 27

A Bat In The Belfry

Mayem woke, parched, on a hardscrabble beach. It stretched farther than he could see in either direction. There were no boats, huts, or signs of life. None other than crabs and gulls scavenging under a torrid sun.

Damn Roulic, damn the dragons, damn those witches, and damn this endless beach!

After trekking miles he began to dehydrate. Uninviting coves, jagged and bony, he left unexplored. But coming to a bay bearing palms and hearty shrubs, he took time to investigate. He sought his treasure inside a tiny inlet walled by steep cliffs. Searching the fjord, he claimed his treasure: fresh water trapped in leaves and crannies along the cliffs. Climbing high, he saw a three-masted brigantine anchored a mile up the beach on the other side of the peninsula. He could make out people on a dock loading a cargo vessel and a few structures on the cliffs overlooking the port. Rushing back to the beach, he limped along the sand, questioning the scene as a mirage. When it clearly wasn't, he hobbled to the dock and tripping, fell on his back in ankle-deep water beside the ship's transport vessel. Digging his elbows into the sand, he sat up and squinted to read the words burned into the brigantine's stern: *Similar Pinch.*

Ha! This can't be the Pinch. I must be dreaming. Or going mad.

"Oh, you're not going mad, friend. Or dreaming," Ozrar slid into his mind. Mayem shook his aching skull trying to wiggle the spirit out. Bliniloth's avenging blue grin blocked the sun from his eyes while Smutch smirked, warming the shallow water around the Ancient's feet.

"You!"

"We're here to collect our spoils," Smutch simmered.

"I've got nothing for you, and you know it."

"Oh, but you have, old friend," Bliniloth swaggered. "Memories! Locked up in that scabby little head of yours. Where the last of your trophies lie. God knows your heart is empty, so we've come along to ease your mind as well."

"Oh, yes, we will, we'll ease it easily, we will," Smutch snickered.

"But don't you worry, we'll leave you a bat in the belfry. Just one, mind ye, one that'll stick in yer craw," Bliniloth spouted.

"One you can never get out," Smutch said.

"Can I at least pick which..?" Mayem begged.

"No! You'll soon forget every thought you've ever had about Grace. Or anyone else, for that matter. Except for Roulic; he'll be with you forever. Your one and only memory will be of him beating you, besting you. Your memory of him will consume you, old friend, just as you've consumed others in life!" Bliniloth raised his hands over his head.

"Wait, wait," Mayem argued, trying to buy time. "Why do you keep calling me 'old friend'? We haven't known each other long. I only met you since you came out of Nina's vase."

"Shut up, you damned fool! You may have been born an Ancient, but you've always been a fool. A fool to chase love. A fool to betray dragons. And a fool for crossing me. Don't think I've forgotten what you did to the pirates of Doth. And you were planning to do to me. But I got killed by the witches first. Drowned me in a ship, they did. But I went to sea with honor. I'll give them that, considering what I did to them."

"I remember what we did to them, Cap'n," Smutch said.

"Shut up, Swig!" Bliniloth flared at Smutch. "If you don't remember me now, Mayem, you're a bigger fool than I thought."

"I wasn't going to hurt you," Mayem pleaded. "We had a deal, remember? You were to deliver the witch boy, and I was going to give you Dandling Oars. It's not my fault the witches intervened."

"Silence!!" the ghost raged. "Time is running out for you to remember who you were. But don't you worry, your old mate, Nagendra, will be with you to show you the ropes. People call him Ozrar these days, but you can still call him Nagendra if you like. Consider that a gift from me old self: Captain Salty. -- So long, mate!"

The shade of Salty raised its arms over the obdurate outlaw. Mayem spat at the ghost, then squeezed his eyelids shut like a scared child. Bliniloth let his arms fall, hexing wind and droplets to rush and spill over the defeated body. "Now, be reborn in the breath of River Lethe," he said. Mayem's body didn't move for a full minute.

W hen he opened his eyes, the ghosts of Onan were gone, but Mayem still lay in the froth of the unknown ship's cargo vessel. He was younger, his skin softer, his countenance lean and agile and he had more hair on his head than he did an hour ago, but he didn't know it yet. He didn't remember the ghosts of Onan, his wounded heel, or yesterday or any day before yesterday. He couldn't remember Grace or Meyrick because all he had ever known and loved were erased, absorbed in the cosmos like grains of sand meeting the sea. His spiritual token had been taken. And now his slate was blank. All except for one lone memory. The memory of someone named Roulic.

Rough banter drew him up from the wet sand. He watched sailors carry crates up the cargo ship's plank. How and why he was there on this beach hadn't entered his mind yet.

"Where are you headed?" Mayem stopped a sailor bedecked in rags, lugging a barrel to the plank.

The sailor eyed Mayem. "Could be anywhere, everywhere, or nowhere. No one knows but the captain. Come aboard and ask him yerself." Mayem waffled. The sailor stepped on the plank. "Well, crack on, then! I'll take you myself. I gets a reward for recruitin'." He took Mayem to a dingy alongside the cargo ship and made Mayem row seaward a quarter-mile to the galleon. Two mates swung a net overboard. Unquestioning his ability to board by rope, Mayem climbed topside like a seasoned sailor.

Onboard, he got pushed and shoved by crew stacking barrels and crates on the deck. Finding the Master's quarters, he tapped on the open door and stuck his head inside. The long-haired captain was mumbling to himself.

"Enter!" he said, his back to Mayem, in a red leather button-back chair. The captain's head raised from the map spread over his walnut desk. "Well, what is it? Another looking for work? You'll only get yer fair share aboard this vessel. And you'd better be ready to leave within the hour. Where are you from?"

The chair swiveled. Mayem teetered, taken aback by the captain's countenance. His discomfiture lay in a sense of familiarity he couldn't place. So, he gave up trying to decode the captain's squinty eyes and long black mustache. The captain, with one look, appraised him to be a willing man in good enough shape to weather work on a ship at sea.

"Well? Where are you from?" asked the captain.

"I'll be ready, I mean, I *am* ready," Mayem said, "--I believe I'm from the sea. But I'm afraid time has disallowed me from reminiscing about noteworthy stories of my time at sea."

The captain got up and grabbed Mayem's wrist. He squeezed the burnt hand and didn't miss the thin red line across Mayem's throat. "Ahh, a seasoned man in a hurry to sail under the black flag. I like that. I can use a man like you. But remember, no purchase, no pay! All plunder is to be kept on board and tallied before it finds port. Any foul play aboard my ship will find you biting the bullet—or worse!" The captain clutched his map. "Do we have an understanding?"

"Yes," the nebbish Mayem said.

"Yes, what!?"

"Yes, sir, Captain."

"That's better." The excitable captain's eyes softened. "Have ye a name?"

"I...I...," he couldn't remember it.

"The tides of time move by her titan fable, do they not?"

"I suppose so. Sir."

"Very well. I'll put you down as...as...", the captain glanced at a piece of paper on his desk, "...as Maccleen...pirate Lance Maccleen. That's as fine a name as any; indeed, it is."

"Yes, sir."

The captain sat, swiveling to his magnifying glass. He flattened the map over his desk. "She'll come back to you. She always does," he said, reaching for a carafe of wine. "In the meantime, you'll have plenty of leeway to chase after her. Find Seaman Swig. He's on deck. He'll get you sorted."

Ozrar wasted no time in whispering the name Swig in Mayem's ear. Lance Maccleen left the cabin with spine tingling chills. "Thank you, Captain."

"Welcome aboard the Hurling Gal."

Chapter 28

To Deliver On That Divine Request

"Oh, their love, destined for that quiet river, took my breath away, just took it away," Raine looked for scissors. Lilith didn't look up. She was busy weaving with her knitting needle. Crafting in Raine's room, waiting for news from Agnes and Madelyn.

"Love's not all that it's cracked up to be; trust me," Lilith pouted.

"Tell me you're not happy for them. At least be happy for him."

"I'll be happy for him if he ever decides to deliver on that divine request. If he ever even got it," Lilith said.

"Oh, he got it all right. Gram made sure of that," said Raine.

"How did she do that?"

"Our little shape-shifter, Natric. He snuck it into Soaring Castle during the wee hours. The scruff-muggin climbed a curtain wall with it in his mouth and dropped it off in the inner bailey. But Roulic hasn't even read it yet, so..."

"So, there'll be no resolution until he does," Lilith fumed. "Because of your damned deception."

"No, no, no, Lilith! I never lied!" Raine said. "You know all this began before I was born."

"What about Jillian's lie to Callian? Demeter's lie about the key to

Roulic, to the fairies—to King Vim? I could count a thousand lies span-
ning a thousand years, but in the end, you always say it's for the best.
Damn! I'm ready for this to end, Raine; really, I am."

"I know Lil, and it will. As soon as Roulic..." Raine calmed.

"How much time do we have left here?"

"Well, that's a timeline thing."

"No shit, Sherlock."

"No need to get pissy about it," Raine said. "Could be a few weeks,
maybe months. We might stay here depending on how it all works out."

"So I've heard. Either way, I won't be staying here. I'll either be dead
a long time ago or live forever—somewhere else. Who knows? Isn't it
rich? The life I lead. I'm 'Destiny' and yet I have no destiny at all."

"You know what they say. It's all about the journey," Madelyn
barged in. Agnes followed up with, "Why aren't you guys in the Craft
Room?" Raine and Lilith continued knitting.

"So, ladies. What gives? What did the hags say?" Lilith snarled. The
witches bit their tongues.

Agnes reported: "The younger one is on his way up."

"Hello, ladies," Jax said in the doorway.

"Jax!" His sisters never seemed to mind him popping in unannounced. As long as he didn't dawdle too long or interrupt their
schemes. Knowing he had news from the elders, they were all ears.

"So, Gram and Demeter have instructed me to tell you that we're in
for a new round of fixities. Signs, challenges, and tests. But we have no
fear, right? As thus far the Ancient has passed every obstacle with flying
colors. Mayem's reign is over. At least neutralized. Like Gram said, 'It's
what you've all known since the beginning: a time will come to eradicate
the cradle of our problem. That time is now.'" He tried to appease their
long faces. "Al and Rora are out now, rounding up allies from our past,
those we can trust. And Uncle Arthur is going to do everything he can
to help Roulic and Ravenna. I know they're asking more from us than
they've ever asked before. But I do believe it's all possible and doable,
not only for the good of Doth, but for the good of us."

"They could have given us a break," Madelyn snapped her fingers.
"A couple of moons would've been nice," Agnes said. No jaws dropped,

and not one witch said another word. But they all believed in Jax. Perhaps more than in themselves.

"So, Jax, what's for dinner tonight? Not eggs and apricots again, I hope." Lilith lapped her needle, giving him the eye contact he craved.

"Have a little faith, dear," he winked. "You might come to acquire a taste for the fruit."

Chapter 29

A Talon's Tale

Alone at last, the Ancients didn't leave Meyrick's castle for a fortnight. When they weren't in the gardens or courts or by the river, they stayed in Ravenna's room, behind the Great Hall, sleeping in on her balmy queen feather bed. Kissing the oriel windows of the chamber, sunlight warmed their toes, draped in silk.

"I used to feel sorry for them," he said. "Such long lives spent alone. But now, after learning how much they are like us, I don't feel sorry for them anymore."

"Or yourself?"

"My ease comes not from liking nor disliking dragons. I'll always fear and respect them. But I know now, because of them, whether mortal or creature, we are all one."

"If only more people pursued that idea," she said.

"The world might find its heart again," he said, "and all the love that it has been missing." His arm cradled her midriff.

"Tell me again how much you missed me," she allured.

"Oh, I suffered every night; I hope you know. Without your touch, the wind didn't blow. I felt you in my heart, even while running scared through dark places. Even when I slept, you were with me, beside me, the entire time. I thought of our stolen moments and your wild beauty every hour of every day."

Ravenna leaned from the other side of their two white terriers. She caressed his stomach, whispering, "Do you think our past could ever spoil our future?"

"Never," he said, fiddling with the talon-whistle over his chest.

"Neither do I. So, why won't you open that letter? It's been sitting on your bureau for days now. It might be an important message."

"Whatever the witches of Doth have to say, I'm sure it's dreadfully important. But they can wait another day. Maybe forever. They've got nothing but time. And as much as I love them," he said, putting the dogs on the floor, "I much prefer spending time with you." She gave him a look within a look, one that reminded him why he adored her so much.

"I'll read it tomorrow; I promise," he said, rolling back to her.

"You'd better," she said, her lips tending to his.

The End

Everlan

Everlan Book Three

Unbeknownst to sister witches, Demeter and Sionann, a devastating curse is born from one regrettable deed. After a century of suffering,

the siblings seek revenge using the power of love found in the hearts of two young lovers who meet in the dragon's land of Doth.Everlan

—>Sneak Peek chapter i

CHAPTER ONE
OF A NOVEL DEATH

They knelt before the effigy melting in Grammy's cauldron. It 'simmered in the magic,' hidden in the heart of the shrubs on Thorny Hill, just like she said it would. The siblings danced and chanted with teenage abandon. Yet they danced unaware of the damning men who would soon cross their path.

After incanting, Sionann focused on the form bubbling in the pot. Demeter stretched her long arms over the milky red broth. Her back arched, then straightened, flinging arms over her head.

"This is taking forever. She should have drowned by now."

"There's no such thing as forever." Sionann fixed on the floating figure. "She will liquefy before the baneberry boils."

"Well, I may 'liquefy' before she does," Demeter said. "After lugging that pot, I've a mind to burn Grammy's grimoire. None of her spells worked. Not a single one. What are we doing wrong? We prepared every prescription to the letter. And to think I thought we'd found all the answers. Ha!"

Fresh yew and holly berries plopped into the pot. Stirring the brew with an iron ladle, Sionann dismembered the beeswax body. "I don't trust anyone claiming to have all the answers," Sionann said. "Even the Masters seem to be lost. Perhaps that's why they never show themselves."

"What about the old gnome king? The Masters showed themselves to *him*. They gave him the Pearlytok after the War of Realms." Demeter said.

"Maybe they did, maybe they didn't. No one talks about *how* they gave it to him. People assume the Masters handed him the key, but there's no proof that ever happened. He also claimed to be alone when he got it. How convenient. Even the story of how the dragons got hold of the key is iffy."

"They dropped it into the endless pit beneath the Bridge of Belief. Didn't they?" Demeter puzzled.

"So the story goes. But how do you explain the faeries finding it in Faelan years later? You should know better than to believe every legend you hear coming from a King's mouth. Let alone what comes from a scribe's hand." Blue eyes ignited watching the glowing glob.

"No need to get huffy," Demeter said. "There could be a portal in the endless pit. Who knows? The key could've portaled to Faelan."

"Hmm. Now there's a thought. It would explain why the dragons flew there in the first place," Sionann reversed her stirring. "Father's moved through portals before, ya know."

"He has? He never told me...when did he tell you about that?"

"Long before we came to Mark's Den," Sionann stared into the wall of burgundy barberries surrounding them. "It was on the day she made you wear those awful shoes."

"Oh, I remember that day. Those shoes were dreadfully ugly and oh so too tight! My toes turned blue. She insisted I wear them to that boring Ladies of Everlan Feast. I didn't hear a word throughout the entire affair. All I remember is being made to sit next to Mrs. Knead in the farthest chair from the lectern. And getting blisters while Dillena tried her best to appear as a doting mother of the realm. She barely touched her food. And I got a stomachache."

Sionann yawned. "Do you even still have them? Maybe we should have our own luncheon at the bridge and give those shoes their final due: a farewell toss."

"I guess tossing them would be a fitting tribute. If I can find them. They're buried in my closet somewhere. But, didn't they close the bridge of Belief? Sounds dangerous."

Sionann stopped stirring. "What happened to your sense of adventure? It'll be fun. We'll make a ritual out of it. God knows we need the practice. Heaving scraps of leather forced upon your feet by a rotten mother sounds like a good idea to me."

Demeter watched the gooey glob dissipate. "Dillena's never been our mother. Mrs. Knead spends more time…"

"*Or* fit for the task. Even to her own boys," Sionann snuffed the fire with handfuls of dirt. "All the more reason to let go of those old soles. And anything else we can think of with her wretched ick on it. I know I've got something I'd like to put into the pit."

"Fine…I guess," Demeter said. "We'll go to the rickety bridge, ridding ourselves of as much of her as we can. Everything she ever gave me is going under that bridge."

"I'd offer to lend you a hand, but you won't need it," Sionann mumbled.

"I heard that," Demeter said.

"Look," Sionann said, "she's gone away." Demeter leaned over, peeking in the pot. Sionann worked the ladle around the bowl. "I don't see any of her, do you?"

"No, I don't. Good. Now we can go."

"Not until you pack up and I put her in these bottles."

Sionann used copper kitchen tongs to dip a bulbous bottle into the pot of poison. She dipped and filled another, sealing each jar with a piece of cork tied to its neck. Wearing cloth sacks like gloves, they tilted the hot pot and dumped the remaining concoction into the dirt. Sionann set the second bottle back inside the cooling cauldron while Demeter gathered the grimoire, candles, and sachets of herbs. She put them in her sack, and they left, creeping through the opening in the shrubs.

Halfway home, Demeter dropped her sack, tripping on a rock. "Ouch!" she hissed in the dirt, rattling like a riled snake. "It's all Dillena's fault. She's going to get hers!" Demeter's eyes flashed like diamonds.

"Yes, she will—during supper. C'mon, get up. It's getting dark; she'll be wanting her soup." Sionann extended a hand.

An hour later, the sisters tried to act normal while Dillena dined by the fireplace at *her* table. They sat opposite one another at *their* table, behind the kitchen wall. Just as they had every evening for the last year. It became *their* table after Dillena sawed the family's kitchen table in half during a rage the night their father left.

Fraser scorned Dillena, leaving. "Arthur and Frane will learn more from the gods by living in a city with me than dying in the country with you. And I *am* coming back for *my* girls!" But he never did. His rescue never came. After a month of waiting, the girls tearfully agreed to give up hope of their father and stepbrothers ever returning.

Demeter led Sionann to admit they would need to rely on each other more than ever if they were to survive Dillena. And Sionann chose her words, reminding Demeter she was the older and wiser one. It wasn't until a visit to see their grandmother that they gave in to the unthinkable.

The *"necessary act"* reared its head while walking home from Sinann's house. An action previously concurred to be unconscionable. Unspeakable. Yet, neither sibling refrained from describing in gruesome detail wild scenarios for the deed.

After all, it was Sinann who lent them her book of spells. And Sinann, who warned them, "If someone ever hurts you, whether mortal, beast, or demon, you have every right to fight back with everything you've got. But when you do, make sure the full power of your intent is behind the force you put forth." They took her words to heart, thinking she must have known all along about their abuse. That mistaken conclusion saddened and angered them for a fortnight.

With a bristly obsession, they plotted their vengeance. After all, it was Dillena's horrid disposition that split the family and forced their father's departure. And Dillena's vicious hand, they now faced alone, without the cover of their half-witch stepbrothers.

Fraser had left them before, yet always returned none the wiser. Dillena mastered hiding their shame behind long frilly sleeves and clever one-piece kirtles. Had Fraser known of their cuts and bruises, he would never have left them behind. But he never saw past what he wanted to see: his mortal bride's pretty face.

While Dillena sipped from her bowl of stew, a rich mist swaddled the cattle land of Mark's Den like a baby's blanket. Sionann poked at her mutton pottage. "Does he live or die is all I'm asking? In the end, does he win the maiden?"

"You'll have to finish it for yourself," Demeter said, tapping the book beside her bowl. "Anonymous never actually reveals the lovers' ultimate fate. '*Hope lives, all the more in torn hearts.*' was the last line. I found it favorable, but that's just how I read it. You need to read it and see. But if he never finds her and he dies, it would have to be of a novel death. And a noble one, of course, but that would lead to an end I couldn't accept."

"It was a simple question," Sionann said, giving her 'the look.'

"Not really. It's like asking, 'Does love prevail over hate?' Look at the world, Sionann, even in the year 1101, all of Doth seems to teeter between the two."

"Maybe they teeter in equal measure," Sionann whispered, her eyes twinkling in the candlelight.

Demeter whispered back, covering her mouth, "I just hope you put more than an 'equal measure' in her bowl."

"Oh, I did indeed. I poured the entire bottle in," Sionann sniggered.

"Promise me we'll never do that again." Demeter got ready to throw an unwanted doll. A pert face emerged from her cloth sack, gleaming in the pink dawn. They watched it vanish into the dank abyss below the Bridge of Belief.

"I won't promise you that," Sionann said. "But just think, now we don't have to beg to go outside. With her out of our way, we can come and go as we please. We're free to make our own decisions now."

"We'll be on our own though and have to fend for ourselves. How will we manage? You know I'm not as strong as you. Is it so bad to want someone to take care of my needs?"

"Need I remind you child," Sionann mimicked Dillena's high-pitched voice, "there are those that need and those that want, and those that want to need, but for those that know they need to want are they that need to want to know!" Demeter giggled throughout the mockery, then blurted,

"Why am I the only one throwing things away? Why didn't you bring anything? Didn't you say you had something to be rid of?"

"I already have," Sionann said. "My memory of her. The thought of her and her wicked ways. I've thrown the essence of her into the darkness where she belongs and can no longer hurt us," Sionann stared into the pitch black pit below. "I swear on my soul as a witch never again to speak her name."

"Someday," Demeter pledged, throwing one shoe at a time, "my daughter will grow up to toss her own hideous shoes off a bridge, but not because she hates her stepmother for torturing her and making her wear the bloody things. She'll throw them away because she chooses not to wear them. Then she'll run through fields of rye like a wild woman, barefoot and free, chasing the seasons until she chooses otherwise."

"Like Artain, the gypsy."

"Just like Artain," Demeter nodded, letting her last store-bought dress go. "I do hope she hasn't left yet. She's more like us than anyone else in Mark's Den."

"Don't worry, we've got time. The caravan's not leaving until summer's end. Now, we must hurry home to get Grammy's grimoire and return it to her before Mrs. Knead comes around this afternoon. God knows what mortalkin would do to us—and Grammy, if they ever saw that book. We'll tell Mrs. Knead that she died in her sleep. Of course, we'll have to tell Gram everything."

"And we'll do exactly what she says," Demeter added, waiting for reassurance.

"First, we fetch the book, then the pot, then we go to Grammy's.

"Then we'll tell Mrs. Knead about...?"

"That's the plan. She'll send for the coroner. And the sooner, the better. The longer we wait, the more questions will arise about why we waited so long to tell anyone."

"We could say that we were distraught with grief." Demeter tossed her empty sack off the old weathered bridge.

"That's funny," Sionann said. "That might work if we don't accidentally say 'relief' instead of 'grief'." They left, waving goodbye to the bridge, while Dillena's body grew cold by the fireplace.

Sinann didn't answer her door. Demeter waited on the porch while Sionann walked around the house to the backyard.

"There you are, Grammy," Sionann said, adjusting her wide felt hat. Sinann, watering a small black henbane plant, turned and smiled. She waved Sionann to join her. Demeter came running around the corner.

"How long were you going to leave me standing there?" Sionann ignored her.

"Oh! What a nice surprise," Sinann said. "My beautiful grand-daughters," Sinann said.

"We wish it were nice, Grammy, but it's not. 'Tis a dark visit, I'm afraid," Sionann took her hand. Demeter nodded grimly.

"Oh, my child, you tremble. Come inside and tell me all about it. Ramil is far and away so we've got plenty of privacy." At the back porch, Sinann's kitchen smelled of warm cinnamon bread. She hung a brass kettle on the corner fireplace. They explained everything to her: how Dillena abused them, how Fraser never knew about it, and how they felt impelled to carry out the deadly deed. By the time their teacups were on the table, Sionann had heard all the details and looked eager to respond.

"Well, it's good to know the purple potion was a success. My aunt Eigyr bequeathed that spell. She was a very good witch."

"Ours came out reddish," Demeter said, returning the grimoire.

"In every witch bends a rainbow," Sinann said, setting the book in her lap, "no matter her method. Thus it worked, and now Dillena is gone to the otherworld, where she will face a costly reckoning. You did nothing wrong in putting her there. Indeed, a great favor to this world by speeding things along, as it were. Had I known about this, she would have met her maker at the start of it." The girls gulped their tea, watching her tap her chin wrinkles. "Now, as far as your immediate future is concerned, I must warn that staying in Mark's Den may bring you more suffering, for the suspicions of mortalkin could intensify once word of Dillena's demise spreads. There are always those seeking wrath." She looked into the fire.

"Where will we go? We don't have a clue as to where father is," Sionann said.

"I will find him and tell him of your whereabouts."

"But Grammy, how? And how will you know where *we* are if we're in hiding, moving from village to village?" Demeter asked.

"We are witches, are we not? First, I will summon a trusted wolf to locate Fraser. And the ensuing conversation between mother and son will occur here, perhaps in this chair."

Demeter passed Sionann a telepathic glance. *She must be really good at mind talk.*

We will be too, with more practice. Sionann raised her brows.

"In the meantime, once her body is brought to rest, you will come here and stay with me. Further arrangements will see you to a safe and suitable place, as you well deserve. A place where you can live unhindered. You've a bright future ahead, and mustn't waste time taking up space with any mortal jobbernowls. Hmm..." Sinann's fingers returned to her chin. "Perhaps the steady presence of a proper witch in your life will do the trick. When was the last time you met with Artain?"

"She's not a witch, Grammy. She's a gypsy," Sionann said.

"But we *are* hoping to see her soon. Before the caravan leaves Mark's Den," Demeter said, "We do so love Artain."

"That's settled then," Sinann said, clearing the teacups. "You'd better be off now before Mrs. Knead calls. She'll be shocked to find a dead body in the house. But she will calm down, and when she does, she'll see to having it removed."

"What do we tell her?" Demeter stood with a worried look.

"Tearfully tell her you overslept and found her that way midmorning. Say you didn't know what to do and were too afraid to do anything. If that doesn't bring Mrs. Knead's sympathy, sob and mutter 'mama.' That should do the trick. She'll try to soothe you. Let her. And when she wonders aloud what to do with you, tell her you want to be with your grandma."

"What if she insists on taking us home with her?" Sionann asked.

"She won't. Mrs. Knead knows Fraser's away, and I'm your closest kin. Tell her you need to stay here with me and wait together as a family for the coroner to arrive. I presume he'll arrive tomorrow evening, as the crown is hasty when it comes to collecting its due. It's too bad your father isn't here to handle these matters. I'm sure Dillena's dowry, and your share of it, will have to be sorted. Now, run along, girls. I'll have a nice meal waiting for you when you return," Sinann said, giving each a tender hug.

Life was quiet in Mark's Den after the coroner's departure. None suspected foul play, not even the most devout villagers eager to root out hidden evil. But Sinann kept on her guard, advising the girls to stay put and refrain from speaking to anyone until she found them a place to stay.

Sionann sighed, sipping peppermint tea in Sinann's parlor. "I still find it hard to believe she's dead and gone."

"Thanks to Grammy's grimoire," Demeter rejoiced. "Without it, we'd still be under Dillena's doom."

"Tell me you'll never utter that name again."

"I hope I never have to. She was never good for any of us."

"I say we skip her funeral and find Artain," Sionann said. Demeter shot a ready look, got up, and changed her clothes.

Acknowledgements

To my wife, Tracy, I am forever grateful for her ongoing support; humming along with the heartfelt acceptance of a saint during my mad process of procrastination. I also thank my son, Gaurabhakta, for being here—and there, speaking his mind with the superb effect of causing reconsideration amid lifts of laughter. And to the inimitable David Rowe go my warmest regards, for if it were not for his great camaraderie, the spirit required to tell this tale would not have appeared.

About the Author

Before writing fantasy, Conor Jest wrote poems and songs and played guitar in a rock band. A lover of dark chocolate and shelling along the Crystal Coast, he lives in North Carolina with his wife and their dog, Gizmo.

Also By Conor Jest

WHERE THE WITCHES DWELL

CHARMING TOMORROW

EVERLAN

EVERLAN TRILOGY OMNIBUS

Available at:

Amazon

Barnes & Noble

Conorjest.com

www.ingramcontent.com/pod-product-compliance
Lightning Source LLC
Chambersburg PA
CBHW022140240626
47153CB00007B/2439